Published 2024 by Vinci Books

OATH TO DEFEND

An Adam Drake novel

SCOTT MATTHEWS

To all the men and women who took a solemn oath to support and defend the Constitution of the United States against all enemies, foreign and domestic, and have kept their word.

Prologue

WHEN THE TRAIL OF AMERICA'S MOST WANTED TERRORIST goes cold in Tijuana, Mexico, and the path of a nuclear device smuggled under the border in San Diego ends at an abandoned and empty van, one man has a hunch the terrorist and the nuke will ultimately wind up in the same place.

And he thinks he knows where. The only question is whether he can find them both in time.

Chapter One

UNDERCOVER AGENTS DO NOT LIKE TO STAND OUT, ESPECIALLY when they're in a foreign country, they don't speak the language, and they're new. Randy Johnson, rookie DEA agent on his first deployment, was no different. But standing six foot seven, with red hair, freckles, and a baby face that reminded you of your fifteen-year-old younger brother, he had no choice.

While on assignment in Cancun, Mexico, Randy chose to accentuate the obvious by wearing shorts, a pink linen *guayabera* shirt, and a red Boston Red Sox hat. His job was to look like a tourist and observe and report on cartel members spotted in and near the Mayan Riviera. He remembered faces. He'd been taught to compartmentalize them, identify features, and then compare them to photos in the DEA's cartel scrapbook.

Randy was waiting for Juan Garcia Salina to show up at the Presidente InterContinental Resort. An informant had reported that he liked to eat lobster and shrimp curry at the hotel's seaside El Caribeño restaurant. Salina was believed to be responsible for the recent torture and execution of a Mexican army general who had cooperated with the DEA.

The man Randy recognized on this muggy, overcast day sitting at the poolside bar and drinking a cold glass of Superior Beer was not, however, a cartel member. Randy had recognized the face of the bodyguard of a man at the top of the FBI's most wanted list, the man thought to be behind the assassination attempt on the Secretary of Homeland Security a month ago in Portland, Oregon.

Jamal James, a former NFL defensive tackle weighing three hundred and fifty pounds and standing six foot eight inches tall, worked for David Barak. Barak had been the CEO of International Security and Intelligence Services, or ISIS, a top international security firm. After the attempted assassination, the FBI had wanted to question Barak, but he and his bodyguard had vanished. Both his corporate offices in Las Vegas and his residential compound in the mountains near Mt. Charleston, north of the city, had been searched. The FBI found evidence on a restored computer hard drive that linked Barak to the assassination team and made him appear to be its mastermind. But they didn't find anything that revealed where he might be hiding.

Randy saw the big bodyguard walk to a table where three men were having lunch and lean down to speak with one of them, who handed him an envelope. The bodyguard then turned and walked back to the hotel lobby.

Although the men at the table were not on the DEA watch list, Randy took a quick picture of them anyway with his cell phone, left money on the bar for his beer, and hurried after Jamal James. The man was moving like a bus through the traffic in the lobby.

A black Range Rover sat idling at the parking attendant's stand. James tipped the attendant and hoisted his massive body into the passenger's seat. The Range Rover settled an inch or two with the added weight before the air suspension restored the SUV's balance. The vehicle drove off.

For a moment, Randy Johnson hesitated. Stay on post as

ordered, or follow? Follow the bodyguard, he decided. If the Range Rover led him to Barak, he'd be able to send a Flash Priority One alert that every DEA agent would envy. Handing the well paid attendant a five dollar bill, he signaled for a taxi.

"Stay with that Range Rover, Carlos, and I'll double your fare," he said, glancing at the driver's ID and picture as he slid into the back of a green and white Camry.

"Not necessary, señor. With this traffic I cannot lose it. Where do you think it is going?"

"No idea, no idea at all. Here, swipe my Visa card in case I have to leave in a hurry."

"Does this involve your wife, señor?"

"Why would you ask that?"

"Couples come here after weddings. Sometimes men follow wives after they fight."

The young agent had to laugh. Carlos Rodriguez, the middle age taxi driver, had probably seen his share of honeymoons gone bad.

"Not fighting with my wife, Carlos. You and I might go a round or two, though, if you lose the Range Rover."

For the next forty-five minutes, they drove down the coast from Cancun. Highway 307 was a four-lane divided freeway and they maintained a steady seventy miles an hour, slowing only for a couple of traffic lights and reduced-speed zones. The towns they passed through weren't much to see, Puerto Morelos and Tres Rios, but the beauty of the Caribbean Sea on the left and the thickening mangrove jungle on the right served to heighten the young agent's sense of adventure.

"Señor, the Range Rover is turning. It's heading into the Mayakoba resort. Do you want me to follow?"

"Let's make sure this is where he's staying. Drive in. I'll check it out. Might have to stay here myself some day."

"A very expensive place, señor. The Mayakoba is one of the best hotels in the world."

Carlos appeared to be right. The Mayakoba was

surrounded by a mangrove jungle and was built around a network of crystal clear waterways and small inland islands next to a white sand beach.

The Range Rover stopped in front of the main lobby. The bodyguard got out, rolled his massive shoulders, and walked in. No luggage was unloaded before the Range Rover drove off.

"Stay here, Carlos. I'll just be a minute."

The rookie agent approached the Mayakoba valet.

"Hi, could you help me? I think that man who just walked by was Jamal Johnson, the best NFL tackle ever. Is he a guest here? I'd pay a small fortune for his autograph."

The valet smiled. "We do not confirm the identity of our guests, señor." He extended an open palm.

Randy Johnson returned to his cab and sent a text message to his DEA supervisor. Flash Priority One.

Chapter Two

Liz Strobel, special assistant to the Secretary of Homeland Security, took the call in her office at the Nebraska Avenue complex from her counterpart in the Drug Enforcement Agency.

"Liz, we have a lead on David Barak. Our spotter in Cancun just reported seeing his bodyguard. He's apparently staying at some expensive resort on the Mayan coast."

"It's about time. Thanks, Phil. Scan me a copy of the report."

"On its way. How do you want to handle this? You want us to send a team down?"

"I have someone we'll send, but I'd like your spotter to meet with him. Give me the contact information and we'll handle it."

"Is DHS flying solo on this?"

"They tried to kill the Secretary, Phil. He was the first on a list. The rest are Americans, too. So, yes, we're handling it ourselves."

"Okay. Dinner sometime?"

She smiled into the phone. "Thanks for the heads up, Phil."

She knew she wasn't winning the award for the most social power person in Washington, but that wasn't her game. Phil was a nice guy, but she just didn't have time for casual dating. She needed the occasional escort for official functions, however, and she could always find one. If she were going to date again, the man would have to be someone who intrigued her, someone special, and she only knew one man like that. Unfortunately, he was mourning a wife he had just lost to cancer. For now, she had a job to do. She picked up her phone.

"Drake, it's Liz. You busy?"

"Just pulling out old grapevines," Adam Drake said. "Trying to get the vineyard ready to replant."

She remembered his farm in the heart of the Oregon wine country, and the one time she'd been there. Drake had killed three jihadists who'd come after him one night, part of the same group that had tried to assassinate her boss. She'd been sent to help him get rid of the bodies. This was a favor to Drake's father-in-law, the senior senator from Oregon.

"Why aren't you at your office?" she asked.

"I'm taking a little time off. The media are still stirred up about those three young Muslim men who went missing. It's hard to maintain a law practice with reporters three deep outside your office."

"We think we know where Barak is," she said.

He didn't answer immediately, so she waited.

"Will the Secretary honor his promise and let me go after him?" he asked.

"That's why I'm calling."

"Fill me in."

For the next ten minutes, she told him everything they had discovered and arranged for him to meet the DEA spotter on the island of Cozumel. It was a short ferry ride from there to the Mexican mainland and the resort where the bodyguard was staying.

"Do you want me to reserve a room for you?" she asked.

"No," he said. "I'll take care of it."

"When you find him, don't kill him. We have a reservation for him at our little resort in Cuba."

He chuckled. "We'll see. I'll call you from Cozumel."

Strobel hoped they were doing the right thing. As Drake had reminded her, Secretary Robert Rallings had agreed to let him go after Barak in exchange for Drake's agreeing to serve as a private contract trouble shooter for DHS. The Secretary had been impressed by the way the former Delta Force operator had acted on his own initiative to identify the assassination plot, and then chase down and kill the assassins.

It had been a close call. Four terrorists had tried to kill the Secretary at the home of Drake's father-in-law, Senator Hazelton, after failing earlier in the day to kill him at a decommissioning ceremony at Oregon's chemical weapons depot. With help from his former sniper partner, Drake had saved the Secretary, the senator, and his wife from a rifle-launched thermobaric grenade attack that leveled the senator's lakeside home.

The agreement with Adam Drake had been made because the Secretary of Homeland Security was occasionally asked for help by defense contractors who, among other things, suspected terrorist probes and didn't want to read about an investigation in the press. After his experience in Oregon, the Secretary had decided that someone outside DHS, someone with a legitimate reason to be involved, like a snoopy attorney with special talents, could be brought in to handle things discretely. When he'd asked Drake to serve as his private trouble shooter, however, Drake had demanded a quid pro quo: let him go after the man who tried to kill his in-laws, and he would agree to the proposition.

Liz wanted to make sure her boss didn't overlook the potential for disaster for the agency. Not only would the Mexican government be outraged if they found an American had killed a terrorist on their turf, but Barak's ties to the drug cartels could also lead to more cartel violence north of the border.

She left her office and walked across the hall to see Secretary Rallings.

"Is he alone?" she asked Mrs. Cameron, the gatekeeper who had served as Robert Ralling's personal secretary from his early days as Governor of Montana and later as a U.S. Senator.

"He's previewing the video for cyber security awareness month that goes out next week," Mrs. Cameron replied. "Go on in, Liz."

Secretary Rallings was sitting at his desk and looking closely at a monitor. His jaw was clinched so tightly the muscles bulged. He waved her over.

"Have you seen this?" he asked. "People will be afraid to trust us with any of their information. This makes it look like China can hack us whenever they want."

"People need to see what we're up against, sir."

"I suppose you're right, but I don't like people knowing we haven't stopped this."

She cleared her throat. "Mr. Secretary, I told Drake about the DEA spotting Barak in Mexico. He's heading down there."

"You still have concerns, Liz?"

"About Drake? No, sir. We've seen how he handles things. I'm more concerned about Mexico finding out we sent a private citizen after a terrorist without telling them."

He nodded, then said, "That's the only way to keep Drake safe. With the cartel's access to the Mexican government, I don't want some drug lord letting Barak know we're coming for him."

"Is that why you're not informing the White House?"

"That and deniability. By the time the White House tells

State what we're doing, Mexico would know it within the hour."

"What will you say if this goes wrong?"

"I'll say I let Drake know we spotted Barak. As a courtesy. His plans thereafter were all his own. I owe him, Liz. He saved my life twice last month. I agreed he'd have first crack at this guy. Hunting terrorists is something he's good at." He rubbed his hands together as if washing them. "This will be okay."

"I hope so, sir, for both of us," she said. She left the Secretary's office thinking of the intriguing man they were sending in harm's way.

Chapter Three

Shortly after his call from the DHS, Adam Francis Drake sat in his old Ford pickup and looked at the lower half of his overgrown, diseased vineyard. Three years ago, a dentist from New Jersey had thrown up his hands, tired of the work a vineyard required, put the place on the market, and moved back east. Drake's late wife, Kay, had fallen in love with the place and convinced him to buy it. Before she died from an aggressive ovarian cancer, he'd promised her he would complete the restoration of the old vineyard. It was a promise he intended to keep, but not until after he had captured or killed the terrorist named David Barak.

Finished for the morning, he parked the pickup in the storage shed behind his gray sandstone farm house and headed for the kitchen, which now served as a temporary office. This was the first room in the old house they had remodeled, adding a gourmet gas range and other new appliances and saving only the fireplace and the plank flooring. He had added the HP TouchSmart computer that was mounted on the wall next to his round, ebony, breakfast table.

Now he booted up the computer and started the Internet video conferencing program. The first person he needed to talk with was his secretary, and while he waited for her to respond, he made notes for the arrangements necessary for his quick trip to Mexico.

"How's Farmer Brown today?" his fifty-something secretary asked without looking up from the something she was reading.

"Tired," he said. "I need a vacation."

Now she looked up. "You've been on vacation for most of the month. You don't get back to work, you'll be closing this office, and I'll be looking for work with an attorney with clients."

"Relax, Margo. This will be over soon. DHS just called. They spotted Barak's bodyguard in Mexico. My 'vacation' in Mexico won't take long, and then I'll get back to work. I need to be there when they catch this guy."

"When *they* catch him or when *you* catch him?"

"It won't be me, if we keep talking," he said. "I'm meeting a DEA agent in Cozumel. Reserve me a room somewhere nice. Better make the reservation for a week."

"Yes, sir," she said, giving him a tight-lipped smile.

Drake recognized the look. Margo had been his secretary, legal assistant, office manager, and friend since his first days in the district attorney's office. When Drake had stumbled onto the assassination plot and almost been killed, she had angrily said he was just playing soldier. He was too old to be chasing terrorists, she'd told him, and foolish besides for thinking he wasn't going to get himself killed.

She was wrong about his being too old. He was only thirty-five. He still ran five miles every morning and, for the last month, he'd been working at getting back in fighting form with daily stretching and an hour-long Krav Maga workout. He'd dug out a pistol range in the hillside behind the storage shed and could again put eight holes inside the ten ring consistently with his Kimber .45, at twenty five and fifty yards, rapid fire. He knew the risks involved in going after a smart terrorist like Barak, but Margo was definitely wrong about his being too old. He was just barely old enough to be president.

He returned her smile. "Margo, I'll be okay. I'm asking Mike to fly me to Mexico and send along a couple of his best men. Now find me a room and while I'm gone, just check messages from home. Catch up on your soaps."

Before she had a chance to say or do something he considered inappropriate, Drake clicked out of the video conference and called his friend in Seattle.

"Mike, it's me. Got a minute?"

"Let me call you right back. I'm interviewing a SEAL who thinks he's good enough to work for me. Shouldn't take long to convince him otherwise."

Drake laughed. Mike Casey had been one of the U.S. Army's best aviators when he was with the 160th Special Operations Aviation Regiment, the Night Stalkers. When his skill with a rifle, developed shooting varmints as a boy in Montana, had caught the attention of Special Operations Command while he flew support for a Delta Force unit in Afghanistan, he'd been invited to selection at Ft. Bragg. After qualification and the six-month operators' training course for the Army's 1st Special Forces Operational Detachment-Delta, he'd been assigned to a team. Another member of that team was a young operator from Oregon named Adam Drake. Their team had been recognized as one the most successful hunter/killer teams to ever operate in the Middle East.

Drake and Casey had left the army after being interrogated by military investigators for three days. A tribal leader claimed that an al Qaeda commander killed in his village had been tortured and humiliated before being executed. But Mike had shot the terrorist from a hill 1800 meters away, with his Barrett M82 .50 caliber rifle, and the team had never been within a hundred yards of the guy. The interrogation and veiled threats of court martial, however, had been the last straw. Both men had agreed it was time to leave.

Drake had enlisted in the army a week after being admitted to the Oregon State Bar and two days after 9/11. After leaving the army, he returned to Oregon and went to work for the district attorney in Portland. Casey had found work with a small security firm in Seattle, whose biggest client was Microsoft. Five years later, after his parents had sold off most of the family ranch and loaned him what was basically his inheritance, he'd bought the business. Since then, he had expanded the services of the firm to include executive protection, electronic surveillance, investigations, and risk management. Headquartered in Seattle, with offices in seventeen cities, Casey's company was now the largest security firm on the west coast, with a fleet of three Gulfstream G280s. Drake's iPhone started playing his ringtone before he even had time to walk to his bedroom and begin packing for Mexico.

"Since you're calling from your own phone," Casey said, "and not from the county jail, I'm guessing you're still a free man."

"For the moment. How'd it go with the swabbie?

"I hired him. Good skill set, recently married, looking for a quieter life. I think he'll fit in."

"You promised him a *quieter life*?"

Casey laughed. "For a while. His wife's three months pregnant. So what's up?"

"Is there a G280 available to fly me to Cozumel?"

"Not the place to go, I hear, if you want to avoid cartel gang fights."

"DHS called. A DEA agent spotted Barak's bodyguard near Cancun. Secretary Rallings is keeping his word and letting me have a shot at him."

Casey whistled. "Letting *us* have a shot at him, you mean. That SOB almost killed me, too, you know. How soon do you want to leave? And what should I bring? Want me to bring the team we had in Portland last month?"

"Mike, I can't ask you to do that. I don't know how long

this might take. And I don't know if DHS will pick up the tab. I offered to go alone."

"That is *not* going to happen," Casey shot back. "We'll work out the finances. This guy's too good, and probably too well protected, for you to get him by your lonesome. Do we know anything about where he's hiding? What protection he might have?"

"I don't know much at this point," Drake admitted. "He's staying at some resort south of Cancun. His bodyguard is the only one they've seen."

"If his bodyguard's there, he's there. I'll round up the team and be at the Hillsboro airport at nine o'clock tonight. We'll red-eye to Cozumel and find our terrorist. Get a couple more rooms where you're staying and tell Margo not to worry. I'm going with you."

Drake appreciated his friend's confidence. Based on their track record, he knew he should feel the same way. But taking down the men behind the terror plot had always proven more difficult than just stopping the foot soldiers.

Chapter Four

David Barak, aka Malik, or Leader to his followers, took the envelope from his bodyguard, nodded his thanks, and looked out over the white sand of the beach and the blue Caribbean water. The view was stunning from the deck of the Presidential Oceanfront Suite he had rented for the month. At five thousand dollars a night and with ten thousand square feet of pure luxury, he doubted his pursuers would think to look for him hiding in the open among the world's elite travelers.

Barak was used to luxury, at least for the last fifteen years or so. But he still felt guilty for living like a king. He had committed himself to a warrior's life at an early age after watching his father gunned down by Jews in Egypt. His father had worked with the Grand Mufti of Jerusalem to liquidate the Jews on behalf of Adolf Hitler. When that war was over, the Jews had found them living under the protection of Gamal Abdul Nasser. At the age of four, young Barak had witnessed his father being beaten and killed in the street in front of their house by a team of Jew assassins. And he had vowed that day, and each night thereafter in his evening prayers, to become just like the young Jews: a merciless assassin killing his enemy.

The message was from a man who called himself Ryan and was his current liaison with the Aryan organization operating out of South America. For a fee, the Alliance, as it called itself, coordinated the enterprise of the drug cartels with the goals of the Islamic worldwide jihad. The Alliance also supplied its clients around the world with armament and materiel.

Not often like the armament Barak had recently ordered, however. He needed a Soviet tactical, nuclear, demolition device. It was designed to be carried in a special backpack by one man. This particular device, which had gone missing after the breakup of the Soviet Union, had been purchased by the Alliance from an element of the Iranian Revolutionary Guard. Iran had been eager to find someone who would use it against America, and Barak was chosen to be that someone. He had a plan that would make the death toll from the Twin Towers look insignificant in comparison. Ryan was bringing him the details of the nuke's voyage to America.

Barak opened the envelope and read the note, which was nothing more than a telephone number for the Intercontinental in Cozumel and Ryan's room number. Barak opened his cell phone to call his contact.

"Hello, Ryan, welcome to the Riviera Maya. I won't be able to meet you today. I suggest you take the nine a.m. UltraMar ferry tomorrow and go see the wonderful walled city of Tulum. When you return, call me and we'll arrange to meet."

"I did not come all this way to see a ruin."

"And," Barak replied, "I did not arrange for you to come all this way so that I could be found by our friends. Make the trip, have a good time, and prove to me that all will be well for us to meet here in Mexico."

"As you wish."

Barak closed his phone, smiling at the annoyance he'd

heard in Ryan's voice. The last time they had met, he (Barak) had been the one summoned to Aruba to receive orders from his Muslim Brotherhood sponsors. The Brotherhood had guided his early career in terrorism, loaned him the money to start his security firm in Las Vegas, and suggested the assassination plot to kill the Secretary of Homeland Security. Barak had understood their need to use a courier to bring him instructions, but he resented Ryan's condescending tone. The Nazis had used the Arabs as their servants in the Middle East to carry out Hitler's commands, but the Nazi progeny seemed to forget they were the servants now.

"Jamal," he called out to his bodyguard, "bring a bottle of Scotch and some ice. Let's discuss your trip to Tulum tomorrow before we have dinner. I'm going for a quick swim."

Barak learned to swim at an early age. Now, at sixty five, he swam whenever he had the chance, especially when it was in the ocean. Walking back across the warm white sand after an invigorating fifteen minutes in the Caribbean, he saw that Jamal had a towel waiting for him on his deck chair and ice in a crystal tumbler on the table beside it.

"Ryan will arrive at Playa Del Carmen ferry terminal at ten a.m. tomorrow," Barak said as he dried off. "Follow him to the ruins and see if anyone is following him. Alliance men are careful, but their enemies are everywhere. It would be ironic, to say the least, if he led the Israelis to us after all these years."

Lowering himself into the deck chair, he inhaled the aroma of citrus and ripening peach from the ten-year-old Glenmorangie Scotch Jamal had poured for him.

"What do you want me to do if he's being followed?" the bodyguard asked.

"Nothing tomorrow. If he's being followed, I'll arrange a meeting with him that will end any trail back to us. Now call the restaurant and have them send over a grilled grouper dinner with a side of garlic shrimp for me and order whatever you want. The possibility of a little action is making me hungry."

As his bodyguard went inside to order their dinners, Barak sipped his scotch. If his Alliance contact was clean, he would soon know if he possessed a weapon that would cripple America.

Chapter Five

THE FLIGHT FROM OREGON TO COZUMEL IN THE GULFSTREAM G280 Casey had borrowed from his company took them less than six and a half hours flying. They landed at the Cozumel International Airport at sunrise and took a hotel van to the InterContinental Cozumel as soon as they cleared customs. The Yucatan Peninsula and the Mayakoba Resort were just twelve miles across the Cozumel Strait.

As they entered the lobby of the five star hotel, Drake pulled his friend aside. "I checked the ferry schedule on my iPhone while we were in the van," he said. "There's a ferry over to the Playa Del Carmen terminal that leaves at nine a.m. I'd like to be on it. Why don't we get checked in and meet in the restaurant for breakfast?"

"Great. My stomach needs attention. I'll let the guys know."

"Your stomach always needs attention," Drake said.

Like a lot of tall, thin men, Casey's metabolism allowed him to eat whatever and whenever he wanted. Lying in a sniper's hideout for days on end had been hell for him, and he'd been making up for it since leaving the army.

Drake put the three pool-view rooms his secretary had

reserved for him on his credit card and gave Casey the room keys for his team. The rooms weren't the most expensive in the hotel, but he knew they'd be more than adequate for men accustomed to far less. He didn't plan on being in them that much, anyway. If they found Barak, this would be over in a matter of days, if not hours.

Twenty minutes later, six men sat a table looking out over the Cozumel Strait. In the custom of men who didn't know when they might eat again, each man had a plate piled high from the breakfast buffet.

As soon as their waiter had filled their coffee cups and left, Drake began his briefing.

"The only information we have is that Barak's bodyguard was seen in Cancun. He was followed to a resort south of there. Each of you has a picture of Jamal James on your iPhone. It's from DHS, taken in the Las Vegas airport some time ago. Not the best, but you'll recognize him. At his size, he'll be hard to miss.

"When we get off the ferry," he continued, "I'll meet with the DEA agent who spotted Jamal. He may have some new information I haven't heard about, but if he doesn't, he'll lead us to the resort. Then we're on our own. Captain Gonzales will then have the honor of finding someone we can bribe and learn where Barak is staying."

Roberto Gonzales, a former Green Beret, had been born in Mexico and had the sharp features that showed his Aztec ancestry. Taking advantage of his perpetual smile that women loved, it would take him less time to find a maid and locate their target than it would take the team to drive around the large resort once.

"Dangerous duty," Gonzales said, smiling, "that I will take delight in. Gracias."

"I asked Steve, our pilot, to meet us at the ferry terminal," Drake said. "He'll have a fanny pack for each of you with a Glock 21, a clip holster, and two mags. The 21s are used by the Mexican Army, so ditch them if you have to. Guns are allowed down here, as you no doubt know. We have no information about what support Barak has, so be careful. Our story, if we're questioned, is that we're here for sailfish and marlin and seeing the ruins."

Their waiter reappeared and refilled their coffee cups, giving Casey the time he needed to make a second trip to the buffet. When he returned, he had a question.

"Should I make arrangements to fly Barak out of the country after we find him?"

"DHS would like to take him to Gitmo. I personally don't think he'll let us take him alive, though, so I'm not worrying about it. His choice, not ours. When we leave the ferry, we'll split up in three teams. Decide among yourselves who you'll work with.

Meet in the lobby in five and we'll leave for the ferry."

Drake signed for their breakfast, and Casey left to arrange transportation. As he walked through the lobby trailing the others, his phone vibrated. He saw that Liz Strobel was calling.

"When do you want to meet the man I told you about?" she asked.

"How did you know I was here?"

"Come on, Drake. I knew when you were wheels up in Oregon. This is your government you're talking to."

"Right. Okay, we're taking the nine a.m. ferry from Cozumel to the Mayan Riviera. Can he meet us there?"

"No problem. He knows what you look like, he'll find you. You need anything?"

"If things go wrong, you can get us out of jail. I understand they don't have TV and WiFi in Mexican jails."

"Then make sure things don't go wrong, 'cause if they do, you're on your own," she said. "That's what you wanted."

"Lighten up, Liz. We know what we're doing, nothing's going to go wrong. I'll call when I know more."

Ending the call, he joined the others getting into a tour bus to the Mayan ruins. He had been on enough missions to know that things never went as planned, but he also knew that Liz had been right to remind him of the stakes. Mexico was sick of the cartels' violence. If six Americans were caught adding to the mayhem, they'd be lucky to ever get out of jail.

The team filled up six seats in the rear of the bus, while couples and a few families took up the rest. It wasn't hot outside, at least not yet, but the driver had the air conditioning on in anticipation of another hot and humid day.

The nine o'clock ferry was a sleek mini-cruise ship that carried 550 passengers to and from Cozumel six times every day. Drake signaled to Casey to lead the way to the upper deck, where they could enjoy the fresh sea air and a little privacy, as most of the other passengers stayed below to enjoy the video showing highlights of the ancient city of Tulum and the surrounding ruins.

When the ferry docked, Drake led his team into the terminal. Groups were forming around tour guides holding signs, and his men spread out to blend in. Gonzalez made his way over to a young woman seated at the information kiosk to find out about transportation to the Mayakoba resort.

"Interest you in a guide for the ruins, Mr. Drake?" a tall red-headed man in a lime green *guayabera* shirt, shorts, and hiking boots asked.

"Actually," Drake replied, "I was hoping to find a friend of a friend here."

"And that friend would be a lady, first name Liz?"

Drake reached out and shook the DEA agent's hand. "Adam Drake, and you are?"

"Randy Johnson. My orders are to help you find the bodyguard, but I'm afraid that won't be necessary."

"Don't tell me they've left already."

"No, sir. What I meant was, he's standing right over there. Large black man with sunglasses. Reading the brochure."

Drake glanced over at the bodyguard. No question, it was Jamal James. "Is he alone?"

"He came in alone. He's been wandering around. Probably waiting for the ferry to arrive."

"Any idea who he's waiting for?"

"No, sir."

"This place you followed him to, the Mayakoba. Were you able to locate which unit he was staying in?"

"I didn't try," Johnson said. "It's a very exclusive resort and spa. I figured they'd be pretty tight lipped about their guests. I didn't want to let them know we knew they were here."

Drake caught Casey's eye and signaled to him to join them.

"Mike," he said, "this is Agent Johnson and that," his eyes went to the bodyguard, "is the man we're here to follow. Let the others know. And make sure we have tickets for whatever tour he's on, if that's what he's doing here."

"Roger that. This is almost too easy, finding him waiting for us."

Casey walked over to the information kiosk and told Gonzalez to position the others.

"Agent Johnson," Drake said, "thank you. We wouldn't be here without your keen eyes spotting him. We'll take it from here. How do I reach you if I need to?"

"My number's on the back of this Mayakoba brochure. Thought you might need it." Johnson touched two fingers to his temple in a quick salute and walked away.

Drake focused his attention on the man he hoped would lead them to their target.

Chapter Six

For the next two hours, Drake's team followed the big bodyguard to and around the Pre-Columbian Mayan city of Tulum. Driving a black Range Rover, Jamal had followed the string of tour buses and taxis along the coastal road south to the walled city. The team watched him walk along the massive wall that had protected the city on three sides, then visit the two remaining temples and the castle, El Castillo, perched on the tall cliffs over the beach. Built like a fortress, the ancient city had also been a trading post for the Mayans, with the highest building serving as a lighthouse for merchants arriving by canoe.

Less than an hour after arriving, the bodyguard walked swiftly back to the parking area and drove off. Drake and the team had to scramble to follow him.

"What was that all about?" Casey asked as he and Drake climbed into the back of a taxi. "The only thing he seemed interested in was following that tour group around. You know, I thought the place was pretty amazing."

"The big guy didn't seem to think so." Drake looked at the taxi driver's ID, which was hanging from his rearview mirror.

"Victor, if you keep that black Range Rover in sight, I'll double your fee for the day."

Victor met his passenger's eyes in the rear view mirror and smiled. "I still have time for another tour or two today. How about you hire me for the day and I will make sure he doesn't know you are following him?"

Drake returned his smile. "How much?"

"Three hundred dollars."

"Two hundred, and I won't tell your wife about the young woman you were flirting with at the souvenir stand."

"Two-fifty, señor. That was my sister." Victor laughed, then said, "Are you interested in a date?"

It was Drake's turn to laugh. "Two-fifty it is, for you, and two for the other two drivers. I haven't seen their sisters."

Fifty minutes later they were back at the ferry terminal in time to see the bodyguard park the Range Rover and hurry inside.

"Victor, I don't know where this guy's going. Stay here and wait for us."

When they got inside, Drake moved to the one side of the terminal waiting area and Casey covered the other. Their man was standing next to the rack of tour brochures, again looking like he was trying to decide which tour he was going to take. As the line for the ferry returning to Cozumel began boarding, he dropped the brochure he was holding back in the rack and stared at the last of the tourists boarding until the gate to the ferry was closed. When no one came back though the gate when the ferry pulled away, he walked back to his Range Rover and drove off.

Victor had the motor running with both rear doors open when they walked out.

"Follow the Range Rover?"

"Follow the Range Rover." Drake turned to Casey. "Mike, he's driving north toward that resort the DEA agent mentioned. If Barak's there, let's end this now."

For the next twelve minutes, Drake and his team in three taxis drove north on Highway 307 until they saw the Range Rover turn right toward the beach and the five diamond Mayakoba Resort and Spa. As they pulled up in front of the reception area, they saw a valet at his post in front of the lobby.

Drake told his driver to have the valet allow them to park their taxis and wait with the other drivers until they returned. He then gathered his men around him.

"We're here for lunch and a tour of this resort," he told them. "If we're asked, Mike's company is thinking of hosting a conference here. Gonzalez, go find a young señorita and find out where the bodyguard is staying. Mike will see about a tour, and when we've looked around, we'll meet up for lunch at one of the restaurants. Any questions?"

"What do you want to do if we spot them before lunch?" Casey asked.

"We've got to do this without attracting attention, so wait until we go over a plan. We're on our own here, and I, for one, don't want to spend time in some Mexican jail. You've all worked undercover, so you know how to do this. Let's do it."

Drake followed Casey into the lobby and walked past him to look out over the lagoon. A canopied gondola motored quietly toward a small island in the middle of the lagoon and electric carts moved along paths between the luxury lagoon suites. If Barak was here, he thought, he was hiding among the world's affluent, judging from the French, German, Russian, and Spanish conversations he could hear behind him in the lobby.

After a few minutes, Drake returned to the three men from Casey's team. "You guys ought to see if Mike can arrange a little R&R for you here."

Billy Montgomery, a former Army Ranger, grinned. "My dad used to have brochures for places like this in his office. He's comfortably retired from his Wall Street firm now, but I don't think he would spend this much on a vacation. This is some resort!"

Lawrence Green, a stocky, black cop from L.A. with a master's degree in criminology from USC, shook his head. "Only guys I know who live like this are the ones who make their money illegally. Like Wall Street, I guess." He stepped back before Montgomery had a chance to respond.

"Okay," said Drake, "if we're right about Barak, he should fit right in. He's somehow involved with drugs and the Mexican cartels. That's one reason to be very careful here. He probably has plenty of protection available."

Casey walked toward them with a smiling young Mexican woman at his side.

"Gentlemen," he said, "please meet our hostess, Angelina, who will show us her wonderful resort and conference facilities. After our tour, she has offered to buy our lunch at her restaurant down on the beach if we'll consider the Mayakoba for the company retreat. Let's go take a look."

For the next hour, Angelina led them through the conference rooms, the spa on an island in the middle of the lagoon, a raw bar and tequila library, and resort shops that were the equal of any on Rodeo Drive in Los Angeles. She ended the tour at a beachside restaurant located on a mile of white sand beach.

"Señores, please enjoy your lunch," she said, still smiling, "and order anything you like. When you leave, Mr. Casey, I will have the information for you at the front desk about arranging your conference. It has been a pleasure to assist you today." She gave a tiny curtsy and left them to be seated near the windows overlooking the beach.

Drake grinned. "Mike, I'm sure your men think you should bring them back for some R&R."

"Bring them back, hell, I don't want to leave! You get DHS to cover my costs, and I'm in."

"Anyone seen Gonzalez?"

"Relax," Casey said. "I'll call him and let him know where we are. It's been four hours since we had breakfast, can we eat now?"

"Unbelievable! We're about to go active, and all you can think about is eating."

"Some men face danger and think about sex. I don't like to mix business with pleasure, so I focus on keeping my lean machine fueled and ready. Shall I call our waiter?"

"Wait," Drake replied. "Gonzalez just walked in. Let's hear what he's got first."

The former Green Beret pulled out a chair and sat down, then opened a map of the resort.

"Despite the danger of my assignment," he began, "I was able to learn that our bodyguard has been seen coming and going from the presidential suite right down the beach from here. It's the last one in the row of beachfront suites. The golf course is on one side," he laid a finger on the map, "here, with some trees providing a little cover. Access from the beach also has some tree cover, but it's open to the suite next to it. Cart paths link all the suites."

"Are there others in the suite besides the bodyguard?"

"She didn't know, but she has taken a cart away from this restaurant with plates and utensils for two."

"What about gardeners, maintenance workers, other people around?"

"She said the landscape crew works in the early morning so no one will be disturbed. She didn't know about anyone else being around on a regular basis."

"Hmm. This looks too easy. Mike, what am I missing?"

Casey looked at the map again. "Other than people who might be around, I don't know. There are no high places to use for observation. This place is as flat as a tortilla. He can retreat to the beach, but we can have someone there. There aren't any roads he can use, only the cart paths."

"So…wait for dark or go now?"

"I'm not sure it'll make much difference. Unless you want to wait until three or four in the morning. We could see if there are a couple of rooms we could book, but without any luggage, it'll look suspicious."

Drake made his decision. "That's too much time. Here's what we'll do. Mike and I will approach from here in one of those electric carts. Montgomery, you look like a golfer. Take Green and rent a golf cart. Tour the course. Get in position close to the suite. We can use the golf cart to exfil with Barak. Gonzalez and Richards, you two will take a stroll down the beach and approach from that direction. We'll go in one hour. If we need to separate, find your way back to Cozumel and the hotel. Fall back is the airport and Mike's plane."

"Can I order now?" Casey asked.

Chapter Seven

It was the middle of the afternoon, and the sun shimmered on the blue Caribbean Sea. David Barak was standing and watching a large white yacht in the distance motoring toward Cozumel. He'd been thinking about buying something like a yacht and making it his floating headquarter in the Caribbean. Expensive but private, a yacht could provide the margin of safety he'd need if the Americans kept looking for him. Hiding in Mexico certainly wasn't what he had in mind for the reward he would give himself as soon as he completed his next mission. The Mayakoba resort was nice, he had to admit, but he deserved more. There was no way he was going to end up like bin Laden, isolated in a grubby villa, cut off from the world. His sponsors might think the "true way" was to live like a nomad roaming around in the desert, but refusing the advantages the modern world offered didn't make any sense to him.

His cell phone came to life with the sound of a Ferrari driving by at speed. He opened it and heard a voice.

"I'm not being watched, but you are."

"What are you talking about, Ryan?"

"I spotted your bodyguard as soon as I got off the ferry,"

said Ryan, "as well as the surveillance team that followed us both to Tulum and back. They weren't watching me. They were watching him. Leave now. Use the number I gave you earlier and tell them to get you out of there. And erase everything."

"Ryan," Barak replied, "I don't need your advice. This wouldn't have happened if you hadn't insisted on meeting."

The line went dead.

"Jamal," he yelled. "Get in here."

His faithful servant ran in, a startled look on his face. He had never been yelled at before.

"What did you do?" Barak asked. "Ryan just called and said you were followed."

"Malik, I did as you told me. There was no one following Ryan. I didn't see anyone following me. You trained me well. I did not fail you. Maybe Ryan is angry because you made him go to Tulum."

Barak shook his head. "I can't take a chance that he's wrong. Download everything on my laptop, then run the incinerator program. I'll call for a ride out of here."

But he waited until his bodyguard had left the room before he called the number Ryan had provided. As faithful as Jamal was, he wasn't in Ryan's league and most likely had been followed. The problem was to escape and make sure Jamal was no longer a risk.

"This is Barak," he said into his phone. "Emergency, extraction now, beach off the Mayakoba."

The call ended, he went into the master bedroom and changed into black swimming trunks picked up his waterproof fanny pack. When he returned to the living room, he found Jamal waiting.

"Your laptop is clean," the bodyguard said. "Here's your thumb drive. What do you want me to do next?"

"You know what I must ask of you, Jamal. You have been beside me all these years, and you know I cannot be captured.

What we have planned must be completed. Tens of thousands will die soon. Because of your sacrifice, you will always be remembered as a martyr. Let no one get by you. If no one comes and Ryan is wrong, call my number and I'll get you out of here. Are you willing to do this for me, my friend?"

"You know that I am, but Ryan is wrong, I promise you."

"I believe you. But this must be good bye for now. Guard the front. I must go."

As Jamal turned and started toward the foyer of the large suite, Barak took his silenced Sig Sauer P226 out of his fanny pack and shot him twice in the back of his head.

"Sorry, old friend, but I think Ryan is right. You were followed."

When he was sure there was nothing in the suite that would lead anyone to him or compromise his plans, he threw a towel around his shoulders and walked out the door.

On the beach, he saw a few couples walking along the water line and several parents watching their children playing in the white sand, but otherwise the area looked safe. He walked to the edge of the trees lining the beach and sat in the shade. If they knew where he was staying, he knew they wouldn't leave the beach open to him. He looked up and down the beach, but saw no enemies approaching. Then he shaded his eyes from the afternoon sun and looked for a signal from his rescuer on the horizon.

Despite the humiliation he knew he would experience if Ryan was right and his man had been followed, at the moment Barak felt only anger. No one but Ryan and the Alliance knew he was in Mexico. Until Ryan had called and said they needed to meet, Jamal had never left the resort. If it turned out that Ryan was responsible for Jamal being followed, he swore that one day he would kill him in exchange for Jamal's life.

When he opened his eyes after a quick prayer for his friend entering paradise, he saw two men walking along the beach from the direction of the Las Brisas restaurant. The shorter of the two looked Mexican, the taller, American. Both were walking more like soldiers than tourists, alert and looking in the direction of his suite without a glance at the blue water.

Barak slowly stood up and walked casually toward the water line. When he felt the surf starting to swirl around his calves, he took three running steps and dove into the first wave high enough to allow him to swim freely. Surfacing, he swam steadily until he was beyond the breaking waves. He kept swimming. From the beach, he was sure, he looked like just another swimmer exercising in the sea.

A hundred yards out, he turned and began treading water so he could watch the two men on the beach. If they had noticed him, they weren't paying any attention to him now. One had stopped and was sitting in the sand near the tree line, twenty yards from the deck of his suite. The other had gone another twenty yards beyond. Another five minutes, Barak thought, and he would have walked right between them.

He turned and swam another fifty yards, then turned toward the beach again. The two men hadn't moved from their positions. Yes, he said to himself, they were waiting for him, or maybe waiting for a signal to rush his suite. It was the way he would have done it. Whoever they were, they were good. He would have to learn more about his hunters, for surely he would face them again.

He heard the approaching roar of a fast boat. When it had pulled alongside and he'd climbed up the ladder that had been lowered to him, he looked again at the two men on the beach. They weren't looking his way.

Chapter Eight

WITH THE TEAM IN POSITION, DRAKE DROVE AN ELECTRIC golf cart down the path toward the presidential suite. Casey, riding shotgun, used their secure personal radios to alert the others that they were moving in. The in-ear tactical headsets with speaker and bone conduction microphones made them, he thought with a silent laugh, look like Secret Service agents protecting the President.

They saw no one outside guarding the suite.

"Gonzalez," Drake asked, "you see anyone on the beach side?"

"Not from here."

"Montgomery, anyone on your side?"

"We're sitting just off the green on 15. Can't see anyone."

"All right, enter on my command."

He stopped the cart on the turnabout in front of the suite and walked to the main entrance. With Casey standing to the left of the massive, carved front door, he took his Glock from the belt clip at his back and rang the doorbell.

After ten seconds and no response, he tried the door. It was unlocked. With a nod to Casey, he gave the command.

"Go."

He pushed open the door and moved quickly to the right of the foyer as Casey moved to the left. Moving forward together, they cleared the media room to the right and then the elaborate bar and game room to the left. The only sound they heard was footsteps running across the terrace.

Drake saw it first, the blood and brain matter on the mahogany floor leading into the main room of the suite. It was Barak's bodyguard, lying face down on the floor.

"The bodyguard's dead," Drake said into his radio. Make sure Barak isn't hiding somewhere in here. Then we'll meet in the main room."

To get so close and fail made Drake coldly furious. They had been lucky to get this close, he knew, but with Barak on the run again, they might not get another chance at him.

"Mike," he said, "how'd he know we were coming? Where did we screw up?"

Casey shrugged his shoulders. "We may never know. Maybe the bodyguard spotted us at some point. Maybe some gardener was a lookout. Remember the goat herders in Afghanistan?"

Drake nodded and said, "If the bodyguard spotted us, he did a hell of a job not letting on. Damn it, anyway. Let's make sure there's no sign we've been here and get back to Cozumel." With a brief curse, he added, "I might as well let DHS know we missed him."

Driving the cart back to the resort's parking lot, Drake called Liz Strobel at DHS.

"We missed him, Liz. We found his bodyguard dead. Two bullets in the back of the head. Body still warm. He had to have been tipped off somehow."

"Did you get out clean?"

"We're leaving the resort now. We're clean."

"The Secretary will be glad to hear it," she said. "How long ago do you think he slipped out?"

"Why?" Drake asked.

"I needed to make sure there were no repercussions. I bought satellite images of Cancun and the Mayan Riviera from a private space firm so no one else in the government would know what you were up to. Give me an approximate time he might have left, and I'll see what we can learn."

"We arrived in Cozumel this morning at 0630 and took a ferry to Playa Del Carmen at 0900. I don't think there's much of a chance he could have known we were here before this morning. You didn't tell me about the lead until yesterday."

"All right," she said. "I'll check the images for that period and call you back. What will you do now?"

"We're heading back to Cozumel. We'll regroup. I'll wait for your call. Good luck and thanks." He ended the call.

"What did she say?" Casey asked.

"She's checking satellite imagery to see if she can find out how Barak eluded us. You have to give her credit for that. Probably more CYA than tactical foresight, but getting satellite imagery was a good move. Why don't you head back to the lobby and pick up your conference stuff at the front desk. I'll round up our rides. No use letting them think we were just here for a free lunch."

"Speaking of lunch…."

"Do not go there."

Drake parked his cart in the lot and led the three taxis back to the lobby, where Casey was tipping the valet and waiting with the others.

"Let's vamoose," he said. "I think they just found the bodyguard, if *hombre muerto* means what I think it means. They're calling the *policia* as we speak."

"Anyone suspicious?" Drake asked quietly.

"The conversation I overheard behind the front desk included the word 'cartel,' so they're probably thinking it's drug related. I didn't stick around to ask."

Drake signaled the other men to load up, and soon they were back on Highway 307, heading south to the ferry terminal. As he stared out the window of his taxi, he thought about what Casey had said about Afghanistan. More than once, after days of surveillance from a nearby hillside, they had approached a target they knew was hiding in a village of mud brick dwellings only to find the man wasn't there. How he'd been smuggled out, or perhaps slipped out through a tunnel they didn't know about, they had never learned. Most likely, as his friend had reminded him, someone had reported their presence in time for their target to escape.

This time, though, no one at the resort knew who they were. Even if Barak had been tipped off, how had he left without them seeing him? Assuming Barak had shot the bodyguard, he might have already been gone before they surrounded his suite. No one had seen him, however, so maybe the bodyguard had been alone and his murder wasn't even connected to Barak.

The bodyguard had to be the key. Drake remembered that when he first saw him at the ferry terminal, he had been looking at brochures for excursions to the ruins at Tulum. If he was staying at the Mayakoba, he asked himself, why wouldn't he have booked his tour from there instead of driving to the ferry terminal?

Because he was waiting for someone on the ferry.

"Mike, when we saw the bodyguard at the ferry terminal, do you think he spotted us?"

"He never looked at me that I remember. He was reading a brochure and then, as the rest of us were getting on buses or in taxis, he got in his Range Rover and followed one of the buses. I don't think he was paying any attention to us."

"He wasn't interested in us or seeing the ruins. Remember how he walked around, following that tour group? He wasn't there for the tour. He was following someone. He was at the terminal waiting for the ferry from Cozumel."

"I didn't see him talking with anyone."

"Maybe he was doing the same thing we were, just following someone."

"That still doesn't explain how Barak knew we were coming."

"The guy he was following," they said at the same time.

"He could have been the one who spotted us and tipped off Barak," Drake said. "If he's the one, he's the only link we have to Barak. If we can access the security cameras I saw at the terminal, we might find out who the bodyguard was waiting for."

"It's worth a try," said Casey. "You can buy your tickets for the ferry online, so I should be able to hack into the system when we get back to the hotel. But that still won't tell us where Barak is now."

"Maybe not. But it might give us someone who can lead us to him. That's all we have right now."

Chapter Nine

Barak was alone in the well appointed cabin of a Gulfstream G450 flying to Tijuana. The jet was owned by Mexico's most powerful cartel, as was the black cigarette boat that had picked him up in the blue waters off the beach at the resort.

For the first time, he felt his life was out of control. When he was running his international security firm in Las Vegas, he had developed a private army of assassins that he kept hidden among the company's other employees. No one had ever ordered him around the way Ryan and the Alliance were doing now. The Brotherhood, which sponsored him, had left him alone to carry out their plan to assassinate American and other world leaders. They had trusted him.

But he wasn't sure they still trusted him.

Now he was being told what to do and when to do it. He knew he was being tested, but he could not let that knowledge interfere with his plan to use the demolition nuke in America. That would put an end to the humiliation of his current order to serve as a subcontracted assassin for Hezbollah in Tijuana.

He knew that Hezbollah had established a base in Tijuana and was doing some of the heavy lifting for the Tijuana cartel.

Many of the two thousand murders in the last two years were the work of Hezbollah assassins, which was precisely why he was uneasy with the order to step in for them now. He was going to have to be very careful in the next few days.

The Gulfstream began its descent through the polluted clouds to the Tijuana International Airport, located just three hundred meters south of the U.S.-Mexico border. It taxied to the general aviation terminal and stopped in front of an idling black Mercedes S600.

Barak waited for the exit door to be opened for him, then walked alone to the Mercedes. The rear door was held open by a young Mexican with a pearl handled .45 stuck in the front of his jeans. Barak got in and found that he was alone in what he realized was an armored vehicle. He should have expected that a cartel flying its own Gulfstream around Mexico wouldn't be driving anything less than the safest car in the world, next to the armored Cadillac the American President used. The cartel moved two thirds of the drugs smuggled into the U.S. and had operations in fifty-two countries around the world. It could well afford the best.

After the Mercedes was waved through a gate guarded by two soldiers, the driver said over his shoulder, "Señor, we have an hour's drive to the villa. There is Scotch in the bar and a basket of tapas."

Leaning forward, Barak opened the panel of the bar and found a crystal tumbler, a bottle of Glenmorangie Scotch (his favorite), and a plate of tapas on ice. As they drove through Tijuana's squalid streets, he savored an olive that reminded him of his boyhood in Egypt and poured two fingers of scotch in the tumbler. He was used to luxury, but it was always nice to be treated with respect.

Most of the drive south and east passed in silence. When they reached the Guadalupe Valley and the Mexican wine country, Barak saw that the paved road they were traveling was lined with vineyards, olive orchards, and small farms.

"Most people don't know we make fine wine," the driver said proudly. "They think only of tequila and cerveza. You will taste our fine wines when you drink tonight at the villa."

"Are we close?" Barak asked.

"See the lights on that hilltop?" The driver pointed to his left. "That is where you are going."

Barak looked out at the lights of an arched veranda that ran along the front of a two-story villa. Small floodlights lined the driveway and illuminated a vineyard on one side and an olive orchard on the other. Two black Cadillac Escalades were parked in front of the villa. As they drew nearer, he saw that the villa was guarded by men wearing paramilitary dress and carrying AK-9s, the new Kalashnikov assault weapon. He counted ten men on the drive up and could see more moving in the shadows around the villa. Whoever he was meeting wasn't taking any chances with his personal safety.

The driver stopped in front of a gravel terraced walkway lined with blooming lavender. With a flourish, a young man approached and opened the rear door of the Mercedes.

"Come, señor, I will show you the way."

Barak stretched for a moment, enjoying the fragrance of the warm evening, before he followed the young man up the steps. The villa, he saw, was magnificent with adobe and flagstone walls and a red tile roof. The veranda was lined with potted cacti. Three men were seated at a table in the middle of the veranda.

"Thank you, Manolito," the shortest of the three men said. "You may go. He turned to Barak.

"Come, join us," he said. He nodded to one of his comrades. "This is Jesus, the head of our armed wing. This is Saleem, our friend from Hezbollah. I am Felipe Calderon. Please have a seat."

Barak sat, facing the three men. Jesus, he knew, was the enforcer for the cartel and a former member of Mexico's elite commandos that had been trained to fight the cartels.

According to information he'd received from Ryan and the Alliance, Saleem was the head of Hezbollah in Tijuana. Felipe Calderon was the top lieutenant for the cartel and reported directly to its leader, a man known as El Verdugo, the Executioner.

"I understand, Señor Calderon," Barak said, "that you have requested my services. May I ask why?" He paused. "Surely Jesus is capable of carrying out your desires."

Calderon gave a thin smile. "Thank you for recognizing that," he said, "but this time Jesus and his men must not be involved. Do you know about the little war that has been going on here in Tijuana with our rival for the last several years?"

"I do."

"Then you know they blame us for the arrests of their leader, the Architect, and his top lieutenant. Which we deny, of course. What you do not know, because we have just learned this, is they have borrowed commandos from our main competition to the east. They plan to kill El Verdugo and as many of the rest of us as they can. We want you to put a stop to this."

Barak nodded. "And how do I do that?"

"We know that Ramon Guerrero, the brother of the Architect, and Antonio Mendoza, the borrowed commando from the east, will be having lunch on the day after tomorrow at the Cien Años restaurant in Tijuana. It's Ramon's birthday. He wants a proper celebration. You will make it his last celebration. His last birthday."

"How am I to do this for you?" Barak asked, wanting to know the cartel's expectations.

"You are the master *assassino*, Señor. That is for you to figure out. Use the assassins you have trained. If there are casualties, they cannot be traced back to us. We do not want to start a war with our competitors to the east."

Barak gave this some thought. "In return, I understand you will help me get my merchandise across the border."

"If you are successful, we will help you. That is why Saleem is here. Our business is feeding the American appetite for our drugs, not killing the Americans. That's what you and Saleem want to do. It would be very bad for us if America learned that we helped you with your 'merchandise.'"

"Then we have a deal."

Calderon nodded. "Now let us drink a little tequila. Then you will eat with us, the finest food, and drink some Mexican wine, also the finest. Then you will get to work."

Chapter Ten

DRAKE WAS STEPPING OUT OF THE SHOWER WHEN HIS PHONE started vibrating on the tile counter. *Caller unknown*, he saw, but he recognized the prefix.

"Hi, Liz. Got anything?"

"What happened to hello, how are you, and all that?"

"You mean foreplay? I don't have time. I just stepped out of the shower."

"Gee, I hope the innuendo was accidental."

He smiled at the phone. "Hello, Liz, how are you, thanks for everything, got anything for me?"

"Better. Your man was picked up in a boat about a hundred yards off shore. Just before you guys went in. He knew you were coming."

"He was swimming out there? Watching us the whole time?"

"That's what the satellite images show. They dropped him off in Cancun and then he was driven to the airport. We can't tell which plane he left on, or if he left at all. Our guess is that he flew out not long after he was picked up."

"We may have a lead you can help us with." Drake said. "We think his bodyguard was following someone he was waiting for at the ferry terminal. While we were following the bodyguard, this someone must have spotted us and called Barak. Mike is searching the surveillance videos from the ferry terminal to see if we can identify him. If we can, you might be able to listen in if he calls Barak."

"You mean ask the NSA for a little Echelon help?" she asked.

"Barak's a threat to our security. He's also involved with the cartels. They should jump at the chance to help."

Drake knew that the global network of computers operated by the five signatory countries of the surveillance agreement —Australia, Canada, New Zealand, the United Kingdom, and the United States—were able to intercept communications anywhere in the world. The system, which allowed governments to monitor citizens and their communications, was controversial. It was very, very effective.

"I'll see what I can do," Liz replied. "Go dry yourself and call me if you ID the guy."

Drake considered her reaction to his use of the word "foreplay" and smiled. Was she flirting with him? He dressed and left to join Casey in his room. It felt strange to think about someone being interested in him, or even noticing it, just a year after he'd lost his wife to cancer.

"Hey, Mike, you want another Dos Equis?"

"Sure. And grab one for yourself. I need another pair of eyes on this security video."

"You got in."

"Did you think I wouldn't?"

"I've never questioned your skill. I just didn't think you could do it this quickly."

Drake fetched their beers and sat down next to his friend. Casey was searching the video one frame at a time. The big bodyguard was standing with his back to the wall reading one of the excursion brochures. In front of him, people were getting off the ferry.

They could see most of the main floor of the terminal on the glare-free screen of Casey's laptop. Casey pointed. "He stands there like that until this group comes off the ferry. This guy, the blond with the sunglasses, blue polo shirt and the linen pants is the only single in the group," he pointed, "but the bodyguard doesn't seem to notice him until," he advanced the frames, "right now. See? He looks down at his cell phone, then he looks right at the guy's face. He's making sure this is his guy. Watch. From then on, he keeps the guy in sight until he walks out with this tour group and leaves for his Range Rover."

"Go back and run it again."

Drake watched the sequence two more times, then slapped his partner on the back.

"Mike, that's our guy. He's right here at the InterContinental. I noticed him on the bus we took from the lobby to the ferry terminal this morning."

"There are two hundred and twenty rooms here," Casey said. "We don't know if he's still here. How do we find him?"

Drake smiled. "You think Gonzalez could find another cooperative maid?"

Casey touched the neck of his bottle to Drake's. "We don't want to wear the lad out, but why not give him the chance?"

After Casey left to meet with Gonzalez, Drake called Liz back.

"Hello, Liz, how are you and thanks for everything."

"Smart ass. Got anything for me?"

"Mike came up with the guy on the security video from the ferry terminal. We think he's staying right here, and we're looking for him right now. If he's here, what do you need to get a fix on him?"

"If you find him, get someone close to him with one of your cell phones. We'll track both phones from that point on."

"Uh, that might be a problem. If he's the one that spotted us following the bodyguard, he knows what we look like."

"Do you have anyone there he won't know?"

"We have a pilot that wasn't with us."

"Use him. Just let me know which cell phone he'll be carrying at least fifteen minutes ahead of time."

"Thanks, Liz. Wish us luck?"

Drake hung up and called their pilot, who had stayed with the plane, and asked him to join them for dinner poolside in an hour. Then he left to see how Gonzalez was doing. He found Casey talking with their Latin Romeo in the hallway.

Casey turned to him and grinned. "Gonzalez has scored again, figuratively speaking. Our man has an ocean suite on the fifth floor. He registered in the name Sven Johannsen. From Denmark. He's up there now, but he's checking out tomorrow."

"That was fast. Good work, Ricardo. I invited our pilot to join us for dinner. We'll use him to get close to Mr. Johannsen. Do we risk being seen together?"

"And pass up a great dinner while we're here?" Casey sounded almost indignant. "I say we draw straws. The loser gets to stake out the guy's room and eat later."

"And if you draw the short straw?" Drake asked.

"Not going to happen. I hold the straws, and they're my men. Short straw, big bonus, no problem."

"All right. Make it happen. But I hope your growling stomach doesn't screw this up."

"Trust me, my friend. Napoleon said an army marches on its stomach. Words to live by."

Unless you're marching to Waterloo, Drake thought.

Casey's young Ranger from New York, Billy Montgomery, drew the short straw and left to keep an eye on the fifth-floor ocean suite. Drake and crew went to the open-air restaurant and took a table for eight. Their view included the white sand all the way to the dark waters of the Cozumel Strait.

After ordering a round of beers for everyone, Drake turned to Casey. "Liz is ready to track our man's cell phone.

She needs a call from one of our phones while we're standing next to him. They'll track him and monitor his calls, one of which we hope will be to or from Barak."

"What do you plan on doing in the meantime?"

"Maybe I'll stay here for another day. Barak's no doubt left Cancun by now, but if we get something right away, we can follow him. Otherwise, I guess we head home and wait. We were so close!"

"We'll get him, buddy. Then we can both get back to our day jobs."

Drake grinned. "Do you miss this?"

"Sometimes. But stuck in a ghillie suit for three days, peeing on myself if I have to go—that I don't miss."

"DHS is putting me on retainer to act as a troubleshooter. We might be doing more of this. You up for that?"

"Will you get to call your own shots, or wind up doing what we did before? Missions that made no sense?"

"I'll be on my own. Just like now."

"I still have a family and my security firm to run," Casey said, "but, sure, the Lone Ranger and Tonto can ride again. As long as we get to live like this some of the time. Have you tried the fresh lobster here?"

Drake just shook his head and smiled. He was reminded of the lyrics from an old Dave Matthews Band song: "Eat, drink and be merry for tomorrow we die." He hoped there was nothing about the man in the fifth-floor ocean suite that might cause any of them to die.

Chapter Eleven

Barak excused himself after an elaborate dinner, and too many rounds of tequila, that left his hosts telling endless stories about torturing and killing anyone who opposed him. He had witnessed great violence in the Middle East, but if his hosts were to be believed, Mexico was keeping pace in both body count and sheer savagery.

Retreating to his upstairs room, he studied the floor plan of the restaurant in Tijuana where the birthday celebration for the Architect's brother was to be held. The place was small, with only one private area closed off. That was where they would hold the party. The question was, should the brother meet the Zeta lieutenant alone, or would he surround himself with a small army of his own men. From what he'd seen and heard so far, the Mexican cartel leaders preferred the superiority of numbers. He'd have to plan for a full room of men protecting the meeting.

Barak's men, on the other hand, usually worked alone and killed boldly. As believers, they embraced their own deaths. Martyrdom gave them an enormous advantage. Two men willing to enter a room and die there were more than capable of defeating a small army of men in a closed, small space. So, he thought, two men armed with MP5 Ks and 900 rounds per minute should be enough.

The problem, he knew, would be getting these two men into the room undetected. The brochure and menu for the restaurant his hosts—his employers—had given him listed a variety of Mexican delicacies he would never try; including ant eggs and cactus worms. There were, however, over a hundred brands of tequila stocked in the restaurant. That many tequilas would surely require more than one tequila distributor. One borrowed delivery van was all he would need to deliver his men to the restaurant.

The other possibility he considered was the hotel across the street from the rear of the restaurant and its loading dock. He knew the rear entrance would be guarded, but all of the restaurant's vendors would use it. Two men walking toward the loading dock without a recognizable purpose, he concluded, would provide too much of a warning to anyone posted there.

No, he thought, the tequila delivery van would provide the best cover. If his men survived, it would also provide transportation away.

He made a call to his best man in Los Angeles and ordered that two men be prepared for a short trip south of the border. Then he went downstairs to talk with his hosts, who were still on the veranda.

"Ah, Señor Barak," Felipe Calderon said, "Help me finish this bottle of Casa Noble, which is the finest tequila in the world. Have you made your plans?"

"I have made my plan. I will need your help to get my men into the restaurant. I will need to borrow a tequila distributor's delivery van. Can that be arranged?"

"Of course. Will you need the driver's uniform as well?"

"Yes, two of them."

"You will use just two men against the Architect's brother?"

"Yes."

"And you think only two men can do the job?"

"I am sure of it. I trained them. They are, shall we say, highly motivated."

"My men are motivated, too," Calderon replied. "They know I will kill them if they fail me." He took another drink. "But they still might fail."

"My men aren't afraid of dying," Barak said. "That's why they won't fail. They want to die."

"No man wants to die, señor."

"That's where you are wrong, señor. Do you know where the word 'assassin' comes from? It comes from ancient Persia, where a man named Hasan-i-Sabbah created the Order of Assassins. This was about the time of the first Christian Crusade. He trained his men to be willing to sacrifice themselves on his orders, so they could enter Paradise. His assassins were highly skilled, intelligent, and well-educated. I have trained my men the same way."

"And you promise your men Paradise if they obey you?"

"Allah promises that. I just help them believe it."

The Mexican smiled. "My priest told me that I would go to hell for wanting sex with a woman who was not my wife. Is it the same, you and my priest?"

"We are both just humble servants helping our flocks believe. Now I must make a few more calls if I am to be successful." He set his empty glass down. "The tequila was excellent. Thank you."

"*Si*, it is excellent. I drink to your success so that you do not journey to Paradise with your men."

Barak returned to his room, wondering if he should give in to the temptation to kill the man. Just because Calderon was feared as a cartel lieutenant, that didn't mean the man would last a minute with him, *mano a mano*, as they liked to say. Any one of his men knew how to kill a thousand ways, and he was their teacher. This man, however, knew only the gun and the knife. What had he gotten himself into, working for men like this? When he had his nuke across the border, he would tell the Alliance this was his last time.

He called Ryan in Cozumel. "Are you enjoying your stay?"

"Are you enjoying yours?"

Barak gave an angry laugh. "You have no idea how much. I should be finished here day after tomorrow. Will you have my merchandise here by then?"

"It will be available when you have completed your assignment."

"Don't let me down. There is too much at stake here."

"For all of us. Do your job and we will deliver, as promised."

"Be sure that you do. Any news about my man?"

"Just that they found him dead at the Mayakoba. Nothing else so far. Call me when you're finished out there."

When I'm finished out here, Barak thought, *and then pull off the devastation I have planned in Oregon, Ryan, then I won't need you ever again. I will be the one calling the shots from now on.*

Chapter Twelve

DRAKE WAS ENJOYING GRILLED SEA BASS WITH A MANGO BUTTER sauce when his cell phone vibrated.

"You may not have to get your pilot close to our friend from the ferry," Liz Strobel said without preliminaries. "We've been monitoring all calls coming from your hotel. A call just came in from south of Tijuana that might be your guy."

"Oh? What did you hear?"

"Caller asked if anything had been heard about 'his man.' Someone in your hotel answered, 'They found him dead at the Mayakoba.' The call came from the Guadalupe Valley south of Tijuana."

"That has to be Barak. Can you track him?"

"We have his phone monitored."

"Keep monitoring the guy upstairs. We need to know how he's involved with Barak. We'll head to Tijuana tonight. Do we know exactly where he is?"

"I'll have satellite imagery for you before you get to Tijuana. DEA has a team working with the Mexicans at the Tijuana airport, I'll see if they know anything that might be helpful."

"Let me know what you find out. I'll call you when we're

airborne." He nudged Casey. "Our ferry friend just got a call from Tijuana. The caller has to be Barak. I need to get to Tijuana. Can you drop me off on your way back home?"

"And miss all the fun? How soon do we leave?"

"As soon as I check us out and we get to the airport. Tell the guys." Abandoning his sea bass, Drake left the table.

An hour later, after a hurried checkout and a dash to the airport, Casey's Gulfstream was waiting for them. His pilot had rushed ahead and filed a flight plan for the Tijuana International Airport.

"Steve says our flight time is three and a half to four hours, depending on conditions," Casey said as they were boarding. "Anything you need from us before we're all sleeping?"

"Liz is working on satellite imagery for us. We'll sort things out when we have that. Go ahead and get some sleep. You'll probably need it."

Sitting in the front seat on the right side of the plane, Drake looked down at the lights of Cancun as they crossed over the Cozumel Channel. Just one night ago, they'd left Oregon to fly to Cozumel, and now they were flying red eye again, chasing the man who called himself Barak. *Who was he?* he wondered. *What was he up to now?*

In the days following the attempted assassination of the Secretary of Homeland Security and the raid on the offices of ISIS, Barak's international security firm headquartered in Las Vegas, DHS and the FBI had found the employment records of felons who had converted to Islam while in prison and met their deaths while trying to kill the Secretary. There were other felons, too, men spread around the world in the ISIS offices, who were also converts to Islam. But it wasn't clear that these other men were involved in Barak's terrorist plot.

They were, however, American citizens who were free to travel back to and around the country without raising suspicion. To a man, they were capable of blending into their surroundings, and as security guards and personal protection specialists, they had almost unlimited access to the very people Barak had targeted on his assassination list, which they had found. As far as Drake was concerned, Barak's felons constituted the perfect terrorist fifth column. They were homegrown, most of them, and members of minority races, often ignored, invisible to most people. They had been raised as victims in a society they hated. Add the promise of Paradise, Drake knew, and you had the perfect clay from which to mold into an assassin.

There had been no other assassination attempts, however, after their raid on the ISIS offices. The employees with adopted Muslim names and prison records had all disappeared. The remaining thousands of ISIS employees went to work for other firms, as the company's contracts were taken over by smaller security firms like his friend Mike's in Seattle.

Barak and his bodyguard had fled without a trace. Why were they in Cancun? Why stop in Mexico, Drake wondered, when Barak could have easily fled further south to Central or South America? And why Tijuana, within spitting distance of the U.S. border? With all the cartel violence in the last couple of years, Tijuana had to be one of the most heavily watched cities in Mexico. The Mexican president had stationed over a thousand *federales* in Tijuana as part of his war against the cartels. The DEA had an office there, too, to assist the Mexican army and provide intelligence. Tijuana was not a city Drake would have chosen if he were on America's most-wanted list.

When they reached cruising altitude, he called Liz at DHS for an update.

"You're putting in some long hours," he said when she answered.

"I have to keep the ball rolling," she said. "This isn't exactly an authorized mission. It's easier for me to ask for what I want directly, as the Secretary's executive assistant, than to pass it along to someone else. Otherwise, someone might ask who authorized our surveillance satellite over Mexico to be shifted to look at Tijuana. When I ask for it, they just assume it's been authorized."

"Isn't the Secretary backing you on this?"

"Of course he is, but if someone has to fall on a sword, it'll be me, not him."

Drake grunted. He didn't like the idea of Liz falling on a sword, but he understood what she meant. "Any luck finding out where Barak's holed up?"

"Sort of. The GPS locator on the phone that called your guy in Cozumel indicates it's in the middle of the Mexican wine country. Looks like a villa, or maybe a replica of an old hacienda. It's about an hour south of Tijuana. Perched on a knoll. It has a clear line of sight for anyone approaching it. We know the phone is there now…along with thirty or forty men guarding the place."

"Hmmm. If it's Barak, he's not taking any chances we'll get as close as we did in Cancun. Can we get intel on the place from the Mexicans?" Drake asked.

"We're working on it. DEA in Tijuana is carefully asking about the place, but the cartels' informants are everywhere, so we have to be careful. The unconfirmed rumors are the place belongs to the Tijuana cartel."

"Terrific. So to get at Barak, we have to take on a cartel the Mexican government can't even crush."

"Well," she said, "you could wait for this to be referred to the Pentagon and let them send in Delta Force. Your old outfit," she said unnecessarily. "Tracking down a lone terrorist is one thing, Drake, but this doesn't look like it's a one-man job."

"Oh, I'm not alone. I have Mike and his guys. They're as good as anyone the Pentagon is likely to send in. Besides, we don't have time to wait for anyone. Any chance we can get Mexico to raid the place?"

"DEA says maybe, but only if we can prove this is a cartel hangout and not just some terrorist we're after."

"Okay, we can work with that. See if you can get permission for us to tag along as advisors if Mexico is willing to raid the place. If they won't, we'll just have to find another way in. And, Liz, thanks for seeing this through with me."

"You're welcome," she said. "Just be careful," she added. "We don't want an international incident down there."

No, he thought, *we certainly do not. Unless it means I've found Barak and put an end to both him and his plans. Then it would be worth it.*

Chapter Thirteen

Barak initiated the assassination of the rival cartel leader's brother and the borrowed commando leader from the east. His men were scheduled to arrive in the tequila distributor's van at 12:30, a little after the birthday party started. They would enter from the loading dock and kill everyone in their way. When they reached the private salon, they would kill everyone else.

He'd been driven to the Camino Real Hotel, across the street from the restaurant, to supervise the hit. His tenth-floor room looked down on the small restaurant, and he could see the loading dock where his men would arrive. Given the veiled threat if this failed, he had decided his personal attention was required. If something did go wrong, Allah forbid, it would be easier for him to escape in Tijuana than from the villa. But he would not fail. He would kill the brother of the Architect himself if he had to.

He watched the invited guests begin arriving at noon. Some were family, a mother, a wife, four children, plus a few friends. Spawn of the devil, he thought, as Americans were fond of saying. For him, they were no doubt Catholic believers, *infidels*, who would die, along with the Architect's brother and Los Zetas hit man. So be it.

He had watched others arrive, too, men he knew were associates and cartel members, given the lack of concern they were showing that any danger might threaten them. Considering the number of cartel men standing beside their black SUVs in front of the restaurant and more likely inside, their confidence was reasonable. It was also why they were vulnerable. Twenty men could not stop his two men once they were inside. They had the element of surprise on their side.

At one o'clock, the delivery van the cartel had supplied him pulled up to the loading dock. His two men, dressed in company uniforms, got out of the van and opened the back, where cases of tequila were stacked. He watched as a restaurant employee and cartel guard approached to sign for the delivery. Both were quickly, silently shot and shoved into the van behind the cases of tequila.

When his men raced inside, Barak couldn't hear the automatic fire from their MP5s, but the guards lingering outside heard. Pulling out their weapons, they rushed in, and Barak saw muzzle flashes flickering in the restaurant's front windows. Then there was no movement, not even on the street outside. Tijuana was used to cartel violence. He was not surprised no one rushed up to help.

Five minutes later, however, Barak felt a cold chill of apprehension as he watched two cartel men stumble out the restaurant's front door and collapse on the sidewalk. If they had survived, then the Architect's brother might also have survived. That was something he could not let happen.

He grabbed his tactical weapons bag and ran to the elevator. If he could get across the street fast enough, before the survivors could regroup, then he might have enough time to finish the job.

When he stepped out of the elevator in the lobby, it seemed to him that no one had noticed the destruction taking place in the restaurant across the street. He crossed the lobby at a fast walk. As he crossed the street, he heard moaning coming from the two men he had seen from his room. He shot them both in the head as he walked by.

Inside the restaurant, he smelled death even before he saw the first group of bloody bodies on the floor outside the banquet room. The cartel's men had been shot as they tried to enter, and blood splatter covered the walls around the door. He went inside the private room. Pools of blood were everywhere, like mud puddles on a rainy day. Shards of crystal and china covered the bodies of men who tried to crawl under the tables, but most of the bodies were still slumped in the chairs and booths where they'd been shot.

Barak saw the bodies of his two men lying in front of the head table. There was a pile of bodies just beyond them. Stepping around the dead on his way through the room, he looked for the Architect's brother.

Lying on his back next to an overdressed, bloody woman, the man once thought to be one of the smartest drug smugglers in Mexico had a line of bleeding bullet holes across his chest. His eyes were open, and his mouth still moved in a silent plea for help.

Barak leaned down and shot him twice in the head. The Architect's brother was no better, no worse, than the man who ordered his death. He didn't deserve to suffer any more than any other person who wasn't an American. Americans deserved to suffer, Barak told himself, but not this man.

He walked quickly out of the banquet room and through the kitchen, where he saw that the restaurant staff had died at their work stations. When he reached the loading dock, he heard the police sirens. He had planned to leave by taxi from the hotel, but now he thought better of it. His men had been told to leave the delivery van's keys in the ignition. He was pleased to see they had obeyed. He stepped up into the cab and started the engine. Driving carefully down the alley to the

Avenue of the Heroes half a block away, he pulled into south-bound traffic. He opened the cell phone he'd been given.

"Leaving now, Felipe. Tell your boss the good news. He alone is El Supremo in Tijuana. See you in five minutes."

"And your men, señor?"

"They are in Paradise, as Allah promised. Tell Saleem it's time for him to keep his promise."

"You can tell him yourself," Calderon replied. "We celebrate tonight. My boss wants to meet you. You have done him a great favor."

"Get me out of here safely, and you will have done me a great favor."

"No problem. The police here are our friends."

Chapter Fourteen

When their Gulfstream landed in Tijuana, where the sultry night air was heavy with the smells of burned jet fuel and pollution, it was met by two black Suburbans and men wearing blue and black fatigues.

"Mike, keep our guys here," Drake said, as he climbed down the ladder. "No use showing them what we bring to the party before we know if there's a party." He walked toward an agent walking toward him.

The agent extended his right hand. "Drake, I'm Special Agent Cooper. Welcome to Tijuana. Have your men join us and we'll talk."

"I told them to stay in the plane until I know if we're staying."

"Oh, you'll be staying, all right. Washington pulled in some favors Mexico owes us. They've agreed to raid the villa."

"Do we get to join you?"

"Only two of you. As advisors, and no guns. They want to be able to take full credit if the raid is successful. My men will be armed, but Mexico's go in first."

Drake nodded. "Fine, but I want to be right behind you.

I'll go tell my guys." He turned and went back to the Gulfstream.

Back in the forward cabin, he sat across from his friend. "Only two of us get to go," he said loud enough for the others to hear. "No guns. And we're only allowed to observe. Mike, you still have those Glock 30's and ankle holsters?"

"Sure do. I thought we might need them."

"Are they here in the cabin or stowed with our luggage?"

"In the back. I'll get them."

As Casey stood up, Drake turned to Gonzalez. "Roberto, you can monitor us on the team radios. Let me know if you hear anything hinky from any of the Mexican army around us. The DEA might trust them, but we don't have to. We'll be too far away for you to get to us in time if we need help, but stay with the plane. I don't want anything missing when we get back."

"You want a vest?" Mike asked when he returned with the Glocks. "The radios are in the vest pockets."

"Only way to dress for a party like this," Drake said as he strapped his Glock on his right ankle and pulled on the bullet-proof vest. "Now let's go see if we can find our terrorist."

Special Agent Cooper stood beside his SUV talking with a Mexican army officer. "Gentlemen," he said, nodding at Drake and Casey, "this is Major Rafael Castillo, head of Mexico's war on the cartels in this region. He will lead the raid tonight."

Major Castillo did not look like a Mexican commando. Tall, with blue eyes and a light complexion, he looked more like a California beach boy than a soldier. Those blue eyes, however, showed the toughness required to fight the cartels in Mexico.

"Gentlemen," he said in almost unaccented English as they shook hands, "Special Agent Cooper has worked with me before and assures me you will not get in my way. Make it so. We know of the villa you have identified. It is owned by a man we have been watching. He has no connection to the cartels that we have found. He is connected, however, to many of our politicians from Baja Mexico. For that reason, we will be very careful tonight. We will also be very careful because an important cartel member and his family were assassinated at a birthday party this afternoon. The cartels will have blood in their eyes for anyone moving against them. You are welcome to observe, but that is all I can allow you to do. Is that understood?"

"It's your call, Major," Drake said. "The man we're after is a danger to both of us, but he's here in your country. We appreciate you being willing to take him on. We won't get in your way."

"Good. My two Black Hawks will be here soon. You'll ride in the second one," Major Castillo said as he turned and walked toward a nearby hangar, where soldiers were mustering.

"Castillo's good," Special Agent Cooper told them. "He attended college at Texas A&M, ROTC, then enlisted in the Marines. He has dual citizenship, but came back home to fight the cartels. He's a good leader, but he doesn't exactly have crack troops to lead. So keep your heads down. What he said about a cartel leader getting whacked is troubling. When the cartels are at war, it's worse than anything the *Godfather* movies ever portrayed."

"Does this assassination have anything to do with our guy?" Drake asked. "Barak had a working relationship with the cartels, and, if our intel is correct, he just arrived in Tijuana."

"Who knows. What the police here say is that the brother of the Architect—the former head of the cartel—was assassinated by two black Muslims with prison tattoos. Who the hell knows how they're involved. An opposing cartel could be trying to throw us off. Make us think this was some outside group that did this."

Drake looked at Casey, who knew enough to keep silent. If Barak was here using his men to carry out a hit, it made sense if he wanted the protection of the cartels for awhile. Or he was joining in their smuggling enterprise as he had before.

When the Black Hawks flew in low and landed in front of the hangar, Special Agent Cooper led them to the second helicopter and motioned them in.

"Since you are their special guests, they saved the window seats for you," he said with a smile. "Of course, they'll probably fly with the cargo doors open."

Drake returned Cooper's smile. He and Casey had flown more times in Black Hawks than either of them cared to remember. Flying with the cargo doors open was routine.

The flight south from Tijuana took less than fifteen minutes. They flew down the Guadalupe Valley and landed in a flat area next to a swimming pool below the villa. No sooner had they touched down than gun fire raked both helicopters as the soldiers jumped out and took positions behind the retaining wall around the pool. Major Castillo gave hand signals to his men to move out in three groups and up a slight hill toward the villa. At the same time, Drake and Casey took cover behind the retaining wall and watched the soldiers advance on the villa, firing controlled bursts from their AK 47's.

Drake frowned. "Mike, there's no sound from the incoming rounds. What are these guys using?"

"Only thing I know of is the Kalashnikov AK-9," Casey said, ducking his head as rounds peppered the swimming pool behind them. "Almost no sound, fires 9 mm rounds that can penetrate bulletproof vests."

"I hope Castillo knows that. If he doesn't, he's going to lose a lot of his guys."

As the soldiers moved in on the villa, the fighting intensified, then suddenly stopped. In the silence, Drake signaled Casey to move to the right end of the retaining wall as he moved to the left end. Either Castillo had won or there would be men moving down to finish them as well.

When he looked up again, the light coming from the veranda revealed Major Castillo turning over a cartel defender with his boot. Satisfied the man was dead, he turned toward Drake and waved.

"Come up and look for your man."

Walking up the gravel path to the villa, they saw that Castillo's pincer tactic had caught the cartel men falling back to protect the villa, where they were mowed down in a crossfire. It looked like Castillo had lost several men.

In the villa's main room, they found two men lying face down at the foot of a staircase and several others that had fallen around the doorway they had defended. Their bodies had been mutilated by the savage fire from the soldiers.

"These two were trying to reach the stairs when we came in," Castillo said. "We haven't been upstairs, so I don't know if anyone is there. Would you like to wait for my men to clear the second floor? Or would you rather go look for yourselves?"

Drake picked up an AK 9 lying next to one of the dead men and headed for the stairs. "We have some experience at this," he said. "We'll go look."

Casey picked up the other AK 9 on the floor and followed Drake up the stairs, at the top of which they moved down each side of the hallway that ran the length of the second floor. There were doors on both sides. The first two rooms they cleared were empty bedrooms, with unmade beds and clothes on the floor. The third room was a den, complete with a massive flat panel TV, a pool table, and a poker table where men had been sitting, judging from cigars left in the ash trays.

Next to the den was a larger bedroom with a balcony. The bed was neatly made, but here, too, they saw a cigar left in an ash tray. There were several magazines and a brochure on a mahogany writing desk. Drake picked up the half-smoked cigar, made sure it was cold, then looked at the magazines.

The first was titled *Mallet, The International Magazine of Polo*, the second was *Polo America*. The brochure announced a charity polo match in Bend, Oregon. Drake didn't know anything about polo, but he pocketed the brochure just in case. He doubted the cartel guys cared about polo in Oregon, but if Barak had been in the villa there might be a connection he could look into.

After they finished clearing the second floor, they returned downstairs and found Major Castillo talking to Special Agent Cooper.

"We were able to have a conversation with one of the *sicarios*, or cartel hit men," the major was saying, "before he unfortunately died. I did not think he was so badly injured, but you know…things happen. He told me the one they call El Verdugo, the Executioner, had been here with his bodyguard and two others he did not know but who were not Mexicans. He said they left in a helicopter, after they got a message we were coming."

"Damn it!" Cooper said. "I'm so tired of them always being one step ahead of us."

Castillo smiled sympathetically. "Until we pay our people as much as the cartels do," he said, "they will always be ahead. But tonight, not all of them got away. We lost a few, but they lost many more."

Drake tapped the major on the arm. "Did the unfortunate *sicario* describe the ones who weren't Mexican?" he asked.

"Only that one was older, maybe sixty, and spoke only English. He said he was only here for several days."

That had to be Barak, Drake thought. Where was he headed now?

Chapter Fifteen

Barak looked down at the silver sea below reflecting the full moon's light. The cartel's Bell 429 helicopter was flying west from the coast of Baja Mexico. Back at the villa, after taking care of the Architect's brother, he had been treated with respect and served a Mexican feast of green poblano chiles stuffed with meat, fruits and nuts, lamb shank with chiles, tequila and garlic and the favorite of El Verdugo, a brick red *mole* served with grilled iguana. Unfortunately, the celebration had been interrupted by a phone call warning them that the army was on its way.

Now, Barak had been informed, they were headed for an island in the Pacific where the cartel sponsored a research station at an abandoned abalone fishing village. Two university students who were sons of his cartel's *familia* were doing legitimate research there, studying the shrinking abalone beds. The true purpose of the facility, however, was to serve as a base for the cartel's helicopters as they retrieved drug shipments from oil tankers from Venezuela headed to Los Angeles. Special shipments like his demolition nuke were also brought in this way.

He had to admit that he had underestimated the sophistication of the cartel. He knew it was international in its reach, but now he was learning it was also a finely tuned business. Violence was a tool it used with great effect, obviously, but its real power lay in its wealth and growing influence both in Mexico and elsewhere. Investments in real estate, the construction of new resorts, marinas and hotels, and even philanthropic involvement all served as legal means to influence local authorities. When that wasn't enough, outright bribes were usually successful. When they weren't, those who refused to cooperate simply disappeared.

The cartel's leader, El Verdugo, wasn't what Barak had expected. In appearance, he was ordinary, a short, thin man with thinning hair who wore round, wire-framed glasses that made him look like a professor. Behind those modest glasses, his eyes burned with a cruel ferocity that was intimidating, even if you didn't know his reputation. Those eyes softened slightly only when he smiled, which was infrequently. As a host, however, he was as gracious as a desert sheik welcoming a weary traveler into his tent.

When they landed in front of a concrete block house at the end of a row of four metal Quonset huts, El Verdugo waved for Barak to follow him as they climbed out of the helicopter.

"Come inside, my friend," he said. "We'll have a drink while I see if we've learned why the army came for us."

Inside the block house that was part office, with desks, computers, and phones, and part laboratory, with fish tanks, metal trays of specimens, and microscopes, Barak examined a wall of underwater photos of brilliantly colored fish and other sea organisms. If this research station was just a front for a smuggling operation, he said to himself, it was a very convincing front.

When El Verdugo got off the phone, he joined Barak in front of the photo wall. "The beauty of this is getting paid by the government to study global warming and its effect on abalone," he said with a smile. "The abalone have not been good here for a long, long time, or the village would not be deserted. They pay us anyway to find out why. Science is a beautiful thing, no?"

When Barak nodded, El Verdugo went on. "My men tell me the army was looking for you, Señor Barak. They say you are a terrorist. That must be worse than a criminal. They never raided my villa before, and like you, I have killed."

"Were Americans involved in this raid?" Barak asked.

"One DEA and two others. You know them?"

"Maybe. They could be the ones from Cancun."

"Then the sooner you are on your way, the better. I know when our army is coming, but America's president likes to use his drone missiles, and I won't know when they're coming."

"Don't worry," Barak assured him. "When I have my merchandise from Venezuela, I'll be on my way. Besides, you work with Hezbollah. You already have a target on your back. But America won't strike here. They can't even stop your violence along the border."

El Verdugo laughed. "They are afraid the ACLU will sue them if they shoot us." He took a bottle of tequila out of a locked cabinet and raised it in a toast. "I *salud* the ACLU, my American friends."

Barak accepted the shot glass he was handed and raised it in a second toast to the ACLU. It was true, he thought. America was afraid to use its power. If he ran the country, every drug smuggler he caught would be executed, every person critical of the government would be in jail, and homosexuals would lose their heads on TV every day until their abomination was erased from the face of the earth. How America remained powerful for as long as it had baffled him.

When he had the device he was waiting for, he would be the one to show America that its days were numbered. One small demolition nuke the size of a small refrigerator would blow a hole in America's confidence and cripple it forever. He would soon have this device. All he needed was a couple more days to get the nuke across the border. He also had to make sure the Mexican didn't try to snatch it for himself.

He sipped and swallowed. "My friend, when do you expect your helicopter will return from the oil tanker?"

"It will be back before daylight. You should get some sleep." El Verdugo put the bottle away. "We'll sleep in the Quonset hut next door and leave in the morning. You go ahead, I'll call the pilot and make sure everything is okay."

Barak left, but he had no intention of sleeping. There were only six people that he knew of at the research station: the two students; El Verdugo and his bodyguard; Saleem Canaan, the Hezbollah commander and himself. When the helicopter returned, the pilot would make seven unless the pilot brought others back with him. If they wanted to take the nuke for themselves, that's when he would have to make a move. He wasn't worried about Saleem, as they were fighting the same war, but a nuke delivered on a silver platter to the cartel without costing them a cent was a huge temptation.

The Quonset hut, which was newer than it looked, was divided into sleeping quarters plus a large open area for the kitchen and one long, wooden table scarred with the carved initials and the cigarette burns left by past guests. A large marine propane heater was mounted to the bulkhead that separated the eating and sleeping areas on one side of a door to the rear of the hut. To the right of the door was a locked metal cabinet that he guessed served as the research station's armory. A couple well-worn couches were positioned in front of the propane heater.

Barak walked through the sleeping quarters, inspecting ten small rooms, five on each side, each equipped with an army cot, a metal wardrobe locker, and a plain wooden night stand with a lamp. All of the rooms were empty. At the end of the hallway was a military-style latrine with two shower stalls, five sinks with mirrors, and two toilets. There were two windows on the rear wall on each side of the row of sinks. These windows opened outward from the bottom as far as short chains attached to them would allow.

He chose the room closest to the latrine on the right side of the hut and lay down on the cot without undressing. He kept the Beretta 92 he had carried throughout the Middle East, from the time he had first served the Brotherhood, in his right hand alongside his leg. His plan was, when the others were asleep, to slip outside through one of the windows in the latrine. For now, he wanted to appear to be tired and unconcerned for his safety. But he still made sure his gun was loaded.

It was midnight when the other men entered the Quonset hut. He heard them laughing, tequila slurring their words, and then heard doors opening and closing in the rooms down the hallway. He heard three doors close. That left two men or boys still up. They were the ones he would wait for.

Chapter Sixteen

When Major Castillo returned them to the Tijuana International Airport, Casey watched Drake thank him and Special Agent Cooper for their help. Then they headed straight for the Gulfstream. Once inside, Drake called Liz Strobel at DHS.

"We missed him, Liz. We flew in Black Hawks and killed a lot of cartel soldiers defending the villa, but Barak wasn't there. He'd been tipped off, and I have no idea where he is now. Unless you have something, I'm heading home."

Casey took off his vest and sat down across from Drake, who was angrier, in a cold, silent way, than he'd ever seen him.

"So where is he now?" he was asking Liz. "If your satellite tracked the helicopter to the coast, where did it go from there?" Drake stood up. He looked like he was about to hurl his cell phone at the bulkhead in front of him. "With a hundred satellites at your disposal," he said, "you only had *one* trained on the villa? Unbelievable! I thought you agreed this guy was top priority."

Drake walked to the rear of the plane's cabin and back. When he sat down again, Liz's voice was loud enough for Casey to hear.

"… *ever* talk to me that way again! I helped you every step of the way, and I don't need your whining. *You* missed him, not me. Maybe if we had used our people, he'd be on his way to Gitmo by now."

Drake shook his head at the phone. "Fine," he said. "Go find someone to drop everything and chase Barak like I did. By the time you guys got your act together, he could be on the moon!" He slammed the phone shut.

Casey waited for him to calm down. Finally, Drake took a deep breath and turned.

"DHS used a satellite to monitor the villa all right," he told Casey, "but when the helicopter left and flew west, it reached the coast and then went out of range. They don't have a clue where he is now."

"You really want to go home?" Casey asked. "We're closer than we were three days ago, you know. Maybe we'll catch another break while he's still around here somewhere."

Drake shook his head. "No, I don't want to go home. But I don't want to waste your time down here, either. I know you want to get back to Megan and the kids and get your guys back on the job."

"Another day won't hurt," Casey said. "Why don't we find a place in San Diego, give Liz a day, and if nothing turns up, then head home. Megan will understand." He paused. "Besides, you owe me that dinner I didn't get to finish in Cancun."

Drake had to laugh. "All right, one more day. And we'll find someplace with an all-you-can-eat buffet so you won't go hungry."

Not that Mike Casey had ever really gone hungry. He'd grown up on a ranch in Montana and had always been able to eat steak and potatoes or anything else he wanted without gaining weight. When he ran track at the University of Montana, the training table also ensured that he was well nourished. The only times he could recall being somewhat hungry were on missions in Afghanistan with Drake that involved weeks of following a target, days spent in a hideout waiting for a shot with his 50 caliber Barrett rifle, and then a careful exfiltration with nothing to eat except what he'd carried in weeks before.

AS FOR HIS BUSINESS, Casey knew it was in good hands and could run without him for another few days. His good friend had enlisted in the army after his father's death and wound up fighting beside Drake to save the world. When he'd returned home and met and married Megan, they had moved to Seattle, where he'd found a job with Puget Sound Security. After five years doing threat assessments, risk analysis, and personnel protection for high tech firms he'd bought the small company when its founder retired. Now PSS, Inc. was a smooth running company. He had surrounded himself with the best talent available and was comfortable letting them do their jobs.

He hadn't been completely honest with Drake, though, when he said he only missed chasing bad guys some of the time. Although his work provided some of the old excitement, it wasn't the same. The danger was still there some of the time, sure, but he wasn't at the front line any more. He was stuck in an office, meeting and greeting clients and running the business. The money was fantastic, and he'd been blessed far beyond any dream he'd had growing up in Montana, but he knew he belonged back in the fight. And in the process, staying in nice places. If DHS came through and picked up the tab for their little outsourced adventure, that just made it all the better.

"Drake," he said, breaking out of his reverie, "I was just thinking…if you don't have a place in mind, there's a little inn north of the San Diego airport I stayed at once for a conference. You might like it. I can call them and see if there's room for us."

Drake was still staring out the jet's small window. "Sure," he replied. "Give them a call. And tell Steve to get us out of here. I'm beginning to hate this place."

Wait until you see where I'm taking us, partner, because if it doesn't cheer you up, you can't be cheered up, Casey thought, as he rapped on the cockpit door to get his pilot started on the short junket across the border. Then he pulled out his iPhone to search for the Rancho Bernardo Inn, one of the coolest places he had ever stayed. A great golf course, world-class dining, and two beautiful pools, one adult only, Drake was going to love it.

Chapter Seventeen

WHEN THE SNORING IN THE THREE OCCUPIED ROOMS DOWN the hallway was steady for an hour, Barak made his way to the latrine and used the stiletto switchblade in his pocket to unscrew the base plates of the chains on one of the windows. Then he slipped outside. It was dark along the rear of the hut, but light from the windows of the office and lab next door allowed him to make his way across an open area behind the buildings to a grove of junipers at the base of a small ridge that circled the cove. The wind was steady from the north and whispered through the needles of the junipers. Even though there were lights still on in the lab, he couldn't tell if there was anyone in there. But he knew only three men had entered their rooms in the Quonset hut to sleep.

It was almost four o'clock in the morning. He expected the helicopter to return from the oil tanker within the next hour. Apart from the waves pounding the hard gray sand of the beach, nothing moved and the research station remained quiet.

Most people believe the best time to attack another person is just before dawn, when they are sleeping most soundly. That is why Barak wanted to be out of the Quonset hut, just in case they chose that time to come for him. He knew, however, the common belief is wrong, that the deepest sleep occurs in the first two non-REM cycles and diminishes as the night wears on. If he had been sleeping, their chances would have been better earlier in the night.

Now he waited patiently behind one of the junipers, and when the sky to the east started to lighten, he heard the first faint sound of an approaching helicopter. At the same time, he saw light from the front door of the office building splash the ground as two figures darted toward the Quonset hut.

Covered by the sounds of the helicopter and ocean waves, Barak ran to the far side of the Quonset hut and looked around the front door, which was now partly open. Inside, he saw the two students from the lab standing in front of the door to the sleeping area, apparently building up courage to move in for the kill. He waited until they had opened the door, then moved in behind them, as they tried to silently cover the distance to his room.

Before the second student got halfway down the hallway, Barak moved like a jungle cat, grabbing him from behind and covering his mouth with one hand as he drew his stiletto and cut the boy's throat. A small gurgling sound was all the noise the boy made. Lowering him to the floor, Barak took three quick steps and caught up with the other student, who was standing with one ear pressed against his door. He was holding a large revolver. Barak silently cut his throat and dropped him to the floor, then backed down the hallway until he was through the door to the sleeping area.

In the stillness of the predawn, Barak sat on top of the old dining table with his Beretta drawn and waited for the sleeping men to get up. Before anyone came into the dining area, however, the helicopter pilot rushed in, leaving the helicopter idling outside. As soon as he was aware of the gun pointed at his head, he froze, then raised both hands above his shoulders.

"Go to the door," Barak told him. "Tell the others to slide their weapons out and walk out slowly. Or they will not leave here alive."

The pilot did as he was told. Then he addressed the leader. "Señor Verdugo, he says to slide your weapons out on the floor and walk out slowly or—"

"I heard him," Verdugo said. "Señor Barak, why did you kill my researchers? They were just coming to tell you the helicopter was coming."

"For the same reason I want to kill you," Barak said, not moving from the table. "Betrayal is an unpardonable sin. Someone had to die for that sin, especially the ones you sent to kill me. Atonement for that betrayal is another matter."

A shot rang out and a body fell behind the door.

"Would my dead bodyguard atone for the sin?" Verdugo asked. "I believe he was responsible for your betrayal."

Barak despised the cowardice of a man so willing to kill his own devoted servant to save his life.

"It will for now," he growled. "Know that if you ever betray me again, in any way, at any time, I will personally chop your children into little pieces and feed them to dogs. I will hang every member of your family before your eyes and then make you beg before I cut off your head. That is the way we guarantee loyalty where I come from. Now, before I change my mind, walk out here and get on the helicopter."

Two revolvers and an Uzi slid into the dining area, and a smiling Verdugo and a solemn Saleem, the Hezbollah commander, stepped out. Without a word, they followed the pilot to the helicopter. Barak walked behind them with the Uzi and his pistol aimed at their backs.

The pilot took his seat and checked his instruments. He looked only straight ahead.

"Verdugo," Barak gestured with the Uzi, "you sit beside the pilot. Saleem, take the seat behind Verdugo. I'll sit in the back next to my merchandise. Where I can see all of you."

His merchandise, as they had been calling it, was strapped to the floor of the helicopter where a passenger seat had been removed. It was contained in a wooden shipping crate, thirty-six inches high and thirty inches wide, with yellow and black warning symbols for dangerous chemicals stamped on all four sides. The nuclear device was itself housed in a canvas transport container that weighed one hundred and fifty pounds. It had been originally configured to allow troops to carry it as they parachuted behind enemy lines to destroy power plants, bridges, and dams. The demolition nuke that he had purchased from Ryan and the Alliance was a Russian weapon that had been in Iran, then Venezuela, before being sold to the highest bidder. The only requirement beyond the steep purchase price had been a promise that it would be used against the West.

With help from his Hezbollah friends, the next phase of his plan would begin as soon as they landed. This phase would include a short trip in one of the smugglers' tunnels under the border, a careful drive north to his target, and then a few days to train the four men Saleem had selected to plant the nuke. The most difficult part of the trip, he knew, would be the hundred yards or so under the U.S. border.

Not that the tunnel itself would be a problem. His friends had perfected their tunneling skills long ago as they had engineered massive tunnels into Israel, tunnels from Gaza that were large enough for trucks to pass through. The problem was avoiding detection by the WMD border sensors. Although the tunnel the Alliance had sponsored was supposed to be fifteen feet below the surface and deep enough to prevent detection, Barak knew that America was always creating new technologies he and his friends hadn't heard about. Even with lead shielding, his people couldn't guarantee that the nuke wouldn't raise an alarm. For that reason, the railroad tracks in the tunnel had been built to accommodate a mine locomotive towing a convey rail car that had been purchased in China.

With a speed of thirty kilometers an hour, the nuke would be across the border before the border guards could respond to any alarm.

As the cartel's helicopter approached the Mexican coastline, Barak used his cell phone to alert his men to be prepared for the cartel to make another attempt to steal his nuke. All the careful planning in the world couldn't prevent human error or greed from screwing things up.

Chapter Eighteen

THE SMALL INN CASEY HAD CHOSEN FOR THEIR R&R TURNED out to be a five-star resort thirty minutes north of the San Diego International Airport. Drake had been too tired to argue with his friend when they'd checked in a little after midnight. After a restless night and being awakened at four o'clock by the sprinklers on the golf course, he was still in no mood to spend a day lounging around a swimming pool or playing golf.

What he needed was some evidence they hadn't lost track of Barak, that the last three days hadn't been a waste of time. He knew that someone smart enough to build an international security firm and train a cadre of assassins, someone bold enough to try to assassinate a cabinet member, could be anywhere in the world. But Drake didn't think Barak was anywhere in the world. He would not run away and hide. He was here someplace.

With the drug cartel helping him, Drake reasoned, the terrorist was probably just across the border laughing at them. Drake's imagination saw Barak taunting them like a matador waving his red cape in front of the bull's nose. Like a mad fighting bull, Drake was feeling his anger crowding out the icy control that had kept him alive in Afghanistan and Africa. Maybe Mike was right, he told himself, maybe he did need to step back a bit and think things through. Barak had been one step ahead of them all along. As long, as they were chasing from behind, he would stay ahead.

Drake put on a pair of workout shorts and started through the morning exercise routine he used whenever he was away from home. Ten minutes of stretching were followed by twenty-two minutes of body weight exercises that included explosion pushups, squat jumps, reverse crunches, and shadow boxing until he was ready for a hot shower. After shaving and dressing, he called Casey's room.

"What?" his buddy said. "I'm sleeping."

"No, you're not. We need to talk."

"*You* need to talk. *I* need to sleep. Go back to bed."

"It's oh five hundred. Meet me in the restaurant and we'll have an early breakfast."

"They don't serve breakfast until six. I checked. I'll meet you then." Casey hung up.

Drake knew nothing he could do or say would get his friend out of bed until six o'clock, so he called Liz Strobel in Washington, D.C. With any luck, she would be in her office with something new on Barak.

"Good morning, Liz," he said in his best cheerful voice. "Long night or an early morning?"

"Both. Thanks for asking." Her voice was marginally less angry than in their last conversation. "You're up early."

"I didn't sleep very well. We parked Mike's plane here in San Diego and decided to hang around for another day in case you turn up anything on Barak."

"Well, if that's the only reason you stayed, you may as well go home," she replied. "We have nada, zip, nothing on the man. Once he got beyond the focus of our satellite out over the ocean, we lost him. DEA's reaching out to all of their sources in Mexico, but so far nothing has turned up. We're still monitoring the phone of his friend from Cancun. That friend, by the way, made his roundabout way to South America and the Tri-Border Area via Stockholm, Berlin, Rome and Sao Paulo, Brazil."

"Did he have business in all those places?"

"Might have. But he never stayed long enough for us to find out. Never left the airports. Just moved from one plane to the next."

"Liz, we need to know more about this guy. Whatever connects him to Barak, he sure went out of his way not to lead us back to the Tri-Border Area. There's a big Muslim population down there. You think this guy's involved in terrorism or drug smuggling?"

She gave a short laugh. "They're one and the same today. That's what's going on in Mexico. Hezbollah is working with the cartels to fund their efforts. Helping them build tunnels under the border so they can use the cartel's smuggling routes into the U.S. for human trafficking and getting Other Than Mexicans—that's OTM's—and other illegals across the border."

"Do we know if Barak has any ties to Hezbollah?"

"Good question. But you know as much about Barak as we do at this point. Other than what we turned up from his offices in Las Vegas, we don't know anything about him. Mexico did arrest the head Hezbollah guy in Tijuana not long ago. Maybe they can get someone to 'talk' with him and see if he'll give us anything about Barak. Mexico is not real good at treating their prisoners well. He might want to trade information for a nicer cell."

"It's probably worth a try. I wonder if they'll let me talk to the guy."

"I don't think the Secretary would approve that," she said. "We let you go after Barak in Cancun so we didn't have to ask permission to operate in their country. Asking permission to get you in to talk with their Hezbollah prisoner, well, that might get them curious about that dead body that turned up in Cancun while you were there."

"Okay. Then how about getting Special Agent Cooper to talk with him? DEA has a legitimate interest in whatever he might know."

"I'll ask the Secretary and let you know. When will you be back in Portland?"

"Tomorrow, why?"

"The Secretary got a call from a firm that's being repeatedly hacked. It's developing technology to protect our infrastructure, mainly our electrical grid. They don't want the FBI charging in and making waves. He thought you might be able to help them, like you did at Martin Research last month. Are you available?"

"Is this what he had in mind when offered me a retainer to be his private trouble shooter?"

"Outsourcing is the future of 'limited' government…yes, this is what he had in mind. The CEO of the company is an old friend who doesn't want to lose the confidence of his shareholders if they learn he can't protect their research."

"Okay," Drake said. "Send the information to my office. I'll go see him if you'll keep looking for Barak."

"You know we will. Stop by sometime and meet the team, and I'll treat you to dinner."

"The dinner would be a treat, but I need to get home. Rain check?"

"Sure, any time." She paused. "Oh, I have a meeting in a few minutes, I should go."

She sounded disappointed, he thought, but he wasn't ready to cross that line, not even with someone as attractive as Liz Strobel. It just didn't feel right. He wasn't sure when or if it ever would. No one could replace the love he had just lost a year ago when Kay died, and right now he had no interest in trying. He was interested in only one thing at the moment, and that was finding the terrorist David Barak.

When Casey finally sauntered into the restaurant, Drake had already finished his second cup of coffee and was ready to order without him.

"If you were Barak," he asked before his friend was even seated, "where would you go?"

"Let me guess," Casey replied. "You couldn't sleep and you decided to make sure my morning was ruined, too." He signaled to a waitress. "Could I get some coffee, Miss? Extra strong please."

Drake grunted. "No reason for us to waste the day waiting for something to happen. I talked to Liz this morning. DHS doesn't have a clue where he might be."

"Well, maybe we can order breakfast first. Let my mind catch up with my grumbling stomach. Then we can discuss the possibilities. I find it hard to think when I'm hungry."

While Casey studied his menu, Drake watched a foursome of golfers getting ready to tee off outside. Stretching, taking their practice swings, and preparing to enjoy four hours on a picture-perfect day, they were enjoying themselves in a way he hadn't been able to for a long time. Perhaps not since the day after 9/11, he thought, when he had enlisted in the Army. Or after his time in Afghanistan and the Middle East. More probably, not since the day Kay was diagnosed with cancer. But there was a war going on that men like those golfers didn't think of. That was because no one was willing to call it a war.

How, he wondered, did a country forget that one of its first wars had been fought against Muslim pirates off the shores of Tripoli during the administration of Thomas Jefferson? How did a country forget that Muslim terrorists had brought down the barracks in Lebanon in 1983? Took down Pan Am 103 in 1988? That Muslim terrorists had bombed the World Trade Center two decades before they attacked the Twin Towers and had vowed to destroy us every day of the year?

Drake knew who the enemy was, and he wasn't afraid to

say so. Nor was he afraid to do whatever had to be done. He was no longer a soldier, but his oath to defend and protect his country hadn't expired when he left the Army.

He looked up. "Mike," he said, "Barak was hiding in plain sight in Cancun and protected in Tijuana by one of the cartels. He knows we're looking for him. Where does he go?"

"Why would he need to go anywhere? The cartel obviously has the cooperation of the police and the army. I'd stay in Mexico," Casey said as he waved the waitress over. "Huevos rancheros, an order of ham, a fruit bowl, toast with some strawberry jam, and a refill on my coffee, please. I might also save room for a pastry later. What are you having, Drake?"

"Scrambled eggs, whole wheat toast, and grapefruit, thank you."

"If he stays in Mexico, we'll get him sooner or later," Casey added as the waitress left. "We've had to be patient before. We've waited days for our target to appear."

"I know. But this guy is different. He thinks big. I don't see him backing off. He could have fled to anywhere in the world, so why Mexico?"

A few minutes later, when Casey was enjoying the huevos rancheros, Drake answered his own question. "Because it's easy to get back here from Mexico. He's not running away, Mike. He's taking a time out. He's waiting over there to hit us again."

He took out his cell phone and opened his contact list to call DHS. He wanted to tell Liz to watch the border. Barak was coming at them again. He was sure of it.

Chapter Nineteen

As the Bell 429 approached the building site for the cartel's new marina and hotel development in Rosarito, just south of Tijuana, Barak looked down and saw his team of eight men faced off against an equal number of cartel men. Both sides had their SUV's and trucks positioned for a quick getaway.

At least they were able to agree to the number of men each side would bring, Barak thought as he considered the obvious truce both sides recognized.

"Verdugo," he called from the rear passenger seat of the helicopter, "make sure your guys know we're friends. They may be afraid of you, but you have many more reasons to be afraid of me. Make sure they don't act stupidly. I will forgive your one stupid act, but not another. *Comprende*?"

"Don't insult me," Verdugo said without turning around. "They're here to make sure I return safely. Once they see I'm safe, and you're on your way, there will be no trouble. I am a man of my word."

"As am I. Remember my promise. If I find you have tried in any way to interfere with my work, you and your entire family will regret it. Now let's get down there and be on our separate ways."

When the helicopter touched down on the improvised landing site, they waited until the dust settled, then got out, saying their farewells with tight smiles and handshakes. While Saleem stayed inside with the pilot to make sure he didn't lift off with their precious cargo, Barak waved his men over and gave them instructions on how to carefully unload his nuke to secure it for transport.

"Saleem," Barak said, as they stood together and watched four men lift the crate into the back of the waiting Suburban, "how do you put up with these cutthroats?"

"I put up with them because they serve our purpose. They have learned to make vast amounts of money in America. We need to do the same. They use their money to indulge their vulgar ways, while we use the money we take from America to buy the weapons we need." He gave an elegant shrug. "It works for both of us."

"Well, watch your back, brother," Barak growled. "They remind me of Jews. The only thing you can trust is their greed. How long will it take us to get to your tunnel?"

"From here, two hours. We use a distributing business and its delivery trucks to move things to the warehouse. We'll transfer the crate to one of the trucks in south Tijuana and then drive along the truck's regular delivery route until we get to the warehouse."

When Barak's men were ready to leave, he signaled the helicopter pilot to take off and joined Saleem in the lead Suburban for the ride up the coast to Tijuana. The town of Rosarito was trying hard to remake itself into a classy resort by drawing tourists to the Pacific Baja coastline. It was beginning to look as if the effort was paying off. Tall hotels were being built and new golf courses lined the highway to the east. How much of the cartel's money were involved was unclear, but he guessed a substantial amount was being washed clean in these new developments, just as it had been in Las Vegas when organized crime built its oasis in the Nevada desert.

But Tijuana was another story, he saw as they passed through the ugly border town's industrial district a short time later. Even though it was one of Mexico's largest cities, it lacked character and any semblance of class. Like so many of the creations in the Western world, it was just another spot on the earth without purpose, without soul. Barak wasn't a devout Muslim, far from it, but when Islam had ruled the world many centuries ago, great cities had been built and great inventions had been made. What did the West have to show for its two hundred years of supremacy? Disneyland? Television? Texting and Twitter? He wouldn't be around to see the world change, but it was worth fighting for. And worth dying for.

At the distributing company's headquarters, Saleem directed them around the building to the loading dock and a delivery van parked beside the cyclone fence surrounding the back lot.

"Back up to that truck and unload the crate," Saleem said. "The drivers are out making other deliveries, so no one should see you. I'll go in and let my manager know I'll be using the truck for a while."

Barak watched his men move the crate from the SUV to the delivery van. He beckoned them to gather around him.

"When we head to the warehouse," he said, "one of you drive the delivery van. We'll let Saleem lead in one Suburban with me, and the other Suburban will follow behind the delivery van. I trust Saleem, but we're still in cartel country, so stay alert. If anyone tries to stop us, we'll fight our way through, understood? Allah has trusted us with this work. We will not fail him."

Eight of his best men stood silently in front of him until Walid spoke.

"Malik, why are we using Hezbollah men to get this crate across the border? We have our own ways. Why them?"

Barak appreciated that Walid, the youngest of the eight men he had chosen for this part of the mission, used the honorific Malik, or Leader, when he asked his question. He was disappointed, though, that a question had been asked at all. He wasn't prepared to explain how the Alliance was using Hezbollah to create chaos in the world they would profit from once the devastation they were planning was blamed on Hezbollah. And he wasn't about to tell Walid why he wanted the crate to be smuggled into the country by someone else in case they were caught. All he could do in front of the others was put Walid in his place.

He stepped in front of the young man and slapped him in the face. "Don't ever question me again. I trained you better than that. You'll sit in the van with the crate until we get to the warehouse. Don't make a sound. We'll talk when this is over."

When Saleem returned, the convoy of the delivery van and two SUV's set out and drove for an hour, taking the same circuitous route the delivery van took every day until it reached a metal building located north of the main runway of the Tijuana International Airport.

"Honk three times, then three times more," Saleem directed the driver. "A guard will come out. When he waves us in, drive to the far end of the warehouse."

Barak watched from his Suburban as a guard dressed in combat fatigues walked out, carrying his assault rifle across his chest, and motioned for Saleem to lower his window. After a quick exchange of Farsi passwords he recognized, the guard spoke into his lapel mic and the overhead door slowly opened, revealing a concrete floor and largely empty warehouse.

At the far end, another guard stood next to an enclosed office, waiting for them.

"The stairs down into the tunnel are in the office," Saleem

said. "Back the van up to the office and get your men to carry the crate inside. There's a hydraulic lift they can use."

At the bottom of the tunnel entrance, forty feet down and next to a hydraulic lift, a flatbed cargo car sat on railroad tracks hitched to what looked like a small locomotive engine. The tunnel had electric lighting and cool air circulating through it.

When the crate had been lowered and secured on the cargo car, Barak asked the guard how long it would take for it to reach the warehouse across the border in the Otay Mesa industrial district of San Diego.

"The mule, as my men call it, travels at thirty miles an hour. Your crate will be across in a couple of minutes."

Barak nodded. "And when it reaches your other warehouse, how long before the crate will head north?"

"You and your men will drive the crate through San Diego to the meeting place we agreed upon. As soon as we load up, I'll leave with my men and head out. It should take thirty minutes or so."

"Excellent. We should go now." Barak waved to his men and sat on the front of the cargo car beside Saleem. "Take me across."

Chapter Twenty

WHEN CASEY DROPPED HIM OFF AT THE HILLSBORO EXECUTIVE airport in Oregon the next morning, Drake bailed his Porsche 993 out of the long term parking lot and headed south to his farm in the rolling hills west of Dundee. He'd been gone four days, but with all the miles he had traveled searching for Barak, it seemed longer.

The familiar purr of the engine behind him and the sense of control the car provided him as he wove in and out of traffic were a sharp contrast to how he felt about his life in general. He hadn't been in his law office in weeks. The imams of Portland were still crying for the head of the man who had killed three young Muslim men, even though they were assassins sent to kill him, and he wasn't sure how far the FBI would go to keep his name a secret. And despite his fondness for his long-suffering secretary, Margo, he wasn't even sure how much longer he wanted to work as a lawyer. He'd been in a fog of sorts since Kay died, and nothing seemed important anymore. Maybe it was because without Kay, nothing *was* important anymore.

He was still driving, lost in his thoughts, when his cell

phone vibrated on its hands-free, black leather KUDA mount on the dash.

"Drake," he said.

It was Liz Strobel. "Where are you?" she asked.

"Checking up on me, Strobel? Worried that I'm still in San Diego, waiting for you to find Barak for me?"

"Checking to see where you are, yes. Worried about you, hardly. But I am worried. Border Patrol detected a nuke coming across the border in San Diego yesterday. They found the tunnel the thing came across on, and then NEST—that's the Nuclear Emergency Support Team—located a deserted van that was hot. We don't have any idea who's behind this or where the thing is now."

"Tell me about the tunnel."

"New. Costly. The kind of tunnel the Border Patrol thinks Hezbollah has been building for the cartels. They build them in a month, use them for about that long before they're found, and then they just build another one."

"Where did they find the deserted van?"

"They found the van," she said, "a rented U-Haul, in a field near the San Diego Polo Club."

"Anyone see anything?"

"We're working on that. There was a celebrity polo match there yesterday, a cancer fundraiser, so there were a lot of people in and out. Our investigators are taking statements from everyone we can find who attended."

"Are there any big events there that terrorists are likely to target?" Drake asked.

"None that stick out. But San Diego itself is a pretty good target. Drake, we're only guessing at this point. There's no chatter about a big strike, nothing to suggest something's in the works."

"Why are you telling me this?"

She paused for a second, then, "I'm clutching at straws,

okay?" Another pause. "Is this something that Barak could be involved in?"

"He was—*is* all about assassinating America's leaders. Nothing that I know about him suggested he wanted to use WMDs or cause mass casualties, but the guy's a terrorist. It's possible, I guess."

"Look, I've got to go. Things are pretty hectic here. Call me if you think of anything, okay?"

"Okay," he said. "And you do the same."

It was just a matter of time before someone smuggled a nuke into America. So far, they had been lucky, checking at border crossings and monitoring shipping containers at the ports. But there were too many ways to bring things into the country. Ways like tunnels under the border in San Diego.

The country's resources, he knew, would be on full alert by now. Once the NEST response team got a hit on the deserted van, the FBI would be in charge of the search for the nuclear device, whatever it was, and they had full legal authority to kill anyone in the unauthorized possession of a nuclear weapon. But intelligence that helps to locate the nuke is the key to success; without it, Drake knew, you truly are looking for a needle in a haystack.

Detection was only possible when gamma and neutron detectors came within twenty to thirty feet of the device.

But without information about the terrorists behind the threat, it was next to impossible to head off the threat. Like the type of information Liz had been hoping he might have about Barak.

There was something, though, something he couldn't quite identify, buzzing for recognition in the back of his mind. What had she said about San Diego? He tried to focus on her words, but he couldn't quite pull the something to the front of his mind. He knew it would come to him in time, but he needed to remember it *now*.

For the next few miles, he let his mind wander as he enjoyed the familiar glimpses of snow on the upper reaches of Mt. Hood in the distance, and the green rows of grape vines on the hillsides along the highway. He was thinking about stopping to buy produce at the Red Horse Farm roadside stand for dinner when the stand came into view. And then it hit him.

Horses. The San Diego Polo Club. The brochure for the celebrity polo event in Bend. An Argentine polo star.

Was there a connection between Barak, the smuggled nuke, and a polo match or the polo star? Coincidences happened. Usually, they were just that, random events that appeared to be connected but weren't. But, he said to himself, this might be one to take seriously. He didn't remember the date of the polo match in Bend, but he knew where to find it. He had kept the brochure and when he'd gotten back to Mike's Gulfstream, he'd put it in his duffel bag that was now in the bonnet of his Porsche.

Drake steered to the side of the road, stopped, pulled the release, and jumped out to retrieve his duffel bag. The brochure was still in the outside pocket, just where he remembered putting it. In bright blue and green lettering, it announced the inaugural Pacific Polo Invitational to be held in Bend, Oregon, next week. One of the two polo teams competing in the charity event would include an international polo star from Argentina.

Nothing in the brochure had any reference to David Barak or ISIS, of course, and Drake knew there was no reason to connect Barak to the brochure just because it had been in a room in the Mexican villa. But the U-Haul van had been abandoned near a polo field that had just hosted a celebrity event. If this Argentine polo star had been at the San Diego polo charity event, maybe there was a connection after all.

Drake put the duffel bag back in the bonnet and took out

his cell phone, waving off a Good Samaritan who had started to pull over to see if he needed help.

"Liz," he said as soon as she answered, "I might have an idea where that nuke is headed."

Chapter Twenty-One

Approaching his destination in Oregon, Barak looked at Mt. Bachelor through the port-side window of his Raytheon Hawker 400XP executive jet. At nine thousand feet in elevation, he knew, this American mountain was not half as high as the Pamir Mountains in Afghanistan, but it was still a thing of beauty. He wondered again why Allah had allowed such a depraved people to inhabit such a bountiful land.

Perhaps, he thought, it was the abundance of the place that made its people so lazy and allowed them to be so pampered. If Americans had to suffer hardships like the rest of the world did, maybe they would be better prepared for the long war ahead. Then again, maybe not. Hadn't they already mortgaged their future to China rather than endure a little financial hardship? No, he thought, the fight had gone out of this paper tiger. It's our time now.

The Hawker descended from its cruising altitude and began a turn for the approach to the Sunriver Airport and the Skypark development, where he had rented a hangar house for the month. While he stayed in the area to coordinate the attack, he didn't want to make it too easy for anyone to find him. The Hawker was owned by one of the dummy corporations he had used to hide assets while he ran ISIS, his security firm, and the hangar house was rented to one of the new identities he had been forced to adopt after the fiasco involving the assassination attempt.

The ranch he was using to stage the attack, however, was owned by a liberal supporter, a rich Hollywood producer who thought the Palestinians were brave freedom fighters and had offered his assistance to their cause. There were no ties that could be found between them, other than an indirect connection to the foundations to which they had both contributed generously over the years. It wasn't necessary to expend your own resources, he had found, when there were plenty of allies in America who hated the Jews as much as he did.

Hearing his pilot telling him to prepare for landing, Barak fastened his seatbelt. As the Hawker touched down and began to taxi to the hangar house, he spotted the resort's main lodge a mile away to the east and the resort homes across a small river to the north and south of the lodge. It was perfect, he thought. He was isolated from the resort as much as he could be, and there was only one road leading to the hangar house from the airport.

When the pilot stopped the Hawker and let down the cabin's stairs, Barak stepped out into the brisk morning air. He used the controller he'd been given to open the overhead door of the hangar on the first floor of the five-bedroom, five-bathroom vacation home. He and his pilot would be the only ones staying in the house, which had been built to accommodate large groups for getaways and corporate retreats. But that's the way it had to be. There was no way he could risk having the team from Hezbollah be seen around the resort.

Once the Hawker was rolled into the hangar and the overhead door closed, Barak walked upstairs and went out onto the wraparound deck. It was time to check on the progress of the convoy driving north from San Diego. The route he had chosen for them used the lesser traveled highways of Nevada up to Reno, then went across to Susanville, California, and north to Klamath Falls, Oregon. By now, he calculated, Saleem should be somewhere near the Oregon-California border.

Barak accessed his satellite GPS tracker app on his smart phone that allowed him to use the Low Earth Orbit satellite data network to monitor the progress of the team. This was a system that provided global asset tracking and eliminated the need to use a cell phone or other means of communicating that could be monitored.

The display showed the tracking device he had secured to the demolition nuke moving past Tulelake, California, on Highway 139, just south of the Oregon border. By his calculation, that meant the small convoy of two trucks and the horse trailer would reach the ranch in about four hours if it made no stops. Figure five hours, and the team would be on the ranch and secure by early afternoon.

That would give the men a full three days to practice delivering and detonating the device. It would also give him time to meet with the Argentine and make sure he understood the loss he would suffer if he said anything about being forced to come to Oregon with his polo ponies.

The young man's father had been a famous Argentine polo player who had fallen on hard times and made the mistake of borrowing money from a bank owned by the Alliance. The cattle ranch the man owned in the Pampas grasslands produced some of Argentina's best beef, but he had difficulty competing with the large feedlots that were opening all over the country and destroying the nation's reputation of prime, grass-fed, Argentine beef. Without his son's knowledge, he had helped the Alliance transport various items along with his son's polo ponies as they were shipped all over the world for polo matches and charity events like the one in Oregon. This was the first time the father had been asked to assist with anything so risky, but he wasn't in a position to say no.

The young man had been a different story. Raised from his earliest years to be a polo star, he had taken advantage of his good looks and consummate skill at the game to become a celebrity while he was still in his teens. By the time he was twenty-five, he had a following on four continents and spent as much time in Europe, the Middle East, and Asia as he did in South America. Getting him to agree to appear in the celebrity event in Oregon had required making him an offer he couldn't refuse: cooperate, or see your father, mother and siblings die painful deaths along with your reputation and pampered life.

In the end, the young polo star had cooperated, if grudgingly. Since leaving Argentina on this last polo tour, however, he had been drinking heavily. It was probably time to pay him a visit, Barak said to himself, and remind him what was at stake for him and his family.

Chapter Twenty-Two

Liz Strobel listened while Drake told her about the brochure he had found in the Mexican villa and why he thought the celebrity polo match in Bend, Oregon, might have something to do with the search being conducted in San Diego. When he finished, however, her silence told him he was wasting his time.

"Look," he finally added, "I know it's a stretch, but you have to admit the U-Haul left near the San Diego Polo Club and the brochure I found are a suspicious coincidence. Barak wasn't successful the first time in Oregon. Maybe his ego makes him want to try again. Or he might just want revenge for the men and company he lost."

She waited another minute before replying. "Drake, I know I didn't listen to you when you thought the Secretary was in danger at the chemical weapons depot last month. But I can't walk in to him now and suggest we focus our search for the nuke in Oregon. We have hundreds of people in San Diego searching on foot and in vans and helicopters. They're going in and out of buildings with gamma and neutron detectors concealed in carrying cases so people don't panic." She paused again, but he didn't reply. "Every threat profile we've done points to San Diego as the target," she said. "There are ninety five thousand military personnel there, and the Navy and Marines have seven separate bases that would attract a terrorist. The Navy SEAL BUD/s training is on Coronado Island. After the SEALs took out bin Laden, what better place to bomb and make the place uninhabitable for God knows how long!"

"Liz, I'm not suggesting that you quit looking in San Diego. I'm just saying you might want to consider another possibility."

"Drake, the protocols established by NEST in 1975, when someone threatened to detonate a nuclear device in Boston unless they were paid two hundred thousand dollars, are constantly being refined and fine-tuned. So far, the NEST teams have been successful in at least thirty different deployments. Nothing I say will change the way they search for a nuclear device. If you come up with some credible evidence the bomb is in Oregon, let me know. I'm sorry, but I have to go." She hung up.

Drake sat for a moment on the side of the road before he drove off. She was right, of course. He didn't have any credible evidence a nuke was on its way to Oregon or that David Barak was involved in any way. Still, he always trusted his perception of patterns and connections.

Barak was a terrorist. He had operated in Oregon. Then there was the connection Barak had with the Mexican drug cartels. If the cartels were building tunnels under the border, aided by Hezbollah, how hard would it be to ask that a nuke be smuggled in with the next load of cocaine? And then there was the brochure he'd found in the Mexican villa, the one advertising a celebrity polo fundraiser in Oregon. Even if it wasn't Barak, someone connected to the cartel was interested in the event or the featured Argentine polo star. Liz might not see a connection, Drake thought, but his gut told him it was there and that it needed to be pursued. If he found something, she could call in the NEST teams and take the credit. If he found nothing, she could take credit for ignoring him and he would have had a nice trip to the high desert of Oregon. Either way, he decided he was going to check it out. If there was any possibility he could find something that pointed him to Barak, the trip would be worth it even if there was no connection to the missing nuke.

Drake drove the rest of the way home making a mental list of things he needed to do before he left for Bend. First on the list was a call to his secretary. The last time he had called her, when he'd been on his way to Cancun, she had complained that he needed to get back to work if they wanted to keep any of his clients. Hearing that he was back from Mexico, but off again to Bend, was likely to produce a threatened resignation from his loyal assistant.

Next would have to be a call to his friend and future vineyard manager, Chuck Crawford. Chuck and his wife Laura lived up the road from his farm and had offered to take care of his dog, Lancer, whenever he was away. For starters, he'd have to ask if they could keep Lancer a little longer.

Chuck managed some of the smaller vineyards in the area and served as a consultant for a number of the larger ones. He had a master's degree in viticulture and enology from University of California, Davis, and was eager to help plant a new vineyard just as soon as Drake finished pulling out the old diseased vines. Chuck hadn't convinced him yet to start his own winery when the new vines bore fruit and was even offering to be a partner, if that's what it took.

His last call would be to his father-in-law. Senator Hazelton and his wife, Meredith, owned a log cabin at Crosswater, a golf club and resort south of Bend. He had a standing offer to use the cabin, but a call to the Senator was still in order before he took him up on the offer.

After parking the Porsche behind his old stone farmhouse, Drake went in through the back entrance and dropped his duffel bag in the mud and coat room that also served as his laundry room. He probably needed to run a load of wash, he reminded himself, if he was going to be gone for any length of time. Keeping a closet full of clean clothes was becoming a pain. Maybe it was time to find a part-time housekeeper, someone who could keep on top of the household chores that were starting to take up more and more of his time.

When the clothes from his Mexico adventure were in the washing machine and he had some Jim Beam in a glass, he sat down at the kitchen table and called his secretary.

"Hi, Margo, I'm back."

"For how long this time?"

"Well, hello to you, too."

"Fine," she said. "How was Mexico?"

"Cancun was beautiful. Tijuana, not so much. But the weather was okay."

"You know what I mean. Did you get him?"

"No, we missed him twice. How have you been?"

"I'm not used to staying home all day," she said. "So I'm bored. Paul takes off every morning, and by nine o'clock I'm climbing the walls. I don't like to shop and I don't watch soaps. Where did you get that idea, anyway?"

"Just trying to be funny. Any news about the imams and the investigation?"

"It's been pretty quiet," she said. "Paul thinks the FBI may have had a heart-to-heart talk with them, and the imams chose to keep the lid on this. Drake, when do I get back to work?"

"How about right now?" he replied. "DHS wants me to visit a company in California and help them deal with a problem they're having. The company is Energy Integrated Solutions, Inc. Find everything you can about the company and its management. You can do this from home. Then we'll get back in the office next week."

"Is this going to be like Martin Research? I'm not sure my

husband will let me keep working for you if you get involved with terrorists again."

"Absolutely not," he said. "EIS, Inc. is having a problem with some research they're doing for the government. Hackers are messing with them and they're afraid their investors will react poorly if they can't shut this down. The SEC told them they can't continue to hold back the details of these incidents on the 10-K reports they file. They're supposed to identify any significant risks they're aware of.

"So what are you supposed to do about it?" she asked. "You're not a cyber security expert."

"The Secretary of Homeland Security is just asking me to look around and make sure this isn't a bigger problem than the company is willing to admit. The research EIS, Inc. is doing is for a new component of the Smart Grid that will help protect our electrical power system. Don't worry. I'll be in and out in a couple of days, and the retainer we'll get will put a smile back on your face."

She sighed. "All right. I'll research EIS, Inc. How soon do you need this?"

"Not for a couple of days. I have to go to Bend and check something out. I'll call you when I get back."

"Well, I guess a trip to Bend is safer than a trip to Mexico chasing a terrorist. Enjoy yourself."

The call had gone better than Drake had expected, but then he wasn't telling Margo everything about his new agreement with Secretary Rallings. He would have to make it a priority to do so when he got back.

The next call was an easier one.

"Hi, Chuck. Adam Drake here."

"Got those old vines pulled out yet?"

"Working on it. I should be ready for you to lay out the new vineyard by next month. That's not why I called, though. I need to ask a favor. Can you keep Lancer for a few more days?"

Crawford chuckled. "Tahoe will be delighted. He and Lancer are quite a pair. No problem."

"Are you and Laura available for dinner tonight?" Drake asked. "My treat? I'm heading down to the Dundee Bistro in a bit."

"We'll have to take a rain check on dinner, Adam. Our daughter is bringing our grandson over for barbequed hamburgers and Laura's mac and cheese."

"Rain check, it is. Thanks again, Chuck."

Drake saw that it was six fifteen and time to call the Senator in Washington, D.C., about using his cabin for a couple of nights. If he was lucky, tonight would be one of the nights his in-laws weren't out on the D.C. social circuit.

Senator Hazelton answered on the first ring. "Good evening, Adam. I heard Mexico was a bust."

"We missed him twice. DHS is monitoring the phone of some guy he called in the Tri-Border Area. Maybe that will turn up something. Are you and Mom in D.C. for awhile?"

"Are you coming here?"

"No, I'm headed to Bend and wondered if I could stay at Crosswater for a couple of nights?"

"Of course, Adam. I'll call John at Deschutes Property Management and tell him to give you a key. His office is right on Highway 97, just as you're leaving Bend. You have business in Bend?"

"I'm not sure yet," Drake admitted. "When Liz Strobel called about the events going on in San Diego, I remembered that when we hit the villa south of Tijuana, I found a brochure for a celebrity polo fund raiser in Bend. I thought it was strange that a cartel leader, or Barak if he was there, would be interested in a polo event way up in Oregon. With the tunneling the cartels are using to smuggle drugs across the border and the U-Haul they found near the polo club in San Diego, I thought there might be a connection somehow. It's probably a long shot, but I thought I'd check it out."

"Let me know immediately if you find anything," the Senator said. "The trail's gone cold in San Diego and the President is considering going public with the whole thing. That would be a major a disaster, in my opinion. I don't think the public is ready for another attack here at home."

"Let's hope we get lucky then."

After Drake repacked his duffel bag, he drove to the Bistro, where he enjoyed a Cobb salad, grilled tuna and a bottle of 2006 Ponzi Tavola pinot noir for dinner. For dessert, he had a serving of pinot noir-marinated Oregon berry cobbler with his coffee. His search tomorrow might be another bust, but with a wonderful meal and the allure of the hunt, he was feeling better than he had in days.

Chapter Twenty-Three

The next morning, Barak called his man watching the young polo star, Marco Vazquez.

"How is our celebrity?" he asked.

"He is still in bed," the watcher said. "But unless he rides today, he will head to the bar for his breakfast."

"Has he had any visitors?"

"Only ones asking for his autograph or women seeking his bed. He keeps to himself mostly, watching soccer matches and drinking. He makes everyone angry when he won't let others watch baseball, but he doesn't care. He just gives the bartender money. For a big star, he doesn't look very happy."

"I need to talk to him," Barak said. "How long will he be in the bar?"

"If today is like yesterday, until he has lunch."

"I'm on my way. Follow him if he leaves."

Barak left the Sunriver Resort and drove north to the Pronghorn Resort. The high desert of Oregon, with the snow capped peaks of the Three Sisters on his left and range land and sagebrush on his right, made the drive north on Highway 97 pass quickly. Except for the heavier traffic on the bypass around the city of Bend, he was able to keep the big SUV at sixty miles an hour the whole way as he considered his options for dealing with the polo playboy.

The celebrity fundraiser featuring Vazquez was a big deal for the region and the amateur players of the Northwest. It had required a substantial financial commitment to cover the young star's appearance fee and travel expense, but the organizers had eagerly agreed to add such a star to their program. The star's fee, however, did not include the cost of transporting the six polo ponies he traveled with. But that was only a small part of the cost of the entire operation, and it had provided an excellent way to move the nuke north from San Diego. Moving it to the intended target, the last critical stage of the plan, wouldn't be nearly as expensive.

Which was why Vazquez's heavy drinking worried him. One slip of his liquor-loosened tongue could cause all their careful work to go to waste. The young man was vaguely aware of his father's involvement with the Alliance over the years, and he was also astute enough to understand the danger to his father and the rest of his family if he didn't fully cooperate. He wasn't aware, however, of the demolition nuke that had ridden along with his polo ponies all the way from San Diego, or that the crew driving the trucks consisted of Hezbollah warriors. In that sense, he was an innocent involved in a deadly plan. But he needed to be reminded he would be just as dead as the rest of his family if he betrayed Barak's mission in any way.

The Pronghorn Club and Resort where Vazquez was staying fit the young playboy, Barak thought. It was as luxurious as any of the golf resorts he had played in Las Vegas before he'd had to disappear, and it was far more scenic. It was a shame he didn't have time for eighteen holes on the Jack Nicklaus-designed course.

Although the organizer of the polo invitational had offered to let Vazquez stay at his ranch, he had declined and rented a suite. He apparently didn't spend a lot of time there, however. According to reports from the watcher, the young star preferred the bar in the clubhouse when he wasn't in the room of one of several young female admirers. If Barak wanted a private word with him, it would have to be around noon in the bar.

After parking his rental Escalade, he found Vazquez right where the watcher said he would be, seated at the end of the bar in the Trailhead Grill. Barak sat on the stool next to him.

"Your father would be disappointed in you, Vazquez," he said in a friendly voice. "He told you to behave yourself when you came to Oregon."

"How would you know that?" Vazquez asked without looking up.

"Because I told him to tell you to behave. He's a smart man. He cares what happens to his family, unlike you." Now Barak's voice was less friendly.

Vazquez turned and looked into the eyes of the man to his right. "You? You are the one he's afraid of? The one who made me come here?"

"Quiet your voice," Barak said. "Get up and go out to the patio where we can talk."

Barak led the way and stopped at the wrought iron railing. Without turning toward Vazquez, he said, "Don't ever raise your voice to me again. If you do, I will have your little sister kidnapped and raped until she pleads to be killed, and then her head alone will be sent to your mother to be buried. If you continue to get drunk every day and whore around every night, I will have your two brothers hacked to death with machetes and fed to your father's pigs. And if you do not do everything I tell you to do, I will have your mother and father killed, and then I will come for you. Now do I make myself clear?"

Vazquez stared at him.

"I asked you a question. Answer me."

Vazquez continued to stare, but he couldn't make a sound.

He nodded and when he could finally speak, it was a quiet "Yes."

"Good. We understand each other then. Ride your ponies. Show everyone what a star you are. Sober up. And pray we don't have to meet again." With that, Barak turned and walked away.

Vazquez remained on the patio, looking out toward the mountains for a long time before he turned and headed to his suite.

Chapter Twenty-Four

After a morning run and a light breakfast, Drake headed to Bend in his metallic gray Porsche. The last of the air-cooled Porsches, his 1997 Carrera was the gold standard for many Porschephiles. Drake liked the car because it was fast, looked great, and was fun to drive, which was the main reason he was looking forward to his time on the road to Bend. It was a chance to drive as fast as he wanted while his radar and laser protection system kept him from getting a speeding ticket. The concentration the drive required would also give his mind a chance to sort out why he thought an international polo star might be involved in nuclear terrorism or with his arch enemy, David Barak.

One brochure about a polo match, left in a Mexican villa that Barak might have stayed in, didn't exactly link the Argentine polo player, who happened to be in San Diego when a nuclear device was possibly detected, with a nuke in Bend. Or mean David Barak was involved in any way. Still, it was a coincidence that Drake couldn't overlook, even if the feds could. If a short road trip was required to check things out, well, that was just great.

One detail still had him puzzled. The piece that was missing from the mosaic of his intuitive masterpiece was the reason Barak would take the time to smuggle a nuke of any sort to Oregon. Bend, if that was his target, had a population that didn't top a hundred thousand or so. Portland, the largest city in the state, had a metropolitan area with just a little more than two million, and San Diego, where the nuke was thought to have crossed the border, had about three million residents in its metro area. Well, Drake thought, if a target of three million wasn't big enough, there was always Los Angeles with sixteen million residents.

So, he asked himself, what kind of target would attract a terrorist like Barak? If he was still intent on killing the Secretary of Homeland Security, he would have to get the nuke all the way across the country to Washington, D.C. Which didn't make any sense. If he was out for revenge because Drake had foiled his assassination attempt, he didn't need a nuke to take him out. A car bomb or a sniper would suffice. No, the target had to be something that would further the jihad in some big way. Killing one meddlesome attorney would hardly accomplish that.

Drake let his mind shift into neutral as he pulled off the I-5 freeway and turned east on Highway 20 toward Bend. Ahead on the two-lane highway that cut through the Cascade mountain range was the little city of Sisters, named after the three snow-capped, extinct volcanoes called Faith, Hope, and Charity by Oregon's early Methodist missionaries. Sisters was the first city you drove through on the other side of the mountains. Beyond Sisters, the high desert country of Oregon ran from the border with Washington in the north all the way south to the California border. Ranching and wheat farms dominated the northern reaches of the high desert, while resorts and golf courses surrounded the central plains city of Bend and the arid desert running south of Bend to the border.

Drake's father-in-law had grown up in Bend and loved his cabin at Crosswater, a golf resort south of the city. Just north of Crosswater was the mega-resort and private residential community of Sunriver, which had its own airport, two golf courses, and a private school, among other attractions. Both resorts straddled the Deschutes River, where Drake had learned to fly fish under the tutelage of his wife two summers ago.

Driving through central Oregon had always been an adventure for Drake. The highway cut through the Cascades amid forests of fir on the western slopes and Ponderosa pine on the eastern slopes. The road was twisty in sections and challenging at speed, with enough passing zones to let you open your car up from time to time. The only dangers you might encounter were deer running across the road and impatient motorists too eager to pass slower cars or trucks. To those limited risks, Drake usually added another by setting an arbitrary time limit for getting from Point A to Point B. Today, he was shooting for a time of two hours and fifteen minutes to cover the one hundred fifty eight mile distance. With a fifty-five mile an hour speed limit most of the way, though, he would have to exceed the legal limit a little.

After two hours of exhilarating driving fun and listening to the raspy exhaust notes of the Porsche, Drake slowed the car to a crawl as he drove through Sisters. With its 1880s frontier theme and variety of shops, the town was a favorite stopping place for tourists traveling to central Oregon. For him, it was a favorite place to stop for a burger in Bronco Billy's Ranch Grill and Saloon. Today, however, he continued on to the outskirts of Bend and turned north on Hwy. 97 toward the Red Lava Ranch, the home of the High Desert Polo Club and the host of the Pacific Polo Invitational.

Drake followed a line of semi's headed north until he turned off the highway and followed the directions from his voice-activated navigation Garmin to the white-fenced equine ranch and polo facility. The ranch got its name, he could see, from the red lava rock road leading to the clubhouse and offices of the polo club. On the south side of the road were sectioned pastures where horses, he assumed were polo ponies, grazed on green pasture grass. On the north side of the road was an incredibly flat polo field with white goal posts at each end. On ahead, behind the clubhouse and office building, were two stables with stalls and turnout paddocks and several outbuildings. All of the stable facilities and outbuildings were painted a soft red and had white roofs. The clubhouse itself, with a river rock façade, was a rich chocolate color.

Drake parked in front of the clubhouse and walked in. At one end of an empty great room stood a floor to vaulted ceiling fireplace made of river rock that matched the façade out front. Dark brown leather sofas and armchairs provided conversation islands near the fireplace, and a magnificent antique bar stood silent duty along one wall, waiting for thirsty patrons. An opening on his left led to a dining area, and on his right, a small office and reception area greeted visitors and members on their way to their lockers. A young woman wearing jeans and a white T-shirt sat behind a desk, checking off names on a list while she twisted the end of her pony tail.

"Hi," she said when Drake stopped in front of her desk. "May I help you?"

"I thought I might attend your polo match this weekend. Do I need to buy a ticket here, or will tickets be available at the gate?"

"Tickets are ten dollars per person. You can buy them here or at the gate Saturday."

"Great, I'll buy one now and see if I can round up some friends to join me. He handed her a ten dollar bill. "Are there practice sessions or preliminary events? I don't know much about polo."

"The Pacific Polo Invitational match starts at eleven Saturday morning." She sounded like she was reciting memorized text. "That's what you'll want to see. We're extremely proud to have Marco Vazquez on one of the teams. He's one of the top-rated polo players in the world, and he came all the way from Argentina to be here. There will be some junior events earlier in the morning, but the Invitational is the big event."

"So Saturday is when all the polo players show up? Or do they get here before then?"

"Most of the players and their ponies will arrive fairly early Saturday morning, but Mr. Vazquez is already here. He's keeping his ponies over at the Wyler Ranch. That's Mr. Abazzano's place."

"Is that where this Vazquez fellow is staying?"

She shook her head. "I think I heard he's staying at the Pronghorn Resort, but he's probably over at the Wyler Ranch making sure they're feeding his ponies correctly. Polo ponies need to be fed differently than those thoroughbreds Mr. Abazzano breeds. Can I help you with anything else?" she said as she looked down at her list of names.

"No, you've been a big help. Thank you."

Drake took his ticket and walked out to his car. Michael Abazzano was a name he knew. He was a rich Hollywood producer who made movies only the Cannes International Film Festival loved and documentaries about the plight of the Palestinians. A big contributor to every liberal cause, Abazzano was famous for fundraisers hosted at his mansion in Hollywood Hills, Los Angeles, and parties before the Kentucky Derby when he had horses racing.

Abazzano's beautiful wife, Nadine, who was from Lebanon, had starred in several of his movies. Drake had seen her interviewed on CNN and MSNBC where she had described living in a Palestinian refugee camp in Lebanon as a young girl and seeing her parents killed during the Shatila massacre during the Lebanese civil war in 1982. She blamed the Israeli Defense Forces, of course, for allowing the massacre to happen.

Drake decided a visit to Abazzano's Wyler Ranch was in order.

Chapter Twenty-Five

Wyler Ranch was a thoroughbred breeding farm located eight miles north of Sisters, Oregon. Telling his voice-activated navigation device to find the ranch, Drake located it easily and followed the directions from the female voice he'd named Lucy.

The ranch was located in a canyon with a good-sized stream running through it. Once Drake left the highway and dropped down into the canyon, he was in a private world of natural beauty. The road followed the stream for a short way, then veered off through a thicket of aspens. Beyond the aspens was a long pasture with high, white fencing like the horse farms of Kentucky. He saw a dozen or more stallions grazing and a group of young fillies and colts racing around with their tails raised high. At the far end of the pasture stood the stables, a long, low building and a cluster of equipment and storage sheds. On a rise halfway to the edge of the rimrock above the pastures a Tuscan-style villa stood watch over the ranch.

Drake drove along the fence and watched as the young horses raced him to the end of the pasture. Even at this stage of their development, they were both graceful and powerful as they ran. They had racing in their blood, that was plain to see.

As he pulled to a stop in the parking area near the stables, he saw several horses being groomed in the private paddocks outside their stalls. The men working on the horses watched him closely as he got out of the Porsche and walked toward a man standing next to the biggest pickup truck he had ever seen.

"Hi," Drake said, extending his hand to the man. "I'm looking for Marco Vazquez. Is he here?"

"This is private property," the man replied. "Didn't you see the No Trespassing signs?"

Drake drew his hand back and casually looked around. The man looked like an old farmhand, but his eyes suggested he was younger than he looked. "You in charge here?" he asked.

"I'm the ranch foreman. Who are you?"

"I'm here to speak with Marco Vazquez. Is he here?"

"You from the polo ranch?"

"Just came from there. Can you get him for me?"

"He isn't here yet. He usually checks on his ponies after he's had a liquid breakfast at the Pronghorn."

"Isn't that what big stars do these days?"

"Big star, my ass. Mr. Abazzano's a big star, and he doesn't wobble around like this guy does. He might be good looking and can ride a horse, but he's no star in my book."

Drake smiled. "I take it you don't care much for him or his horses?"

"I don't have to like him or his horses," the foreman said. "Mr. Abazzano's doing a favor for a friend, letting him keep his horses here. Vazquez brought his own guys to take care of the polo ponies, so it doesn't matter much to me."

"Those the guys over there? The ones he brought with him?" Drake glanced in their direction. "The ones giving me the evil eye when I drove in?" They were still looking at him.

"Those are the ones. They don't talk much. I'm not sure they know much about horses, but, again, not my problem."

"Well, I should be going if I want to catch him at the Pronghorn. Thanks for your help," Drake said, and turned away.

The two men grooming Vazquez's horses continued to watch Drake as they worked.

"You guys know when Vazquez will get here?" Drake called out midway to his car.

Neither answered him, so he walked closer. "I asked you if you knew when Vazquez will get here," he said, raising his voice just slightly.

"*No se*," one of the men said, and continued brushing his horse.

"Did you come from Argentina with him?"

"*No se*," the groom said again.

Then the other man walked around his horse, said something softly to the first man, and they both walked away.

In that moment, Drake knew he was right to check out this ranch. He had heard the exchange. The second man had spoken colloquial Lebanese, a dialect developed from Syrian Arabic that he had been taught to recognize before he deployed in the Middle East. It was the dialect spoken by Jordanians, Palestinians, Syrians, and Lebanese. And Hezbollah.

He left the ranch. Driving back along the road that followed the meandering stream, he called Casey in Seattle.

"I know you miss me," he said in greeting, "so I thought I'd invite you back to Oregon so we could spend a little more time together."

"My, my, my, how the time flies," Casey said. "It seems like it was just yesterday when we said our goodbyes. Oh, wait—it *was* yesterday."

Drake grinned into the phone. "Does that mean you don't miss me as much as I miss you?"

"No. It means I don't miss you as much as I miss my wife. What's up?"

"I just heard a guy say something to another guy in Arabic."

"Where? On Al Jazeera news?"

"No. On a ranch here in Oregon. I thought I'd see if that brochure about the polo match I found in the villa in Mexico had anything to do with the nuke they detected in San Diego. I think it does, and I'm going to need your help to prove it."

"Whoa, back it up a bit," Casey said. "You didn't tell me about a polo brochure you found in the Mexican villa."

"It was in the room upstairs, the one we thought Barak might have slept in. It's for a polo fundraiser here in Bend this weekend, starring some hotshot polo player from Argentina. I thought it was odd that a drug dealer in Mexico, or even Barak, would be interested in polo, so I took it. When I mentioned it to Liz Strobel, she told me if I found it had anything to do with the missing nuke to let her know. So I drove up to Bend today and started poking around."

Casey thought about this for a second or two. "What does the polo star have to do with the nuke?"

"I don't know. The brochure was about this fundraiser. He's the big attraction. They found radiation in a van abandoned next to the San Diego Polo Club. At the ranch I just left, I saw an International RXT truck with California plates towing a luxury horse trailer with the polo star's name on it. The trailer has enough room for four horses, all the equipment…and a nuke or two. No one would suspect an international polo star of hiding a nuclear device in his horse trailer."

"But why would a guy like that get involved in nuclear terrorism?"

"Who knows why the uber-rich do anything. Maybe he loaned them his horse trailer. Maybe he doesn't know anything about a nuke."

"Who are they?" Casey asked.

"Maybe it's Barak. Maybe it's Hezbollah. They dig tunnels under the border in San Diego for the drug smugglers. Maybe it's the guy who owns this ranch, Michael Abazzano. I don't know."

"Abazzano…the Hollywood guy with the gorgeous wife half his age?"

"Beautiful, young and extremely anti-Semitic, yeah. Her parents were killed in the Shatila massacre in Lebanon."

"Home of Hezbollah. What a coincidence! So, buddy, what is it you want me to do?"

"Abazzano's ranch is in a narrow canyon, with rimrock on both sides. Video surveillance of any activity there won't be difficult, but I'm hoping we can get audio surveillance as well. Did you go ahead and buy those Draganflyer surveillance drones you were talking about?"

"I bought two," Casey said. "We equipped one with a Nikon SLR for still photos and the other with a Sony Handycam for video and sound. The Draganflyer's motors don't make any noise so if someone's talking we'll hear them. In hover mode at fifty meters, they won't see it either."

"That's what I was hoping for," said Drake.

"How big a team do you need this time?"

"Are you able to get away?"

"Well, I do need a reason to take my new helicopter on a cross-county flight," Casey said. "Seattle to Bend really isn't cross-country, but it's a start."

"What new helicopter?" Drake asked.

"With all the new customers we're getting since you put ISIS out of business, I upgraded our capabilities a bit and bought a new Bell 525 Relentless. It was delivered when we were in Mexico. Wait'll you see it, Adam. There's nothing like it in the air."

"How many passengers can it carry?"

"Sixteen. You need that many?"

"No, I don't think so. Maybe you and three others. If we find this polo angle has anything to do with the nuke the government is looking for, I'll call in the cavalry."

"When do you want me there?"

"Okay," Drake said after doing a quick mental calculation, "today is Wednesday. How about tomorrow sometime? That gives us two days before the polo match on Saturday. You and your guys plan on staying with me at the senator's place at Crosswater. There's plenty of room."

"I'll land at the Sunriver airport, about noon. You buying lunch?"

"Sure, why not. Meet me at Hola! at the Sunriver marina. We can eat on the deck and watch the tourists trying to paddle the canoes on the Deschutes."

Chapter Twenty-Six

BARAK WAS SITTING IN A RED CEDAR ADIRONDACK CHAIR ON the deck of the hangar house when Saleem, the head of the Hezbollah team, called him.

"Someone just visited the ranch, looking for Vazquez," Saleem reported. "Want me to find out who it was?"

"Yes. But discreetly. It could be someone from the polo club. Check it out and call me."

It wasn't unexpected that someone would be looking for Vazquez. But with all that was at stake, it would be foolish to ignore any approach to the weakest member of his team. His pilot didn't know anything about the plan, and the Hezbollah men were used to keeping their mouths shut. In their world, life ended quickly for someone who talked too much. Vazquez, on the other hand, loved to talk to his fawning fans and the press. The only secret he was good at keeping was which rich man's wife he was sleeping with in any given city. It would give Barak great pleasure to dispose of the young infidel when he had served his purpose.

Until now, Vazquez had not been aware of the arrangement his father had made with the Alliance. The respect he had for his father, and the financial backing his father provided for his polo career, had been enough to persuade the boy to do whatever his father asked him to do. But the addition of the amateur polo match in Oregon, which was such a departure from the circuit the elite polo players of the world traveled, had led to an ill-tempered rebellion on the part of Vazquez. To quell it, his father had threatened to withdraw his sponsorship and reclaim the four polo ponies he had purchased for his son.

Since then, Vazquez had been behaving like the spoiled man-child he was, drinking and womanizing his way along the polo circuit until he arrived in Oregon. Barak had passed along a request for Ryan to instruct the father to tell his son to start behaving or there would be consequences. That hadn't worked, so he had added his own warning.

SALEEM CANAAN, the leader of the Hezbollah task force in Tijuana, had replaced Jameel Nasr when Jameel's efforts to establish a network in Mexico were discovered and he was arrested. Jameel had been sloppy. He had failed to use different identities to conceal his frequent travels to Lebanon, Venezuela, and the Tri-Border Area in South America to meet with Hezbollah and Alliance leaders. But Saleem, or Sal as he had been known to his classmates at San Diego State University, wasn't going to be so easy to discover.

Saleem's father was Lebanese and had immigrated to America during the Lebanese Civil War. His mother, who was Mexican, had been born in San Diego as a so-called anchor baby and as such was an American citizen. Saleem's father and mother were not aware of his passion for jihad, which had been cultivated at the mosque they attended. Nor were they aware of their son's position within Hezbollah. Although he had received a scholarship from an Islamic foundation to attend the university and obtain a master's degree in computer science, Saleem had never shown any interest in computers before. He had always preferred playing soccer to studying. But his imam had persuaded him that his mission was to prepare himself for a future Hezbollah that would be more sophisticated and able to employ cyber warfare against its enemies. Saleem had been promised that he would be just as useful with a computer as he would be with a gun as a holy warrior.

He was thus the perfect homegrown terrorist. He could travel anywhere and, with his natural good looks and athletic ability, blend into any academic or professional setting involving his field of study. What Hezbollah had discovered in grooming him as a cyber terrorist was that Saleem also liked to hurt people. Especially people he thought stood in the way of a worldwide caliphate and didn't deserve to live long enough to enjoy its blessing.

Which was why Saleem had been chosen to lead the team accompanying Barak to Oregon with the demolition nuke. He was smart, capable, and could slip into any setting without attracting attention. Like the posh Pronghorn golf resort.

Saleem parked his rented Escalade in the visitors lot near the clubhouse and walked into the Trailhead Grill, where Barak had found the polo star drinking. An older couple occupied two places at the bar, laughing at something on the woman's iPad. The only other person in the restaurant was the bartender.

Saleem approached the bartender with a smile on his face.

"Hi, I'm looking for Marco Vazquez."

"He's at the pool," the bartender said and pointed outside. "Working on his tan."

The swimming pool behind the Trailhead was ringed with patio tables with maroon umbrellas and chaise lounges covered in a matching maroon fabric. Vazquez, wearing nothing but a skimpy Speedo and lying on a chaise lounge, was hard to miss. He looked like he would be right at home on a gay beach in San Diego or strolling down Ipanema beach in Rio de Janeiro.

Saleem sat at an empty table near the polo star and motioned for a waiter. Even in the shade of the table's umbrella, it was a hot afternoon. The heat required one to keep hydrated. Beer was good for hydration.

In the first thirty minutes, Vazquez moved just once to turn over. As soon as he did this, a young woman wearing a pair of white shorts and crisp white blouse walked out of the Pronghorn spa next to the pool. She was carrying a white towel and a bottle of sunscreen. When Vazquez waved to her, she knelt beside him and began rubbing the lotion over his back and legs. Saleem stared as she carefully massaged the sunscreen all the way up his legs until her fingers stopped at the narrow band of the Speedo.

Saleem wasn't a virgin by any means, but he couldn't remember any lover rubbing him down as suggestively as this woman was rubbing Vazquez's backside. If this was a prelude to an afternoon tryst, he thought, at least he wouldn't have to worry about any visitor from the ranch meeting with the Argentine Romeo any time soon.

Thirty minutes after being lotioned up and turning over to tan his chest, Vazquez stood up, stretched languidly, signaled a waiter for a drink, and dove into the pool. Two laps across and back and he was out again, toweling himself off and sitting at a table not far from Saleem's. When his drink, which looked like a Long Island iced tea in a chimney glass, arrived, the polo star sat back in his chair and gazed at the mountains in the distance. He seemed unaware of everything around him except the drink in his right hand and the small gold cross on the chain around his neck. He was twisting it back and forth with the fingers of his left hand.

From what Saleem could see, Marco Vazquez might be a big shot polo player, but he wasn't enjoying his stardom.

Chapter Twenty-Seven

DRAKE ALSO FOUND THE POLO STAR AT THE POOL, NOW WITH the empty glass on the table next to him. Wearing his apple green Speedo and wrap-around sunglasses, Vazquez looked every bit the international celebrity he was. After watching him for a moment while polishing his own sunglasses, Drake walked over and sat down across from him.

He gestured to the waiter. "May I buy you a drink?" Drake asked.

Vazquez hardly opened his eyes. "Long Island iced tea with double shots of everything," he murmured with a slight slurring of his words. As the waiter left, he sat up straighter and asked, "Do I know you?"

Drake gave him a self-effacing smile. "I'm just a guy wanting to have a drink with you."

"Okay, then. Why do you want to have a drink with me?"

"You're Marco Vazquez! Doesn't *everyone* want to have a drink with you?"

"They used to. Not so much anymore. Except for the women."

Drake looked surprised. "Don't you have men you drink

with? What about the guys you travel with? The men who take care of your horses?"

"I don't drink with them. They don't drink alcohol. They don't even speak my language. They just take care of my ponies."

"Well, then—fire them and hire men you can drink with."

Vazquez shook his head. "I can't."

"Didn't you bring these men with you from Argentina?"

"No, they were given to me in San Diego. For this match only. I won't have to deal with them after this."

"Why is that?

"You would need to talk with my father about that." His new drink arrived and he stopped speaking.

"I went out to the ranch where your horses are," Drake said. "Are those guys who speak Arabic the ones who came up from San Diego with you?"

Vazquez took off his sunglasses and turned to look more closely at Drake. "How did you know that? How did you know I came from San Diego? And why do you think these men came with me? I flew here. They just drove my horses and equipment here."

"From the San Diego Polo Club?"

Fear flashed in the eyes of the young polo star as he stood up. "I have a massage now. Thank you for the drink."

Drake gave him a cordial nod, then turned and watched Vazquez walk to the door of the spa. As he pulled the door open, he paused to look back, then went inside.

Vazquez wasn't what Drake had expected. For one reason, he was alone at the pool. Drake had thought he would have to wade through a bevy of young lovelies wearing even less than Vazquez and trying to get his attention. There were half a dozen other people scattered around the pool, sunning themselves or reading, but none of them appeared to be paying any attention to anyone else. Drake also recalled that Vazquez excelled at a dangerous sport that required athleticism and steady nerves. But, no, this kid looked like a horse off his feed; listless, out of shape, and jumpy.

Drake sat back and considered his options. If Vazquez had smuggled a nuke into the country, he had good reason to be jumpy. But why would an international polo star get involved with something that would jeopardize his career and his life? A ten-goal player like him made big bucks, a hundred thousand dollars a tournament. He lived the life of a rock star. Most terrorists, at least the ones Drake had come across, were fanatical Islamists and hated everything Western celebrities flaunted; their wealth, their promiscuity, their alcoholic drinks, and especially their scantily clad women.

There was something about Marco Vazquez that wasn't right. Drake needed to find out what it was.

SALEEM WATCHED Vazquez's visitor get up and leave before he called Barak.

"I don't think the guy who just bought Vazquez a drink is a polo fan," he said. "He didn't look like a cop, either, but he asked a lot of questions."

"What kind of questions?"

"Did the men who take care of his horses speak Arabic. Did they travel with him from San Diego."

Saleem could sense Barak's anger during the long silence that followed.

"Describe the man for me," Barak said.

"Six feet tall, maybe a little more, mid to late thirties. Dark hair. Wearing jeans, a white polo shirt, running shoes. He moves like an athlete and looks like he's in good shape. Well tanned. Probably spends a lot of time outdoors."

"Follow him," Barak said. "See if you can find out who he is." He disconnected.

Saleem left ten dollars on the table for his beer and

hurried back through the clubhouse to the parking lot. As he got into his Escalade and closed the door, he noticed a metallic gray Porsche turning the corner out of the lot on the road leading to the gatehouse. A flash of white in the open window of the car matched the color of the shirt worn by the man talking to Vazquez.

Keeping the big SUV at a discrete distance behind the Porsche, Saleem turned on the SiriusXM radio to Hip-Hop Nation and cranked up the volume. He might as well enjoy himself, he thought, as he prayed quickly to Allah that he was following the right car. He increased his speed past the posted twenty mile an hour speed limit at the resort.

By the time he reached the gatehouse, he saw that the Porsche had turned south and was headed toward Bend. Saleem let a car pass, then pulled onto the highway and followed. According to the map on the Escalade's GPS navigation screen, he had fifteen miles to get closer and make sure he was following the right man.

To the right, as he drove down Highway 97, he could see the white peaks of the Three Sisters in the distance. Small acreage home sites, with enough room for several horses, lined the route. Stands of juniper and sagebrush dotted the rolling landscape, with yellow wildflowers and outcroppings of lava and rimrock adding color to the scenery. Having grown up in Southern California, Saleem wasn't used to the feeling of vast space the high desert provided, but he thought he could get used to it. He wondered if the deserts of Saudi Arabia would make him feel the same way. When he made his *hajj* pilgrimage to Mecca, he told himself, perhaps he could find out.

As the city of Bend drew nearer, the traffic increased and forced him to concentrate to keep the Porsche in sight. Five cars now separated him from the man who had visited Vazquez, but the Escalade's height gave him a clear view of the smaller sports car. The afternoon traffic was fairly heavy as it passed through the city, but it was nothing like he was used to in San Diego. Traffic. That was one thing about Southern California he definitely did not miss.

Just as the cars ahead began to speed up as they reached the southern edge of the city, Saleem saw the Porsche turn off the highway and pull into the small parking lot in front of a Deschutes Property Management building. He slowed, too, and drove into the lot of the Rimrock BrewPub and Grill next door. When he turned to look, he saw that he had been following the right man. White polo shirt, jeans, running shoes. The man was now wearing aviator sunglasses.

He turned the volume down on the radio and sat back to wait. In less time than it took to change the radio from SiriusXM to a local station, his target returned to his car and got back in. Before he did, however, he put a cell phone to his ear and talked with someone for several minutes. At one point, the man turned toward the Escalade and seemed to look right through the darkened window at Saleem.

When the Porsche backed up and got back on the highway heading south, Saleem followed again. This time, feeling slightly uneasy with the way the man had stared at him, he stayed farther behind than before. Whoever this guy was, he could not be allowed to interfere with their holy work. No infidel alive could be allowed to do that.

Ten minutes after leaving the BrewPub parking lot, Saleem found himself staring at a cinder volcanic cone that rose from a field of black lava next to the highway. He must have been sleeping when he passed it on the drive up from San Diego, because this was a sight he would have remembered. What a place this must have been thousands of years ago when the volcano spewed its fiery breath for miles around. Volcanic destruction would have been greater, but it probably didn't kill as many people as Barak planned to kill. Saleem grew excited again as he thought of what he was privileged to be a part of.

Focusing again on the car he was following, he saw that it was slowing as it approached the flashing signal of an intersection ahead. There the gray Porsche turned right onto South Century Drive and drove west, past the entrance to a large resort, until it turned again onto a drive leading to the Crosswater Golf Course.

Saleem had played a few rounds of golf with friends and considered the time spent walking around and chasing a ball he could never hit straight a waste of time. If the guy he was following was going to this place to play golf, he would at least know where he was for the next four hours.

Instead of driving to the clubhouse, however, the Porsche drove up to a manned gatehouse. Saleem pulled to the side of the road and took his iPhone from the console to take a picture of the spectacular scenery. What he made sure to include in the shot were the gatehouse and the Porsche sitting next to it. If he couldn't gain entrance to the residential golf community called the Crosswater Golf and Social Club, at least he would have something to show Barak.

And, sure enough, when he pulled up to the gatehouse, the guard politely told him only members were permitted to enter and that he needed to turn around and leave.

Chapter Twenty-Eight

Drake sat still and watched in his rearview mirror as the black Escalade turned around at the gatehouse and drove away. He had seen that he was being followed shortly after leaving the Pronghorn resort. The Escalade had stayed four or five car lengths behind him all the way to Bend and maintained the same spacing as they drove through the city. He had tried to see who was in the SUV when he stopped to get the keys to his father-in-law's cabin, but the darkened windows had obscured his view. He had gotten the Escalade's license plate number and thought the security camera at the gatehouse might give him a better look at his pursuer.

Whoever it was, he or she hadn't done much surveillance duty. Professionals worked in teams on moving surveillance, and they didn't maintain distance and speed like this guy had. It was unlikely, Drake thought, that Vazquez had a bodyguard curious enough to follow him all the way to Crosswater. It was also unlikely the organizers of the polo match guarded their celebrity player that closely. That left Abazzano and the Arab groomers from the horse ranch as possibilities. Everyone else who knew he was in Bend was on his side.

He drove slowly along the golf course, which crossed and

recrossed the meandering Little Deschutes River, until he came to the two-story log cabin on a secluded section of the resort. The Hazelton's summer "cabin," as they jokingly referred to it, was a four thousand square foot showplace of Northwest architecture and materials. When he and Kay had visited, they had always stayed in one of the four second-floor bedrooms, but now the master bedroom on the first floor was available. With the library and study adjacent to it, and the covered porch with a hot tub just through the bedroom's french doors, Drake thought it might be just the place to relax and figure out what to do.

Of course, if he didn't lay claim to the master bedroom before Casey and his team arrived, he knew Casey would make some lame argument that the room's close proximity to the library and study meant that he should make the sacrifice and stay there to run the show. As much as he loved the guy, it was only right that he should be the one to make the sacrifice. Besides, the three guys he was bringing with him would feel abandoned if their boss stayed downstairs in the master bedroom.

Drake opened the door of the detached garage and pulled his car in. Grabbing his duffel bag from the back seat, he walked down the covered breezeway to the entrance through the utility room. When he opened the door with the key the property manager had given him, the lingering smell of the tung oil that had been used to seal the red oak floors greeted him like an old friend. The scent also brought such strong memories of Kay that he stopped to cherish the moment before he moved through the kitchen and into the great room, where floor-to-ceiling windows provided a view of the river past the deck that ran the length of the room. One end of the great room was dominated by a massive river rock fireplace, and the doors to the master bedroom and the library opened at the other end. A dark brown leather sofa sat in front of the fireplace, with two matching leather arm chairs on each end, and a glass-topped coffee table supported by two sets of deer antlers in front. Drake thought he picked up the smell of cigar smoke as he walked over and stood behind the sofa. Running his hand over the leather, he thought the senator just might have used the cabin a time or two for a men-only weekend, as his wife, Meredith, didn't let him smoke when she was around.

He turned, walked to the other end of the great room, and claimed the master bedroom by throwing his duffel bag on the king-size bed. Then he went in search of an adult beverage to take out on the deck while he called his secretary's husband, Paul Benning.

Benning, who had been Drake's favorite detective when he was a prosecutor in the district attorney's office, had been a Marine who had deployed to Beirut, Lebanon, in September, 1982, as a member of a multinational force intended to stabilize the Lebanese government and serve as peacekeepers. The next October, Paul had helped pull the bodies of two hundred and forty-one dead American servicemen out of the ruins of the U.S barracks when it was destroyed by a suicide bomber driving a yellow Mercedes truck.

When he'd left the Marine Corp and returned home, Benning had joined the Multnomah County Sheriff's Office and quickly risen through the ranks to become a senior detective working with the Special Investigations Unit. His wife, Margo, was the first secretary assigned to work with Drake in the D.A.'s office, and so the three had soon become good friends. Benning was good at thinking out of the box. He had also learned how to access information that was not available to most civilians. Which was why Drake was calling him for another favor.

"Paul," he said, "this is Adam. Am I catching you at a bad time?"

"I'm sitting at my desk, trying to find a way to cut the unit's budget by twenty percent for next year. What do you think?"

"Sounds like you need a break."

"Something tells me you're going to offer me an opportunity to do something other than what the county is paying me to do."

Drake laughed. "Just consider this an extraterritorial investigation that will prevent a crime from happening."

"What kind of crime?" Benning asked.

"Breaking and entering. For the purpose of obtaining information regarding the driver of a new black Escalade, Oregon license 294YYZ. It followed me from Pronghorn to Crosswater."

"And the place where this crime might happen?"

"Enterprise Car Rental. Probably somewhere in Bend."

"This will cost you, you know."

"Your usual fee?" Drake asked. "Burger and a beer?"

"For my speedy service, it's now a burger and two beers," Benning said. Give me a moment." Drake heard the sounds of his keyboard. "The car was a new Escalade leased for the week to one Timothy A. O'Neil at the Sunriver airport," Benning reported.

"Is there an address for him?"

"No. I'll attach a copy of the Enterprise registration and email it to you. Will that be all?"

"Thanks, Paul. Tell your wife I'll call her."

Drake sat out on the deck and watched a pair of ring-necked ducks paddling their way up the river. The microbrew he'd found in the refrigerator tasted good in the heat of the afternoon, but its slightly bitter, hoppy taste mated itself with an irritating pinging in his brain. The man who had leased the Escalades was nearby. If he was staying at the Sunriver Resort, they would have to pay him a visit when Mike arrived tomorrow.

As he walked back to the kitchen to get another beer, his cell phone vibrated.

"Hi, Adam." He recognized the voice of Liz Strobel immediately.

"Did you find the nuke?" he asked her.

"NEST is calling off the search," she said. "We've had teams covering a five square mile area on foot, with gamma and neutron detectors, vans driving all over the greater San Diego area, and helicopters crisscrossing Southern California. It's looking for the proverbial needle in a very big haystack."

"Has intelligence turned up anything?"

"Only rumors. And because we're waving dollars at every source we have, who knows how reliable any of it is," she said. "Rumor is, the nuke may have come in from Venezuela."

"From our best friend in South America," Drake said. "What a surprise. Chavez is willing to help anyone interested in hitting us, though, so that's not much of a lead."

"Look," she said, "I'm flying to Oregon tomorrow to brief the Portland FBI office on our final report on the assassination attempt on the Secretary. I thought I might stop by and go over it with you, so we're all on the same page if the FBI wants to follow up with you."

"I'm still in Bend. Can you send it to me?"

"There's nothing in writing yet. Maybe I could arrange a short stopover in Bend if you have time to meet with me."

"Sure, why not. Mike is flying to the Sunriver Airport in his new helicopter tomorrow at noon. If you can get here, why don't you meet us for lunch? There's a little Mexican-Peruvian restaurant called Hola! at the marina, right next to the airport."

"Good. Then I'll see you tomorrow."

Drake grabbed another beer and went back out on the deck. He suspected there wasn't anything that secret about the spin the government was putting on the assassination attempt. It was more likely that Liz Strobel wanted to know if he had turned up anything on the missing nuke and was too proud to ask him directly.

Chapter Twenty-Nine

THE MORNING SKY WAS JUST LOSING ITS FLUSH OF PINK WHEN Drake left the Senator's cabin for a run. The air was crisp at five-thirty and mist was rising over the Deschutes River. The peak of Mount Bachelor, where the U.S. Ski Team had trained in summers past, reflected the pastel sky and the sound of grounds keepers mowing the greens broke the night's silence.

While his breathing adjusted to its normal running rate of four strides per exchange, he mentally sorted through the options for the day. After he fed Casey and his men, he needed to get eyes on the ranch where Vazquez was keeping his polo ponies and learn more about those Arab-speaking groomers. He also needed to locate the guy who had rented the black Escalades and find out why it had followed him yesterday. Abazzano's ranch, where he visited yesterday, and the Sunriver Resort, where Timothy O'Neil was staying, were thirty miles or more apart. But they were connected somehow.

And he needed to meet Liz Strobel and find out what was so important that she needed to see him in person. He had followed the media's reporting of the two attempts on the life of Secretary Rallings, the head of DHS. The pathetic attempt of the Portland imams to paint the killing of the terrorists as another example of the U.S. government's war on American Muslims by luring them into conspiracies they knew nothing about had died a whimpering death in the media. The investigation of the three Muslims killed on his farm had also been quietly closed. The explosion that had reduced the Senator's home to a pile of smoldering rubble had been reported as an unfortunate accident caused by a natural gas leak. The Senator's closest neighbors hadn't believed the story, but after a personal visit from him, they had agreed to corroborate the government's story.

It wasn't that he was opposed to meeting with Liz, he thought as he finished his second circuit around the golf course. He was willing to acknowledge that she was beautiful. And probably a lot of fun if she could ever forget for a minute she was the Special Assistant to the Secretary of Homeland Security. He just wasn't ready to allow himself to be attracted to *any* woman. Kay's death was still a painful memory that crept into his consciousness every day, and although his promise had been "till death do us part," he knew he would never stop loving her.

The sudden thought of her made him slow to a jog, then stop alongside a bench. Five antlered deer were grazing in a meadow on the other side of the river. He could clearly hear the excited squeal of Kay's voice telling him to look, look at the deer. She had loved seeing wildlife, especially deer and elk, whenever they had hiked the Cascades or the coast range of Oregon. She had loved everything about just about everything. She had also believed everyone was naturally good inside. Drake knew better, that evil existed incarnate, but he had loved her innocence and her unblinking trust in mankind. Like the deer, he thought, wild animals that now raised their heads to watch him but showed no fear in his presence.

With a shake of his head, Drake broke out of his reverie

and headed back to the cabin. To clear his mind and focus his energy, he kicked up his pace and sprinted the last half mile.

After a shower and a quick breakfast consisting of a cup of coffee and a protein smoothie, he backed his Porsche out of the garage and drove slowly toward the gatehouse at the other end of Crosswater as the engine warmed up and settled into a throaty burble.

He wasn't sure where to start his search for the man who'd leased the black Escalade, but he had plenty of time before Casey flew in from Seattle. With any luck, the restaurant at the lodge would have a receipt for a dinner or drinks that would provide him an address for O'Neil in the sprawling resort community. It was a place to start and would kill some time before lunch.

As he approached the gatehouse and slowed for the gate to draw open, Drake noticed an old Chevrolet pickup painted camouflage green and black parked off to the side of the road ahead. Gray exhaust rose from it in the morning air and drifted forward over the roof light bar with its four chrome spot lights. He paused for a moment to see if the truck was going to pull out in front of him. When it didn't move, he drove on by. Accelerating ahead, he saw the pickup turn out and come toward him. It soon caught up and matched his speed, three car lengths behind. The jacked-up four-by-four had a massive black brush guard protecting its grill that looked like it could punch a hole in a cement wall.

Ahead, Drake saw a slow-moving flatbed truck loaded with hay in his lane. The two-lane country road was straight for a quarter mile or so, and he anticipated that he had plenty of time to pass it, but when he increased his speed as he approached the hay truck, he saw that the pickup was now only one car length behind.

What the hell? What was this guy doing? Drivers often pulled alongside to get a better look at his Porsche, but they almost always flashed a thumbs up at him. For some reason he doubted the driver of the pickup was an admirer of old Porsches. Drake down shifted into fourth gear to pull into the other lane. Then he saw the bed of the hay truck start to tilt upwards. The bales of hay that had been stacked six high began to slide off and tumble toward him, breaking apart and throwing hay high into the air.

Touching the brake pedal lightly and dodging to the left to allow a bale of hay somersaulting end over end to sail over his roof, he saw the black brush guard of the pickup flashing by on his right, missing his car by inches. The pickup ploughed through the hay bales, and when its left front tire ran up onto the tilted flatbed of the hay truck, it was launched into the air, then plunged into the river beside the road.

Shaking his head, Drake shot ahead of the hay truck and kept on going. From the menacing look on the face of the hay truck's driver, he knew he had narrowly avoided being ambushed by two thugs masquerading as country bumpkins. If one of them was finding he was in over his head trying to be a bad boy, his partner would have to help him out of the river. He wasn't going to stick around and lend a hand.

When his hands began to shake, he knew his sympathetic nervous system had triggered the old "fight-or-flight" mechanism. It was an old and reliable response that had gotten him through more than a few close calls. But he was always glad when it had run its course.

Five minutes later, he turned into the Sunriver Resort and drove to the lodge. The sports bar on the second floor probably wouldn't be open yet, but he knew he could get a good Bloody Mary in the restaurant to calm his nerves.

He parked his car and walked up the stairs, through the lobby and straight to the Meadows Restaurant. After he was seated at the window overlooking the golf course and had ordered his nourishment, he took a pen he borrowed from the waitress and began making notes on a napkin. The pickup truck in the river had an Oregon license plate, 697DTB.

Benning would find out who it belonged to. Its driver looked to have been Latino, but in Oregon as in most of the country, that didn't provide much of an identifier. The driver of the hay truck had also looked Latino. Or perhaps Middle-Eastern. But he hadn't gotten a good luck at the truck itself, except to see that it was old and had faded red paint and a tilting flatbed.

For the second time in as many days, Drake wanted to know why someone was interested in him. And was now interested enough to want him out of the picture. He had his suspicions, but as Liz Strobel kept insisting, suspicions weren't getting them any closer to the nuke they were hunting. So far, it was just a string of coincidences that he couldn't tie together.

Chapter Thirty

A MILE AWAY ACROSS A MEADOW AND A GOLF COURSE FROM where Drake was sitting in a restaurant, Barak was pacing up and down the length of the front deck of the hangar house. He had a cell phone at his ear.

"Tell me, Saleem, how did your men screw this up?"

"They are two of my best men," the younger man replied. "That's why I brought them. They tell me he drove his car like a racing driver to avoid the flying hay bales the way he did. We were just unlucky this time."

"Do not mention luck to me. If this man is who I think he is, luck did not save him from your ambush. If he shows his face again, at the ranch or anywhere near Vazquez, I want him killed. Also the two men who just failed. Are we clear on that?"

"I will take care of it," Saleem said. "Will you be at Abazzano's ranch later?"

"This afternoon. I want to see if your men are ready. You will need two more men to carry out your assignment."

"Replacements from our cell up north are already on their way."

Barak closed his cell phone and removed its pre-paid SIM

card. He would drop the burner phone somewhere on a street in Bend as he passed through on his way to the Wyler Ranch, The pre-paid SIM card itself would be tossed in the creek at the ranch.

He smiled to himself as he thought about Michael Abazzano. The man had all the progressive sympathies they had come to count on—his love of the underdog Palestinians, his anti-Semitism, and his loathing of the values and traditions of fly-over America. But it was his wife, the lovely Nadine, that made Barak smile. She had been one of theirs even before her parents had been killed in the refugee camp massacres in Lebanon. She had been ordered to seduce Abazzano at the Cannes International Film Festival and had married him shortly after. Since then, she was their main contact in Hollywood. She had been instrumental in getting her husband and other movie producers to promote their cause.

The West was so easily misled. The Qu'ran allowed deceit as a tool to conquer the world, and even though the command was there in black and white for all to see, the sophisticated elite in the West still refused to believe they were being lied to.

It was the old enemies who kept getting in the way, he said to himself, the ones they had fought before and knew our ways. Like that attorney in Portland, who had prevented the assassination of the DHS Secretary. After he had been forced to flee to Mexico when his headquarters in Las Vegas were raided, Barak had learned the attorney had been a Special Forces soldier, had trained as a Delta Force operator. He had hunted al Qaeda leaders throughout the Middle East and had been, by all reports, very successful.

Barak worried now that the man Saleem's men had failed to kill was the same man who had spoiled his plan the last time. Whoever he was, it was obvious he could not be allowed to see Vazquez again, or even return to the Wyler Ranch. Sooner or later, the man would probably discover the hangar house and come for him. When he did, Barak would make sure he got the warm welcome he deserved.

Leaving the deck and the warm morning sun, he went back inside to find his pilot, who was sitting at the island in the kitchen and drinking a cup of coffee.

"I'm going to Abazzano's ranch for lunch," he said, "and I'll probably be there most of the afternoon. I want you and the plane ready to fly out of here anytime I say, tomorrow or the next day. I may want to leave earlier than planned."

"Trouble?" the pilot asked.

"It's possible. If you see anyone snooping around, call me immediately.

"Are we still flying to Canada?"

"Yes. We'll mingle with tourists in Banff until things cool down.

Barak took the keys for the Escalade off the counter and walked downstairs to the hangar where the car was parked next to his Hawker 400XPR. One of his dummy corporations the FBI hadn't traced to him had purchased the jet for a song, and he had upgraded its performance and avionics just for this operation. The jet was smaller and faster than most other light private jets, but it wasn't flashy enough to attract a lot of attention. When he got to Canada, though, he planned to sell the Hawker and get something more fitting, like a Gulfstream G550 or a Dassault Falcon. Then he would disappear until the Americans grew tired of searching for him.

The traffic was fairly heavy as he drove north to Bend and then to Abazzano's ranch. The city had apparently grown faster than its ability to build highways. The highway running north and south through the high desert of Oregon ran right through it. Even with the congestion, though, it took him less than an hour to reach the ranch. On Saturday, if things went as planned, it would take ten times as long to cover the distance he had just driven.

When he drove past Abazzano's house on the rise below

the rimrock and toward the stables and bunkhouse, now occupied by Saleem's men, he saw them waiting for him. Four men stood beside the Harley Davidson motorcycles he had shipped to Oregon for the mission. Three blacked-out Iron 883's and a Softail that was hitched to a pull-behind cargo trailer. The men were wearing black motorcycle leathers and in their hands were holding full-face black helmets with smoked visors. Suited up and riding their motorcycles, they would look like mounted storm troopers that no thinking person would want to challenge.

Barak walked to the back of the Softail. "Saleem, is the trailer big enough to carry the package?"

"We had to modify it a little. The sides are raised sixteen inches to carry the transport container laying horizontally. We repainted the trailer black to cover the modifications we made, and added the flames in back to make it look like something a motorcycle gang might tow. Otherwise, the trailer will easily carry four hundred pounds. That's more than the package weighs."

"Have the men show me how they will ride to the target."

Saleem turned to one of the men. "Yousef, show us how you'll ride Saturday."

As one, all four men put on their helmets and mounted their motorcycles. Four V-twin engines roared to life and settled into the unmistakable Harley rumble. Yousef raised his left hand in the air, and when he dropped it, all four motorcycles moved off together, convoy-style. Two of the Iron 883's were in front, with the Softail and trailer next, followed by the third Iron 883 in the rear.

"How are they out on the road?" Barak asked.

"They're a little too cautious to look the part," Saleem admitted, "but we're working on that. They'll go out for a fifty mile ride today and a seventy-five mile ride tomorrow. By Saturday, they should look like they've been riding all their lives."

"Is Talal comfortable arming the device?"

"He's my demolition guy, trained in Iran and experienced. He's built IEDs, booby-trapped buildings, and put together massive truck bombs in Iraq. Arming this thing is a piece of cake for him."

"Does he have any idea we've set the timer to detonate as soon as he arms it?"

"There's no way he could know that. Even if he did, he's volunteered for martyrdom. He'll do his job. They all will. Don't worry."

"*Inshallah*, Saleem, *inshallah*. Have you heard from your man watching Vazquez today?"

"An hour ago. He's having breakfast in his room. Alone."

"That's a change. Have your man keep watching him. If his visitor returns, have your man kill him. We only need to keep Vazquez quiet until the polo match. After that, your little distraction will eliminate any risk he poses."

Barak sat in his Escalade for a quiet moment before driving up to Abazzano's villa for lunch and watched as the convoy of motorcycles drove by. They filled the normally quiet interior of the SUV with the roar of their engines.

Chapter Thirty-One

It was a short drive from the lodge to the marina restaurant, where Drake had invited Casey and his team to meet him for lunch. Although there were a few cars in the parking lot already, he saw that he was early enough to still get one of the tables out on the deck. As he was getting out of the Porsche, he heard the approach of a helicopter overhead. When he looked up, he saw that it was the most aerodynamically designed helicopter he had ever seen. Painted red and black, with a bullet nose and a sleek tail boom, it looked like it could fly faster than most winged craft. If this was Casey's new toy, Drake was impressed.

He entered the restaurant and was taken out to the deck overlooking the river. The restaurant was located in the old Trout House, where he had eaten a number of times in the past, but he was unfamiliar with the nouveau Mexican-Peruvian cuisine Hola! featured. Bright colors and lively Mexican music created a festive atmosphere, and Drake was looking forward to lunch.

He was studying the menu when Casey and his team walked out onto the deck and gathered around his table.

"I guess *hola, amigos* is appropriate," Drake said, as he

stood up and shook hands all around. "Mike, was that spaceship that just flew over yours?"

His friend grinned. "That spaceship, as you call it, is a Bell 525 Relentless, the most advanced general aviation helicopter in the world. It flies like an angel and makes me forget all my earthly woes. But, no, strictly speaking, it's not mine. It belongs to the corporation of which I am the majority shareholder. Pretty cool, huh?"

"This is the first time I've ever heard you talk about something other than food in a restaurant," Drake said. "Why don't we get our orders placed and I'll tell you what I have in mind for your little vacation. Ricardo, this place is supposed to have good food. You see anything on the menu you recommend? I don't know much about Peruvian cuisine."

"Give me a minute," the former Green Beret replied. "Mike doesn't care if it's good or not. There just has to be a lot of it."

Everyone laughed, and Drake said, "How well I know. How about a round of margaritas before we get down to business?" He waved at a waitress to take the order. "Five Patron Margaritas, *por favor*."

While Casey and his team took their seats around the table and admired the view of the river and a family of ducks drifting alongside a human family in a canoe, Capt. Gonzalez studied the lunch menu.

"Would you like me to order for us and eat family style?" he asked.

"Go ahead, Ricardo," Casey said. "Just keep my appetite in mind."

When the waitress brought their margaritas, Capt. Gonzalez obeyed his general's orders.

"Señorita, please bring us two orders of ceviche mexicano, two orders of guacamole and plenty of chips. Five orders of ensaladas mixta. Three orders of enchiladas rojas. Three orders of enchiladas mole." He glanced down at the menu again. "And five orders of Baja burritos. Put it all on the table and we'll sort it out."

When she finished writing down their order, she left with a big smile.

"Adam, before I get busy eating," Casey said, "tell us what you've learned so far."

Sitting with his back to the other tables, Drake leaned forward and briefed the team on the events of his time in Bend, from his arrival to the incident on his drive to Sunriver an hour earlier.

"What I need to do," he concluded, "is to get eyes on Wyler Ranch and find out what's going on out there. I'm going to pay our polo star another visit. I picked up a tail leaving Pronghorn, so I know they were watching him the first time."

"We can get eyes on the ranch for you," Casey said. He turned to the men sitting to his left. "Billy still has pretty good sniper eyes, and Ricardo knows how to use the Draganflyer drones. If you can get something more on those Escalades, Larry can run it down for you." As the three men nodded, Casey added, "And I can go with you to see this polo star."

Drake saw all three men raise their eyes and look over his shoulder. Liz Strobel was coming toward their table.

"Greetings," she said. After they caught her up on their conversation, she said, "Adam, I'll be happy to ride along with you. From what I've been reading about the polo star, he has an eye for the ladies. Maybe I can help."

Her brown hair was shorter and her face more tanned than when Drake had last seen her, but her ice blue eyes still sparkled. Wearing a pink polo shirt that showcased her well-packaged form, and jeans that clung to her long shapely legs, there was no question she would catch Vazquez's eye.

"Liz, I'm glad you're able to join us," Drake said. "Would you like a margarita?" He stood up to greet her and reintroduce her to the men at the table.

Casey borrowed a chair from another table and set it next to Drake's. "If you're hungry," he said, "we can order more food.

"Thanks, I'm fine," she said. "I had a bagel and cream cheese on the Secretary's plane before they dropped me off here."

"What are you doing in Oregon?" Casey asked.

"Didn't Adam tell you? I'm here to see if he's found anything that will help us find the thing we couldn't find in San Diego," she said as she glanced over to see if the people at the next table were listening to their conversation.

Casey followed her look and asked, "Are you here in an official capacity or just paying us a social visit?"

"I'm here on my own time, Mike. There's nothing more I can do in California, and I have to be in Seattle on Monday."

"You have a place to stay?"

"Not yet. I'll find something here at Sunriver or in town."

"That won't be necessary," Drake said. "There's plenty of room at the Senator's place. Stay with us."

She nodded. "I accept. If you're sure I won't upset any plans you guys have."

Drake smiled. "If you play poker and won't mind a little cigar smoke after dinner, you'll fit right in. You might even win a dollar or two if Mike hasn't improved his game."

When their food arrived, Drake ordered a margarita for Liz and joined the others passing around the platters of food. He was surprised by how quickly he had asked her to stay with them at the Senator's cabin. A month ago, she had helped him remove the bodies of three terrorists from his farm and then keep the media and police at bay. But they had also exchanged heated words about his meddling in what she had seen as a matter for law enforcement. They had exchanged more heated words about what he believed was her agency's incompetence in dealing with terrorism. Now, however, she seemed to be willing to accept his help...unless there was some other agenda behind her decision to pay him a visit.

As the abundant food on the table was quickly consumed, due in large part to Casey's apparently insatiable appetite, Drake suggested that they drive to the Senator's cabin, unload the team's gear, and get Liz settled in her room.

"Liz," he said, "do you have your things here, or are they back at the airport?"

"I left everything at the airport and took a cab here."

Drake nodded. "Mike, why don't you drive her to the airport and get her luggage while I pay the bill here? My car probably doesn't have enough room for all her bags."

"Ouch!" she said. "I have one duffel bag. You probably have more than that for your toiletries."

"Touché! You can ride with me, then. I'll pay for lunch and meet you all outside."

By the time he walked outside, Liz and four adoring men were standing around his Porsche. But it wasn't his automotive pride and joy they were adoring. All eyes were on his passenger.

"Mike," he said, "if you can get your guys to leave this lady alone long enough to mount up, follow me to the airport and then to Crosswater. We're going to waste the day if we just stand around here."

When they were seated in his car and Liz was buckled in, he drove past the team as they walked toward the two white GMC Yukon XL's Casey had rented at the airport.

Drake slowed down. "You seem to have charmed the men, Ms. Strobel."

"All in a day's work, Mr. Drake. It never hurts to know who your friends are in case you run into trouble."

"I didn't think you expected to find any trouble in Oregon."

"I don't. But you do have a habit of creating it. I was just hedging my bet in case I need someone to come to my rescue and you're not around."

Drake accelerated out of the parking lot, wondering if he should feel flattered that she thought he could rescue her or uneasy that she assumed he would want to.

Chapter Thirty-Two

THE EARTH-FILL, OR EMBANKMENT, DAM HAD BEEN BUILT IN 1951. It was two thousand and fifty-five feet long and stood three hundred and ten feet tall. The reservoir behind the dam covered sixty five hundred acres and was eight and a half miles long. If the dam failed, the subsequent wall of water rushing down would overwhelm two other dams downstream. As a result of the failure of three dams, a wall of water a hundred feet high would reach the valley below five hours later. Estimated casualties were two hundred to three hundred thousand people. The infrastructure of the area would be destroyed for years to come.

All Barak had to do was get his demolition nuke to the dam, and make sure Saleem's men detonated it in the exact place on the dam to break it open.

There were more than seventeen hundred hydroelectric dams in America, and when this one in Oregon was blown, the nationwide panic that would follow, Barak knew, would be a delight to watch. Security was almost nonexistent at these dams, so the government would have to send in the army to protect the remaining dams. Citizens who lived in the inundation zones below the dams would demand assurance they and their families were safe. U.S. Army Corps of Engineers inundation studies would be carefully scrutinized and found to be outdated and inadequate. The panic would thus ratchet up another notch.

The end result would be a nation shaken to its core. The United States would learn that it was inescapably destined to bow before the will of Allah.

That was the goal. Barak had been chosen by the Brotherhood to make it happen. If he failed again, as he had when he failed to assassinate the Secretary of Homeland Security, he knew he would be the one bowing to the will of Allah. The swift sword that would surely be raised over his head would guarantee that he would not have another opportunity to please his sponsors.

Barak stood over the map on the desk in the office of the hangar house and traced the route Saleem's men would take to the dam. From Wyler Ranch, they would follow Highway 97 south through the city of Bend. He put a forefinger on the city. That was the area he worried about the most. If the convoy of four Harleys moved too fast or two slow, they risked being stopped. If they got bogged down in traffic or ran into some road-raged idiot, they might not control their frustration. They were hard men, heavily armed, and shooting their way out of a confrontation would be the first thing they would think of.

Then, if they made it safely though the city, they had a hundred and three miles to travel to reach their target. It was open road that passed through two small communities. Just a couple of stores and gas stations, Barak knew. Nothing to pose any problems. Restricted budgets for most rural counties in the U.S. fortunately meant limited, if any, law enforcement on the roads to interfere with his convoy.

The weakness of his plan, the weakness of any plan like this, he realized, was that he had to rely on men to react to an unforeseen event they weren't trained to face. What if they encountered some off-duty cop on vacation with his family, a cop with a thing about bikers? A hick with a rifle in his pickup? Anyone who flags one of his men down to ask for directions and spooks a deadly reaction from a man trained to shoot first and ask questions later?

Saleem's men were Hezbollah terrorists who had traveled up and down the West Coast as enforcers for the drug cartels. But they were also simple men who were never asked to think beyond the instructions they were given. They were willing to die, but simply dying wasn't enough to guarantee the success of this mission.

What Barak really needed was for Saleem to lead the men himself. The young Lebanese-Mexican American was smart, brilliant in fact, but he was also far too valuable to Hezbollah to risk his loss. Barak had thought about leading the mission himself, but his face was on wanted posters everywhere. Just being in Oregon was a huge risk. But it was a risk he had to take.

No, Barak thought, he'd planned this carefully. Now he had to trust Allah, peace be upon him, to bring success to the mission. He had failed last time because the man he had chosen to oversee the assassination had attracted the attention of a man with the experience and exceptional skills to defeat them. That, however, was fortuitous. It would not happen twice. Which was why he had decided the man who had visited Marco Vazquez and escaped Saleem's ambush could not be the attorney from Portland.

But he couldn't afford to take any chances. He walked out onto the deck and sat down under the patio umbrella that provided shade for an elegant teak table and four chairs. He opened his phone.

"Saleem," he said when his lieutenant answered his call, "I don't want to risk having this man, whoever he is, interfere with my plans. Do you know where he's staying?"

"He was followed to a resort just south of you. Crosswater. It's a gated golf community. My man couldn't follow him in."

"See if you can find out exactly where he's staying," Barak said. "Maybe we can get a clear shot at him from a distance. Or have one of your men sneak onto the golf course. The whole place can't be gated."

"If I locate him, do you want me to kill him?"

"Call me first. It has to be a clean kill that can't be traced to us. We're too close."

Barak ended the call and sat quietly in the shade, enjoying the warm afternoon and the pots of flowering red geraniums and assorted annuals that adorned the deck. The thought of revenge brought a smile to his lips. If the man staying at Crosswater was the same man who had interfered last time, he was about to become a very satisfying casualty in their war on the West.

Chapter Thirty-Three

AFTER HE COLLECTED LIZ'S BAG AT THE SUNRIVER AIRPORT, Drake led the way to Crosswater, a short drive away. The two white Yukons followed him past the gatehouse and around the golf course before parking beside his Porsche in front of the Senator's cabin.

Liz got out and looked up at what was really a rustic mansion. "Are you sure this place is big enough for all of us?"

Drake led her up to the front door. "I'm sure one of the guys will share a room with you if you ask nicely," he said. "But if you want your own room, I suggest you go upstairs and pick the one with the queen bed. The other three rooms have two twin beds each."

Casey and his men trooped in behind them. After everyone found his sleeping quarters, they came back downstairs and Drake led them into the kitchen.

"The Senator had the refrigerator stocked for me," he said, "and there's a well-supplied bar, too. Help yourselves to anything you need. I know Mike will. We'll pick up more steaks for tonight, and if you think of anything else we need, tell Mike. He's the grill master. Okay, now grab a beverage of your choice and let's go out on the deck and coordinate our afternoon."

Liz selected a bottle of wine from the dual-zone wine cabinet that stood at one end of the black granite bar in the great room. The men all grabbed bottles of beer from the stainless steel cooler under the bar.

"I recognize that it's a long shot the nuke Liz is looking for is here," Drake began as the team joined him outside. "But if it is, then the man who brought it here has to be the one we were hunting in Mexico. He was cozy with the cartels down there and maybe Hezbollah, too. There are too many dots that connect for it not to be him. So it goes without saying, but I'll say it anyway—be careful. He's a fanatic who has to be stopped."

"Do we know what Barak looks like?" Larry Green, the former L.A. cop, asked.

Liz answered this question. "We have his driver's license photo and some video of him coming and going from his office building in Las Vegas and passing through the executive air terminal at McCarran International the day they tried to kill the Secretary," she said. "They're on my iPad, but who knows what he looks like now."

"Do we have any idea where he's staying here in Bend?" Green continued.

"The only two leads we have are Wyler Ranch and the resort where Marco Vazquez is staying," Drake answered.

Bill Montgomery, the young Ranger sniper had some questions. "And Mike said you think this polo player might have brought the nuke to Oregon? Why is that? And how'd he do it?"

"The van that was found abandoned near the polo field in San Diego was positive for radiation," Drake said. "We know that. And I found a brochure in the villa in Mexico advertising the polo match here in Bend. Using the big horse trailer

Vazquez uses to haul his polo ponies around in would be one way to get a nuke up here."

Ricardo Gonzales, the Green Beret captain, turned to Liz. "Ms. Strobel, if we know where the horse trailer is, couldn't you test it to see if it carried that nuke up here?"

"I'm here on my own, Ricardo. DHS doesn't think Drake's evidence is worth pursuing. And the trailer's on private property, so we'd need a search warrant. But we can buy radiation detection devices. There are companies that supply them to law enforcement and first responders."

"Mike," said Drake, "if we can buy a detection device, could you use one of your drones to fly it over the trailer at Wyler Ranch?"

"I don't see why not," he said. "We put video cameras on them, so we should be able to outfit one with a small detection device. I'll call my purchasing agent and see how quickly we can get one here."

Drake summed up the meeting. "That's it, then," he said. "I'll show Ricardo and Billy how to find Wyler Ranch. Guys, find a place to set up video monitoring, then we'll launch a drone to get a closer look. Larry, I've got a friend running down the license plate on the pickup that tried to run me off the road. He's also searching for an address for the black Escalade. After I call him, why don't you and Mike see where that takes us." The ex-cop nodded. "Okay, men. Liz and I will talk to Marco Vazquez. Let's all meet back here tonight for dinner, say six o'clock, and watch Mike burn us some steaks."

As his team walked back inside, Casey signaled to Drake they needed to talk. "Liz said she was here on her own," he said, "but she's still a fed. How much of what we're doing do you want her involved in?"

"She knows why I'm here," Drake replied. "She invited herself to join us. I'll let her decide how involved she wants to be. Besides, your guys aren't complaining that she's here." He grinned.

"Neither are you, as far as I can see."

"Come on, Mike. I agreed to help the Secretary from time to time. She's my liaison with DHS. Nothing more."

"Whatever you say, buddy."

Drake just shook his head. What had he done to make his friend think he cared, one way or the other, that Liz Strobel was there? He and Casey walked into the cabin's great room, where he showed Ricardo and Billy how to find Wyler Ranch. After they left, he called Paul Benning in Portland.

"Paul, any luck with the license plates?"

"Luck has nothing to do with efficient law enforcement."

"Yeah," Drake said, "but it has everything to do with knowing the right people."

"There is that. Okay, here's what you need to know. The one Escalade Timothy O'Neil rented is actually one of *two* he rented. Both are the same make and model from Enterprise Car Rentals at the Sunriver airport. Maybe they can tell you where he's staying. The pickup pulled out of the river was stolen from a farm near LaPine earlier in the week."

"So the pickup is a dead end," Drake said. "I've asked Larry and Mike to locate where O'Neil's staying." He paused. "You and Margo okay?"

"I'm fine. She's getting harder to live with, though. She needs to be back to work, full-time. Any chance of that happening any time soon?"

"I'll be back in the office next week. I've got a couple of things to do here, including attending a polo match on Saturday. Then I'm driving back."

"You must have mentioned that polo match to Margo. She's reserved a room for us at the Eagle Crest Hotel. Said it would do us good to get out of town. I suspect she plans on running into you to make sure you're coming back to work."

Drake laughed. "I'll keep an eye out. See you Saturday. And thanks for tracing those plates for me."

He stopped in the kitchen to make a list of the items he

needed to pick up for dinner and wondered if Liz was ready to drive to the Pronghorn Resort. He didn't like to wait for a woman, any woman.

Chapter Thirty-Four

HE FOUND HER STANDING NEXT TO HIS CAR WHEN HE WALKED out of the cabin.

"What mountain is that?" she asked, pointing at the snow-capped summit of a distant volcano.

"Mount Bachelor."

"It's beautiful. Do they ski there?"

"Most of the year. I think they still operate a chairlift during the summer. Get in. Let's find out if Vazquez can help us find your nuke."

As he started the Porsche, Drake couldn't help but remember skiing on Mount Bachelor with Kay. Why is it, he thought, that whenever I'm around this woman I think of my wife and feel guilty? Liz is just a colleague. A coworker. A contact person assigned to me by Secretary Rallings. It's not like I'm taking her out on a date or something.

He did a quick, three-point turn out of the parking area in front of Senator Hazelton's cabin and sped down the road along the golf course.

"When we find Vazquez," he said to Liz, "let me do the talking. I didn't tell him who I am, so let's let him think whatever he wants. Then I'll introduce you as someone from the government who has some questions for him. You can ask him about the men who are taking care of his horses. Ask him about who hired them for him. Ask him if he knows if they have criminal records. He should start to feel uncomfortable by then."

"Isn't there a speed limit here?" she asked. "You're driving awfully fast."

He slowed down. "There is a speed limit and I was breaking it," he said. He steered the car past the security guard, who had stepped out of his booth and was motioning for him to slow down.

"Look, Drake, if you don't want me here, just say so."

"What does my driving fast have to do with not wanting you here?" he asked. Nodding at the guard, he turned onto the highway and accelerated until the tachometer soared toward seven thousand rpms in third gear. "I never said I didn't want you here."

"No, but your face did. It's registering somewhere between anger and disgust. I once taught a class in emotion recognition from facial expressions for DHS agents."

Pondering what she had just said, he continued to exceed the speed limit. He knew there had been a lot of studies of human facial expressions and that computers were now able to read and catalog emotions. That she was able to peg his emotion from the look on his face didn't surprise him at all. What surprised him was that he was angry and didn't know why.

"Look, there's a lot going on right now," he dissembled, turning to look out the driver's side window for a moment. "You think there's a nuke loose in the country, and I think the guy who tried to kill me is the one who brought it here. Sure, I'm angry. But I'm not disgusted. I'll get him."

"And if you don't?"

"Won't happen."

"I want you to understand something" she said. "When

we first met in Portland, I thought you were a cowboy who represented all the things I hate. But then I saw what you were willing to do when you thought we weren't doing anything. Then you saved Secretary Rallings' life and took out his assassin. So now I'm your fan. I just don't think you're right this time...but I don't want to be wrong again."

"For your career or for the country?"

"You don't know much about me," she said, "so I'll let that pass for now." She paused to let that sink in. "I will do everything possible to protect this country, regardless of how it might impact my career."

Neither of them spoke the rest of the way to the Pronghorn Resort.

Drake dropped her off in front of the Clubhouse to look for Vazquez while he parked the Porsche. When he joined her poolside, the polo star was nowhere in sight.

"Stay here in case he shows up," Drake said. "I'll see if he's in the bar," Drake said.

Liz walked toward an empty table and motioned for a waiter.

When Drake entered the Trailhead Grill, he found the same bartender behind the bar who had pointed out Vazquez before.

"Is Vazquez around?" he asked, sliding a Jackson across the bar.

"If he's not at the pool, he's probably in his room."

"And which room would that be?"

The bartender looked down at the twenty dollar bill on the bar.

"Which room?" Drake asked.

The bartender shrugged, took the twenty, and said, "He's in Unit Ten. Follow the path."

Unit Ten was a second-floor suite overlooking the eighteenth hole of Pronghorn's championship golf course. Drake noticed a foursome putting out on the green. Another four players stood by carts, waiting to make their approach shots. They all looked to be serious golfers, judging by the way they were studying their score cards. Either that, he thought, or they were playing for money and were calculating how much the round was about to cost them.

Drake turned off the path and started up the stairs that led to the second floor, Units Ten and Eleven. When he reached the top of the stairs, he saw that Unit Ten was on the left and that an elevator faced the two second floor units across a red-tiled hallway. A rustic log railing ran the length of the hallway on each side of the elevator above the golf course and a paved path. A man was standing, leaning against the railing and gazing at the mountains in the distance.

The carved oak door of Unit Ten had an etched, oval, glass panel at eye level. Next to the door was a round, wrought iron door bell button that Drake pushed as he studied the pronghorn logo in clear glass panel. He was starting to raise his hand to push the door bell again when he saw the man at the railing reflected in the etched glass. He had moved silently toward Drake and was holding a knife, blade down, in his right hand.

Drake pivoted on his right leg toward his attacker and blocked the knife strike with his right hand, deflecting it away from his body. At the same time, he threw a hard left jab at the man's face, striking him between his eyes and knocking him back several steps.

The attacker shook his head and squared off. Drake recognized the knife he was holding. It was a Gerber fighting knife. He's had one himself in his paratrooper's kit. It was a survival knife sold in Army PX's around the world.

Drake waited in his fighting stance for the man to strike again and sized up his enemy. Five-seven, dark hair, Middle-Eastern in appearance. The attacker was in his late twenties, with darting eyes and a sneering smile on his lips.

Without a sound, he lunged, aiming the knife at Drake's chest.

Drake stepped out of the line of the attack and blocked the thrust with his left forearm. As he grabbed the man's wrist above his knife hand, he landed a smashing kick to his groin with his right foot. Then he added his right hand in a wrist lock and, using his planted left leg as a fulcrum, spun to his left and threw his attacker back.

Trying to regain his balance, the man fell against the log railing and flipped over it.

Drake looked over the railing. His attacker was lying on the cart path on his back, his head twisted to one side. Drake ran down the stairs at the end of the hallway and knelt beside the man. He found there was no pulse and looking around saw that no one appeared to have seen the man fall. Pulling the knife out of the hand that still gripped it, Drake walked quickly to the visitor parking lot. When the body was discovered, it would look like he had accidentally fallen to his death…if the damage to his right eye was overlooked.

Drake held the knife against his leg, and when he reached his car, wrapped it in a white cloth he kept in the glove box. The man's fingerprints on the knife might identify him and probably confirm what Drake suspected; the man was on someone's terrorist watch list. His knife fighting style was the fighting style of the Russian Special Forces, but the man was not Russian. More likely, he was Hezbollah and trained by the Russians.

Chapter Thirty-Five

A FEW MINUTES LATER, HE FOUND LIZ SITTING WITH MARCO Vazquez near the deep end of the pool. From the way the polo star was looking at her, Drake could see she had quickly charmed the young man. He hoped that would work to their advantage when they played good cop, bad cop, because he did not intend to be nice to someone who might have just tried to have him killed.

"Marco, may I join you?" Drake pulled out a chair without waiting for an answer. "We need to talk."

"A gentleman does not interrupt a lady when she is talking," Vazquez said without looking at him. "Please go away."

"Sorry, Marco. Not today. Not until I know why you had a man outside your room who tried to kill me."

Now Vazquez looked at him. "I don't know what you are talking about. I have no one at my room." He started to stand up, but Drake put a hand on his shoulder and pushed him back down in his chair. The look in his eyes said, *Liz, let me handle this.*

He looked at Vazquez again. "Remember when I bought you a drink out here and asked you about the men who were grooming your ponies? The ones I saw at Wyler Ranch who spoke Arabic? One of them, or one of their buddies, tried to knife me outside your room a couple minutes ago. I want to know who those men are and why they're working for you."

"I told you, they are not working for me." Vazquez's voice was rising. "They are with the transport company my father hired to bring my ponies here."

"Marco," Liz leaned in toward him, "don't make a scene, okay? You need to tell us what you know about these men."

The polo player looked back and forth. "Who are you? Are you with him?"

"I'm with the Department of Homeland Security," she said. "Mr. Drake is helping me with a matter vital to our government."

Before he said anything else, Vazquez looked around to see if anyone nearby was listening. Then, "Could we have a drink? People are watching us. I don't want them to think I'm in trouble or something. I'll tell you what you want to know."

Drake waved a pool waiter over. He took their orders and left.

"Did someone really try to kill you?" Vazquez asked Drake.

"There was a man standing at the elevator when I came to see if you were in your room. He tried to stick a knife in my back and wound up dead. He looked like one of the men I saw at the ranch."

"Do I need to go and see what's being done?" Liz asked.

"I don't know if anyone's found him yet," Drake said. "He fell from the second floor and broke his neck. It'll look like an accident, and I don't want to get mixed up with the police again. It'll be okay."

When their drinks arrived and the waiter had left, Liz took over questioning Vazquez.

"Tell us about the men your father hired."

"They were waiting in San Diego to bring my ponies here. I don't know much about them."

"Have they worked for you before?"

"No, I usually bring my men from Argentina. But Papa didn't want them to come this time. He said he owed someone a favor."

"Did he say who he owed the favor?"

"No," Vazquez said quickly. "It might have been someone from his bank. A man came to our *estancia* just before this tour. Papa told me when he left that my guys couldn't come with me."

Drake looked at Liz. She was watching the young man's expressions intently.

He assumed her role as interrogator and began asking rapid-fire questions. "Where did you meet the men who came with you from San Diego?"

"They met me at the polo club there," Vazquez explained. "After my match. We loaded my ponies in my horse trailer and they left to drive up here. I flew here the next day."

"How many men brought your horses here?"

"Four men. There were two who drove off with the trailer and two more who followed in another truck."

"Are these four men the ones at the ranch here?"

"Yes. And one other man who came later."

Drake leaned in closer. "What does he look like?"

"He is younger, maybe twenty five. Handsome like me, but I think he's American."

"How do you know he's an American?"

"He talks like you. They call him Sal. That's American, no?"

Drake nodded. "You're a smart man, Marco. Have you seen anything at the ranch that looks like these guys are doing something illegal?"

"You mean like being here illegally?"

"No. I mean do they look like they're doing things that might be illegal or criminal?"

"They just take care of my ponies," Vazquez said with

frustration, "How should I know what they do when I'm not around."

Liz started to ask a question when Drake held up his hand and turned to look at someone talking excitedly with their waiter.

"I think they've found the body," he said. "Marco, when they ask you about the man found dead on the ground in front of your unit, tell them the truth. You don't know him and you didn't see him fall. Don't tell them about me, or that you talked to someone from the government. Understand? This will get you in a lot of trouble if you do. You won't be allowed to leave the country. Maybe never get to play polo again."

"We're going to leave now," Liz said. "If you think of anything else you think we should know, call me. Here's my card. My cell phone number is on it. Remember, I'm counting on you to keep our talk a secret."

She stood and kissed Vazquez lightly on the cheek. As she walked away with Drake, she saw the poolside waiter heading for the young polo player's table.

"He's not telling us everything," Liz said.

"I got that, too. It's not his father's banker that's behind this."

Chapter Thirty-Six

Marco Vazquez tried to remain calm as he walked back to his suite. The waiter had said a man from resort security needed to see him and could he return to his unit immediately. He knew what they needed to see him about. He thought he probably knew the dead man.

From the time he had checked into the resort, he'd noticed a man watching him. He wasn't one of the men he'd seen at the ranch, but he looked like them. Ever since the other man had come and threatened his family, the watcher had made his presence obvious.

He knew who his father was taking orders from, just as he knew that telling the woman from the government about him would mean his family would be killed. There was no mistaking the danger he was in. The eyes of the man who would come for him had burned with hate. The things he'd said he would do, he would do.

When he got to his unit, he found men gathered around a body lying on the cart path. Two men had patches on their khaki shirts that identified them as resort security, and another man who introduced himself as the resort manager. He answered the questions the security men asked and told them he didn't know the dead man and hadn't seen him before. After agreeing to give a statement to the deputy sheriff when he arrived, the manager was allowed to go. But Vazquez could not go to his room just yet, they said. The area in front of his unit was being secured as a possible crime scene.

He walked to the Trailhead Grill and stood at the bar, while another Long Island iced tea was being prepared for him. When the drink was in his hand, he took a seat at the small table farthest from the bar and took out his iPhone. It was time to have a word with his father.

"Yes," his father answered.

"It's me, Papa. We're in trouble."

"For what?"

"That favor you owe someone. A man visited me here and threatened to kill our family."

"Why?"

"I think he was worried they'd find out about him."

"Who would find out?"

"Probably the government. A woman from the Department of Homeland Security came to talk with me just now. The man she had with her just killed a man who's been watching me. What do I do now?"

"Do what I told you to do, son. Behave, don't talk to anyone, ride well. You are there to play polo. Nothing else. I'll take care of the rest."

Vazquez waved to the bartender for another round. He would stay here a little longer and then go swimming. When he finished swimming, he thought he might try to arrange for another suite for the rest of his stay.

IN AN EXCLUSIVE NEIGHBORHOOD OF ASUNCION, Paraguay, the man who called himself Ryan sat in the shade of a covered terrace next to a swimming pool with two magnificent waterfalls. The old mansion the Alliance had purchased for its young leader had once belonged to his grandfather, Rainer Walkur.

Rainer Walkur had worked with Martin Bormann in the last years of World War II to move capital, mainly gold, out of Germany to build a new empire. The gold had been the spoils of a war that Germany had unfortunately lost, but it had also allowed his grandfather and other Nazi leaders to lay the foundation for a new financial and industrial empire. Beginning in the early 1950s, banks were bought, hundreds of new front companies and corporations were started, and new alliances developed.

Rainer Walkur had hidden in plain sight as a banker in Asuncion from 1944 until his death in 1973. A Jew assassination team had followed him to Brazil on a business trip and shot him as he walked to his hotel after a dinner with friends. His estate and home had been sold, and Ryan's father, Rolf Walkur, who was attending college in the United States at the time, had inherited the leadership position for the Alliance. After his graduation, Rolf Walkur had changed his last name to a more American-looking Walker and returned to South America to continue to grow the underground empire.

From a ranch in Argentina, he had brought together several of the powerful drug cartels operating from Columbia, a couple of criminal syndicates from Europe, and fledgling terrorist organizations from around the world. These were the basis of the Alliance. Its purpose was to launder drug money through Alliance banks and develop its own paramilitary arm to carry out and enforce Alliance operations.

The drug cartels had been an easy sell. They were sophisticated in many ways, but international finance wasn't their specialty. The terrorist organizations were harder to convince. They were much more suspicious than the South American drug lords, but they had ultimately become comfortable using the Alliance to move their money around the world. In exchange for services rendered, they had agreed to kill people for the Alliance, especially Jews. That was the bond they shared, their mutual hatred of the Jews.

Ryan Walker was proud of the progress the Alliance had made and the power it now possessed. Following his father, his postgraduate work had been done in the States, culminating in a master of science degree in financial economics (MSFE) from Columbia University. His education gave him both the knowledge and the experience to run a financial empire that was now valued at five hundred billion dollars.

The Alliance had started with the gold smuggled out of Europe and the Far East. There was more gold hidden that had not been recovered, but what they had was enough, Ryan believed. It was his mastery of all things financial that allowed the Alliance to add to its holdings.

But he was growing more and more concerned about the risks they were taking on behalf of the Brotherhood. The failed assassination of the Secretary of Homeland Security in the United States that had been planned and carried out by the Brotherhood's man, David Barak, had been a disaster. Now it appeared there might be another disaster on the horizon.

Ryan had just received a call from his communications center, which was hidden deep in the jungle in the Tri-Border Area of Argentina, Brazil, and Paraguay. The young polo player Barak had used to smuggle the demolition nuke into the United States had panicked and called his father in Argentina. His own people, of course, monitored all of the calls to and from the boy's father. It was just good business, as their bank in Argentina had loaned the old man the money that had saved his *estancia.* That was just good business as well. But now that they were more directly involved with the Brotherhood, he couldn't take a risk that any link to the Alliance might be discovered.

His decision made, Ryan picked up the encrypted satellite

phone on the small table at his right elbow. The number he called belonged to the top lieutenant of the Mexican cartel in Tijuana that had lost its leader, the brother of the Architect who had been assassinated by Barak and his men.

"Hector, do you know who this is?"

"Not many men have this number."

"Not many men know the name of the assassin who killed your boss, either. I do."

"Why would I believe you?"

"Because, Hector, I know you were the one who told us where Ramon was going to be to celebrate his birthday in Tijuana."

"What do you want?"

"I want to repay the favor, Hector. To give you a reason to say you should be the one to lead your cartel. And because you need us as partners."

"How would you repay the favor?"

"By telling you where the assassin is."

After telling Hector where Barak was and how he should be revenged, Ryan ended the call and signaled for his *peon* to bring him another iced *yerba mate.*

Chapter Thirty-Seven

DRAKE AND LIZ STROBEL LEFT THE PRONGHORN RESORT AND drove for several miles without talking. For the second day in a row, someone had tried to kill him. He was having trouble controlling his anger. It wasn't that he'd been attacked, per se, although the possible damage to his car had pissed him off when the hay bales were flying over its roof, and it wasn't that someone had tried to knife him in the back. The coward had gotten what he deserved. He was angry because he was itching to water board young Marco Vazquez and discover who his father was fronting for. He was itching to lead an attack on the lefty Hollywood producer's ranch, take no prisoners, and then go home. But he knew the woman beside him would either turn him in or talk him out of it.

"Well?" Liz broke the silence.

"Well what?"

"What are we going to do?"

He still wasn't looking at her. "Depends on how far you're prepared to go."

"Excuse me? Eva Marie Saint's line from *North by Northwest* —'I never discuss love on an empty stomach' for some reason comes to mind."

"Be serious," he said. "Vazquez could be made to talk, but I doubt you would let that happen."

"Don't be so sure," she replied. "We both know enhanced interrogation works. But I'm not convinced we need to use it on him. What about those guys you say are at that ranch where he keeps his polo ponies? Wouldn't they be a better source of information?"

Drake looked at her to see if she was baiting him. It appeared that she wasn't. "You sure you want to be involved in something like that?" he asked.

"I think we're running out of time," she said. "If a nuclear device of some sort is here in Oregon, that may be our best shot at finding it. The polo match is the day after tomorrow. Vazquez will be gone when it's over. We can bet the men taking care of his ponies will leave with him."

Drake had to concede her point. "All right. If you're sure about this, we'll talk it over with Mike and the guys tonight. If you want out, you need to decide before then. You'll be a coconspirator once we start planning something."

"Drake, I have a law degree, too. I'm aware of the consequences." It was time to change the subject. "Why don't we stop somewhere and get those things you need for dinner? I wouldn't want you cowboys making plans on empty stomachs."

"Or discussing love, right?" Drake said with a laugh, relieved that she had decided to mount up with his posse.

They stopped at the Sunriver Country Store and bought extra steaks, baking potatoes, and items Liz needed for a salad. When they arrived at the cabin, they saw that both of the white Yukons were parked in front. Inside, Casey and his team were pouring bags of ice in the kitchen sink and poking a case of beer into it.

Casey heard them coming and turned around. "Thought we should get ourselves in the proper frame of mind for those steaks I hope are in that bag you carrying," he said.

"Seven of the biggest rib eyes I could find," Drake answered. "Delivered as promised. Liz picked out the greens for a salad, so it looks like it's up to you now. But before you get started at the grill, I'd like to hear what you learned today."

"Not much about the guy from Las Vegas who rented the Escalades," Casey reported. "He told the rental agent friends of his were flying in and they were going camping for a week. There's no local address listed on the rental agreement. It just says Sunriver, so he could be anywhere. Larry checked a couple of the area outfitters. None of them rented or sold gear to a Timothy O'Neil."

"Clever. We know he's here," Drake said, "or at least one of the Escalades is here, because it followed me from Pronghorn. And he knew we'd be looking for him, so he said he'd be off the grid camping with friends. Ricardo, what did you and Billy find at the ranch?"

"Same thing you found, for the most part. The guys taking care of the polo ponies don't look like Mexicans. And they keep to themselves. We hiked in from a country road and found a spot on the rimrock above the stable and bunkhouse area. They spent more time working on their Harley-Davidsons than they did taking care of those ponies."

Drake nodded. "How many men did you see?"

"Four men grooming horses when we got in position, and a fifth who seemed to be supervising them," Ricardo said. "There were other ranch hands doing other things away from the stable area, but they kept their distance from these five."

"What about their Harleys?" Liz asked. "Do they all have Harleys?"

"Yep. Four that look new, or are at least very well cared for. One had a trailer hitched to it that had flames and a skull and crossbones painted on it. Made me think they might belong to a motorcycle gang."

"Harleys aren't cheap," Liz said. "I once had a boyfriend who owned one. So how do four ranch hands afford Harleys?"

"Maybe they're well paid," Billy Montgomery said. "If they travel around taking care of a big polo star's ponies, he might pay them pretty well. Those horses are pampered like you wouldn't believe. My dad used to take me to polo matches out on Long Island."

"I think we're missing the point here," Drake said. "Why are they working on their Harleys when they probably have grooming work they should be doing? Mike, you grew up on a ranch. Do ranch hands have that much free time during the day?"

"Not on ranches in Montana, they don't. You're lucky if you can find the time to eat, you're so busy from sunrise to sunset. But I never got paid to take care of a polo pony that costs as much as a luxury car. But it doesn't sound right, does it?"

"So how are we going to find out what these guys are up to?" Drake asked.

"We don't have a lot of options," Casey told him. "If they leave the ranch, we could snatch one and see what he'll tell us. If they stay put, we might try to get Ricardo in there and see if he could learn something. Or we could just keep watching them and see if there's a pattern to their activities that gives us a clue."

"I don't think we have that much time, Mike. If this O'Neil guy is involved, he's returning the Escalades he rented this weekend. The polo match is the day after tomorrow. They may all leave before we've learned much," Drake said. "Have you rigged that drone you brought to eavesdrop on these guys at the ranch?"

Casey nodded. "The Draganflyer X8 now has a wireless video camera with audio function. I'll add the small radiation detection device my purchasing agent is sending if it gets here in time. It'll work with a smart phone that receives and analyzes data related to any radiation it detects. We'll see what the drone is seeing and at the same time tell whether it's hot or not."

"You're kidding," Liz said. "I'm not even sure we have that capability."

"I'm sure you do," Casey said. "It just costs a lot more and you're supposed to get a judge to approve its use before you deploy it. But we don't have to jump through that hoop."

Drake made his decision. "Let's do it," he said. "First thing tomorrow, let's get eyes and ears on the ranch. Liz and I agree that Vazquez isn't telling us everything. We'll just have to come up with something that will make him want to talk to us."

Liz frowned at him. "I'm not sure I like the sound of that," she said.

"Don't worry. If you think it crosses the line, you can help Larry keep looking for O'Neil. With your FBI background and his LAPD experience, the two of you should be able to come up with some ideas for finding our guy. You can also check with local law enforcement and see what they've learned about the guy I killed."

That made Casey look up from the steaks. "Whoa! The guy you killed? When? Today?"

"I didn't really kill him," Drake said. "I was just there when he took an unfortunate fall and broke his neck. And I'm just curious if my name has come up in the investigation. Liz, why don't you get started on that salad while I put the potatoes in the oven and Mike gets our steaks ready to grill. If we're going to get an early start tomorrow, we need to get these men fed."

While Liz was opening cabinets and looking for a salad bowl, Casey nodded to Drake to grab a beer and go out on the deck with him. The other men followed, Drake took the cover off the grill, then walked further down the deck so Liz couldn't see him. Then he turned to Casey and his men.

"Here's what went down today. I went to see if Vazquez was in his room at the Pronghorn. A man was waiting for the elevator on the second floor. When I walked past him and stopped at Marco's door, he tried to knife me from behind. We fought, he lost. I should have been more alert. He looked like one of the guys at the ranch. If I'm asked to give a statement, after what we just went through last month in Portland, they'll keep me tied up for longer that we can afford. So…if the *policia* show up looking for me, I'm not here and you haven't seen me all day. I don't think Liz will interfere, but I can't be sure. She's a pretty straight-shooter."

"Why don't we just go to Wyler Ranch and talk with these yahoos?" Billy Montgomery asked. "I think we can handle whatever they throw at us if things get out of hand."

"Because," said Drake, "if they have the nuke Liz is looking for, we don't want to scare them off. Otherwise, we wouldn't be pussy footing around tonight. Look, I don't know what I got you into here, but we all need to be careful. They've tried to get me out of the way twice and they'll try again if they get a chance. But tonight, let's 'raise up our glasses against evil forces,' as Toby Keith would advise, and prepare for tomorrow. I have a feeling things are going to get interesting real soon."

Chapter Thirty-Eight

Casey grilled the steaks perfectly to each person's preference, and the baked potatoes with toppings could have been a meal in itself. Liz's Caesar salad was a masterpiece of simplicity with hearts of romaine, garlic-toasted croutons, olive oil, egg, lemon juice and Worcestershire sauce and a sprinkle of grated parmesan cheese.

Casey took a big bite of the salad and raised his bottle of beer in a toast. "Liz," he said, "that's the best Caesar salad I've ever had. You can cook with me anytime." The others raised their bottles in agreement.

Liz returned the salute by raising her glass of wine. "Knowing how you enjoy your food, Mike, I'm flattered. My steak was perfect. Thank you as well."

Bottles of cold beer were again raised in agreement.

The six members of Team Drake relaxed comfortably around the dining table in Senator Hazelton's great room. Outside, the setting summer sun turned the tall grass on the other side of the river into a rich shade of gold. The slow moving water of the Little Deschutes River shimmered in the waning light. Soon the solar-powered lights that bordered the path down to a fire pit by the river's edge came on.

"The evening is too nice to waste sitting inside," Drake said. "Leave the dishes and let's enjoy the sunset."

As the men headed out to the deck, Liz walked to the bar near the fireplace to refill her glass of wine.

What an unusual group of men, she thought. They were all warriors, but they weren't like the men she had competed with when she was with the FBI. These men were respectful of each other and certainly respectful toward her. She had seen none of the one-upmanship she was used to. The team members were all comfortable with themselves, and each other.

Especially Casey and Drake. They were like brothers, she thought, and not just brothers in arms, but best friends. Pity the fool who harmed either one of them. That person would pay a heavy price for his mistake.

She looked out toward the deck. Drake talking to the team. He was good looking, she had to give him that, but looks weren't what she found herself attracted to. What appealed to her was his quiet strength and his confidence. The other men acknowledged these qualities in the way they deferred to his leadership, even though each of them was capable of leading if called upon. It wasn't something Drake had to work on or consciously assert. He was just a natural leader. And a lethal one.

She knew how dangerous he could be from the events a month ago in Portland, when he had dealt with the terrorists who had tried to kill her boss. And she knew it from the record of his military service Secretary Rallings allowed her to see before offering Drake a role as a consultant of sorts, a position as an off-the-books privateer to assist in dealing with issues of national security. As an attorney, Drake could look into matters defense contractors and corporations didn't want the world, or their shareholders, to see when they suspected there were being probed or threatened.

Yes, she told herself, the Secretary had made the right

choice when he'd reached out to Drake. She just hoped she had made the right choice, too, when she'd told him about the nuclear device they were searching for. She had to be back in Washington on Monday and was running out of time to prove Drake's hunch was correct that the nuke was in Oregon.

She suddenly realized she'd been watching Drake for longer than she intended. Her second glass of the wonderful Oregon pinot that Drake had insisted she try was half gone. She refilled her glass and walked out to the deck to join the men.

Drake was talking about the huge steelhead trout he'd caught while fly fishing right here in the river last summer. She couldn't help but ask if she'd interrupted another 'fish story'.

Drake stopped talking, stared out over the river for a second. The last thing she heard was his shout, "Down!" as her glass of wine exploded in her hand.

"Rifle, twelve o'clock, across the river. Get inside!" He crawled toward Liz. Her face and neck were covered in blood.

"Liz, can you hear me?" He searched for a pulse on her neck. She was unconscious, but he saw that her chest was rising slowly with each breath. Her pulse was weak but steady.

"Mike! Help me get her inside. She's been hit, but with the red wine all over her, I can't tell where. Or if it's wine or blood"

When they had pulled her across the six feet to the door, which was partly protected by the heavy log railing that ran the length of the deck, Drake let Gonzalez take over. His secondary training as a medic on his Green Beret A-team had trained him to treat gunshot wounds.

"I saw a flash off a scope directly across the river," he told Casey in a hurried whisper as he headed inside. "Fifty yards deep in the tall grass. Go upstairs and see if you can spot the shooter. As soon as we know how Liz is, we'll go look for him. Larry, Billy, bring the weapons down from upstairs. We might need them."

Drake ran to the kitchen and grabbed two clean hand towels from the pantry and ran hot water over one of them before taking them to Ricardo. He saw that Liz had regained consciousness and was responding quietly to Ricardo's questions.

"I think she hit her head when you pushed her down," Gonzalez told him. "She has cuts on her neck and face from the glass, and I suspect more cuts on her arm and chest. I'll know more when I clean off the wine and blood."

"Okay. I'll go see if Mike's spotted the shooter." As Drake ran up the stairs, he intercepted Montgomery and Green coming down with their weapons. Montgomery was carrying a HK416 carbine and wearing a holstered Colt .45. Green also had a Colt .45 and was carrying a Remington tactical shotgun.

"Cover the front and rear," Drake said. "I'll see if Mike sees anything across the river."

He found his friend standing to the left of the window he had opened in his upstairs room. He was looking east across the river through the scope of his Remington M24A2 sniper rifle.

"I don't see him," Casey muttered. "He could be in the tall grass, but there's nothing he could be hiding behind. If he's good, he could have taken the shot from the far side of the meadow."

"The reflection from his scope was in the middle of field, not behind it. Why just one shot?"

"Maybe he thought his target was down. Liz's wine glass exploding probably looked like a head shot from where he was standing."

"I'll ask Billy to go search the area. There's a dirt road from the highway that runs along the river right to that meadow. If that's the way he got in there, maybe Billy can cut him off."

"If he isn't long gone by now." Casey lowered his rifle.

"Snipers don't wait around for their escape route to be blocked."

"Why do you think it was a sniper?"

"From where you say you saw the reflection from his scope. It's four hundred and forty yards from here. Most hunters won't take a shot from a quarter of a mile away. Besides, hunters don't shoot toward houses. Killers do. Buddy, I suspect you were the target."

Drake had to chuckle. "If I was, they've missed me three times today. It must have rattled them when their guy didn't make it back from Pronghorn. You know, I think it's time for us to rattle them a little more. Whoever they are."

Chapter Thirty-Nine

David Barak stood on the deck of the hangar house at Sunriver, looking south toward where he now knew the meddlesome American attorney had just been shot. He swirled his favorite Glenmorangie scotch in his tumbler and listened as his shooter recounted the kill.

"It was an easy shot," Jameel said. "Straight across the river from the meadow. They were out on the deck of the log house drinking beer. His head exploded. Blood everywhere. But you were right, the other men have been in the army. They took cover as soon as he went down. I couldn't get another shot off. By the time they realized what had happened, I was half way back to the ATV I rode in on."

Barak gave a satisfied nod. "You did well, Jameel. Return to your men in Boise and wait for me there. As soon as I finish here, I'll join you and we'll move everyone to our new base in Canada."

One more day, Barak told himself as his sniper left the deck, and a couple of minor adjustments to his plan, and this phase of the mission would be completed. He had to smile. It would be a hundred times more deadly than the attack on the Twin Towers. His strike in America would be the standard that all others would envy and, hopefully, copy. The underbelly of America was its infrastructure. Bridges and highways, power grids, and, of course, dams.

That was the genius of his plan. Simple targets. Well-placed demolition devices. The unleashing of the most destructive power on the planet, nature itself. A hundred foot wall of water would rush downstream and inundate everything in its path for a hundred miles. That was an awesome weapon that he couldn't wait to use. As he had been taught, a warrior uses the weapons at hand. In America, water and the reservoirs that collected it for hydroelectric power and irrigation were everywhere, just waiting to be used against the people who built them.

But he was growing more and more concerned about his celebrity polo player. He had been visited twice by the attorney, and even though the attorney was now dead, the woman who accompanied him was not. Perhaps worse, the men who were there when he was shot had the training to cause him trouble. If they came for Marco Vazquez, who knew what he would tell them? It was very worrying.

Barak found the number for Saleem, his Hezbollah commander, on his cell phone and waited for him to answer as he walked inside to refill his tumbler with Scotch.

When Saleem answered, he said without greeting him, "I think it would be wise for you to take our Argentine to the ranch to be with his horses until the polo match Saturday. Keep him away from people. Take his phone. I don't want him talking to anyone. Tell him it's in the best interest of his family if he concentrates on playing well. That he needs to focus on why he's here."

"That may be a problem," Saleem said. "There's a charity fundraiser and dinner tomorrow night. He's supposed to attend."

"Well, he'll have to miss it. Call from the ranch and tell them he has the flu or something. If they want him to play on

Saturday, he'll need to rest. Tell them whatever you want. Just get him there and keep him quiet until Saturday. All I need him to do is arrive at the polo field with his ponies and the trailer they came in. He will have served his purpose."

"Will you be at the ranch tomorrow?"

"Yes. I want to talk with the men when they return from their last practice ride. I'll be there by sunset for the *Maghrib* prayers. Bring Vazquez to the ranch first thing tomorrow and keep an eye on him. I don't want the attorney's friends talking with him before Saturday."

"Is there anything you need from me after I'm finished at the polo match?" Saleem asked.

"No, my friend. You and your men have served us well and I look forward to working with you for many years to come. Leave as planned and return to San Diego. Just avoid crossing the mountains unless your car can float."

Saleem laughed. "Don't worry, Barak. As much as I would like to witness your success in person, I'll wait to watch the carnage on the news. *Inshallah.*" He disconnected.

Barak took his tumbler of Scotch and went looking for his pilot. He found O'Neil playing pool in the rec room downstairs.

"Tim," he said in a jovial voice, "I'm feeling good tonight. Let's celebrate. Drive over to that restaurant at the marina and get us two orders to go of their grilled baby back ribs, some ceviche with the Mexican prawns, a couple salads, and some fried ice cream. I'll be busy tomorrow night and we're leaving Saturday, so we'll make this our farewell dinner."

"Would you like me to arrange for female companionship as well?"

Barak shook his head. "I don't need the distraction. But go ahead if you do. As long as you have my plane ready to go on Saturday, I don't care what you do between now and then. As long as you're discreet and don't attract unwanted attention," he added.

As O'Neil left, Barak walked out to the hangar and opened the exterior luggage compartment of his Beechcraft Hawker and removed two padlocked, twenty-four-inch, black nylon duffel bags. Each bag held five pounds of Semtex.

He carried these bags to the closet in the master bedroom and set them next to the smaller black nylon range bag that held his Glock 21 and HK MP5K submachine gun. It never hurt, he told himself, to have too much fire power. He knew that from experience and because most of the world's law enforcement agencies were looking for him. The guns in the range bag were only backup, of course, if he found that he needed more than the Glock 30 he always carried in a horsehide holster on his right hip.

The Semtex was also a backup of sorts. Sooner or later, he knew they would discover where he had been staying. Before they did, he planned to level the hangar house and destroy any trace of evidence that would link him to the most lethal terrorist act in history.

Chapter Forty

When he walked into his bedroom, Drake found Gonzalez using saline to irrigate the wounds on Liz's face. She was on the bed, trying to lie as still as possible. He was impressed that she didn't flinch when the medic dabbed at the skin around the cuts on the right side of her face.

"She was lucky," Gonzalez said without looking up. "She was holding her glass of wine at her side, level with her shoulder, not her face, when it exploded. Most of the small glass shards hit her upper arm. Only a few shards hit her neck and right cheek. If you hadn't pulled her sideways, there would have been lots more of these shards to remove."

Liz spoke up. "I guess that means I should be happy you knocked me down and gave me a concussion," she said. "All I remember is how good that wine tasted and that I was glad I was the only one drinking it."

Drake smiled. "I'll save the rest of the bottle for you," he said. He came closer to the bed. "How are you feeling?"

"Other than a headache, not too bad right now. When he starts removing those little pieces of glass with tweezers, I think I'll be feeling a lot worse." Gonzalez had found tweezers in the bathroom cabinet and had already removed several small shards.

"When he gets the bleeding stopped," Drake said, "we should get you to the hospital."

"No. Then we would have to get the police involved, and I don't want to spend a whole day answering questions about what I'm doing here. Ricardo assures me I'm not going to need major plastic surgery...although," she admitted, "I was kind of looking forward to a little touch up. And you need my help if we're going to get these creeps. I want to find that nuke. Adam, I'm starting to feel that you're right that it's here."

"What about your boss? Want me to call the Secretary and fill him in?"

"Not yet. I'd like to be the one to tell him what happened. *After* I tell him we found the bomb, or whatever it is. You go do what you need to do. I'm fine. I've been hurt worse than this and lived."

"Ricardo, are you okay with this? Does she need to go to the hospital?"

"Her wounds are bloody but superficial," the medic said. "I'll keep an eye on her concussion, but if Ms. Tough Guy says she's okay, I can't argue. She wants to finish this. She's earned the right to do it."

"Okay, then. I'll go check on Larry and see if Billy was able to find anything across the river."

Larry Green, the former LAPD officer, was patrolling the perimeter of the cabin when Drake found him.

"How's Liz?" Green asked.

"Being brave while Ricardo picks the glass out of her face. She refuses to go to the hospital. Doesn't want the police involved."

"She's tough," Green said. "Some FBI guys I've met are wimps, too used to wearing suits and not getting their hands dirty. But FBI women are tough. They have to be, to put up with the BS they get from crashing the federal boys club. I think she's right about not getting local law enforcement involved. If they found out the DHS Secretary's executive assistant was here and wounded on their turf, they'd be changing their diapers every five minutes and taking statements from now to Christmas."

Drake laughed out loud. "Big fan of the F.B.I., are you?"

"Got tired of fighting with them. We'd do the work, they'd take over and get all the press."

As they rounded the front of the cabin Montgomery, the former Green Beret sniper, drove up in one of the white Yukons. Like Green, he held his HK416 rifle down against his right leg as he approached them.

"I found where he shot from," Montgomery said. "Right where you said he was. He was a little too anxious to get out of there, though. I found this in the deep grass." He held up a rifle cartridge. "Seven-point-sixty-two millimeter, hollow point, boat tail. I'd say he was using a Dragunov, the Soviet SVD sniper rifle. That wasn't a stray shot from some hunter."

Drake took the cartridge. "Favorite sniper rifle used by the terrorists in Iraq and Afghanistan," he said. "I've been shot at with one of those before. Let's get inside and talk. We need to come up with a plan to flush these guys out. I'm tired of being in their sights and not knowing for sure who they are."

He stopped at the bedroom to check with Gonzalez and found that Liz seemed to be resting. The medic had used the tweezers, and now the side of her face and neck were covered with small red cuts that had been treated with antiseptic ointment. Her right arm and shoulder were bandaged. Her lips were pressed together and her jaw was clenched, but her eyes were closed and she was breathing evenly.

"She needs some pain meds," Gonzalez said, "but she says she doesn't want anything. What she said is she doesn't want to be doped up and miss all the fun. That's one tough lady. I used the medical adhesive glue that I always carry on her cuts.

It's better than stitches and there's less infection." He smiled down at her. "She may have some minor scarring, but she can get that touched up later."

"Join us in the kitchen," Drake said. "We've got some planning to do."

The others were waiting for him. Their weapons were lying on the marble kitchen countertop behind them and Casey was brewing a pot of coffee.

"It's time we go on the offensive," Drake started. "We know about the bunch at the ranch, and we know where Marco Vazquez is staying. But we still don't know where the guy is that rented the Escalades. What I want to do is stir the pot and see what bubbles up. See what we can learn. Ricardo and Billy, you think you can get back to the ranch tonight and set up surveillance?"

"Sure we can," Montgomery said. "Although parking the Yukon all night where we did last time, it might be spotted in the morning. Better to have someone drop us off and we'll hike in."

"I'll take them," Green offered.

Drake nodded. "Fine. Mike and I will trade off and guard things here tonight and keep an eye on Liz. Tomorrow, I want to put some pressure on Vazquez. He knows more than he's told us. He might run back to the ranch. If he does, we can use the drone to listen in on conversations there. I also want pictures of the guys taking care of his polo ponies. Liz can run them through the facial recognition and iris scanning biometrics they have at DHS. Its database will tell us if these guys are terrorists or innocent polo pony grooms. I'm betting on the former."

"What about that O'Neil who rented the Escalades?" Casey asked. "What are we going to do about him?"

"Good question. Any ideas?" Drake asked the rest of the men.

"I'm not sure how we'd do it,' Casey said after a moment's

thought. "But Escalades come with OnStar. The rental agency can locate its vehicles that way and block the ignition or slow down a stolen car. I might be able to get one of my IT guys in Seattle to hack into the Enterprise Car Rental computer at the Sunriver airport and locate those two Escalades."

"Do it," Drake said. "We need to know who this guy is because he's involved in some way. Anything else? What am I forgetting?"

"Me." The men turned to see Liz standing just outside the kitchen. With one hand on the wall to steady herself, she came forward. "What am I going to do while you boys are finding my nuke?"

Although she looked like the right side of her face had been attacked by a swarm of angry bees, her glued-together wounds did little to hide the smile on her face as she watched the men's reaction to her appearance. Drake was the first to reach her. He took her hand and led her to a chair.

"How's the headache?" Gonzalez asked.

"Not too bad. I'm not dizzy or nauseous." She sat up straighter. "What do I get to do?"

"Nothing tonight, except get a good night's rest," Drake said. "If you're up to it, you can go with me to see Marco tomorrow." He smiled. "Your wounds might scare him into telling us what he knows."

"Thanks for confirming what I didn't want to know," she said, gently punching him in the stomach. "I was going to hide under a ton of makeup, but if you insist, I'll go *au naturale*."

"Where I come from," Gonzalez began, "that means—"

"It means without makeup, Ricardo. Most of your women…."

"All right, gentlemen," Drake said. "Let's leave Ricardo's love life out of this. It's time to get Ricardo and Billy ready to go to the ranch. Larry, why don't you stand guard for now while Mike calls his guy in Seattle and I get Liz a cup of coffee. Tomorrow's game day."

When the rest of the team had left the kitchen, Drake handed her a cup of coffee and said, "Are you sure you feel up to going with me tomorrow? No one will blame you for taking a day to get back on your feet."

Liz took a moment to savor the sweet mellow taste of the Kona coffee Drake preferred. "I have a confession to make," she said, looking up at him. "When I called to tell you about the detection of a nuclear device in San Diego, I really just wanted to know how you were doing. I wanted to thank you again for what you did in Portland. I never intended to get you involved like this. I never meant to put you in harm's way again."

He wasn't sure how to reply. Then, "You gave me the tip about Barak being in Mexico. I'm just returning the favor. Besides, if we find your nuke and I get Barak, we both win. I used to do this kind of thing for a living. You're the one I'm worried about being in harm's way."

"Adam, do you know why I joined the FBI after law school?"

"No, I don't"

"I joined the FBI for the same reason you enlisted in the army the day after 9/11. I chose the FBI because I knew it would be tasked with counterterrorism duties here at home. I wanted to fight them here, just like you wanted to fight them over there. I haven't regretted my decision, either, so don't you worry about me being in harm's way. It's where I want to be."

"What about getting married?" he asked. "Having a family and kids? Do you regret missing out on that?"

She gave him a tiny smile. "I haven't given up on that just yet. When I meet the right guy, well, then I guess I'll have to make a choice. Hopefully, there's a little time before I have to choose."

"You'll find your guy, Liz. You're young and beautiful. I'm sure you have a hundred guys in D.C. who would love to settle down with you and raise a family."

"Not so young and not so beautiful, especially with all these cuts on my face." To cover feelings she felt stirring somewhere down deep, she took another sip of coffee. "You really think my face will scare Vazquez into telling us what he knows?"

He shrugged his shoulders. "I just said that to encourage you to stay here and rest. You watch the way you turn heads at Pronghorn tomorrow. Tonight, you need to rest and get rid of that headache. You go ahead and sleep in my bed tonight. I'll find a bed upstairs."

"I'm fine," she insisted. "Go get Ricardo and Billy on their way. I'll finish my coffee and then get some rest."

After he left, she relaxed against the back of the chair. With a little luck, she might have to make her choice sooner than she had expected.

Chapter Forty-One

IT WAS TWO THIRTY IN THE MORNING, THREE HOURS BEFORE sunrise, by the time Gonzalez and Montgomery reached their observation post on the rimrock above Wyler Ranch. Both men were equipped with night vision optics. Gonzalez was using ATN night vision goggles, Montgomery, an ATN night vision rifle scope mounted on his M24 sniper rifle. They were concealed beneath camouflage netting that matched the brown hues of the rocks and grasses around them.

Nothing moved below them. The polo ponies were in their stalls, and the ranch hands were asleep in the bunkhouse. But they had already spotted four men sleeping on the ground in sleeping bags beside the long horse trailer.

"Wonder why these guys are sleeping outside," Gonzalez muttered.

"Maybe they don't get along with the ranch hands," Montgomery whispered back. Drake said he overheard a couple guys speaking Arabic. A couple of *no comprendes* from the regulars might have hurt their feelings."

"Or they're practicing for their *hajj* pilgrimage. Don't they sleep on the ground under open sky one night before they get up the next morning to gather pebbles to throw at the devil?"

"Something like that," Montgomery said. "How good are you with that drone? Will you be able to get it close enough to hear what they're saying?"

"I should be able to. With any background noise at all, they won't hear the seventy-two decibels the drone makes. I can put the thing right over them and the built-in zoom mike on the Sony Handycam will focus the audio recording right on them. Yeah, we should hear them loud and clear. Then we'll just feed the recordings to Drake and he can translate whatever they're saying."

"Good." Montgomery took another look around. "We won't need the drone for awhile, so why don't you get some sleep. I'll keep an eye on things. There's enough moon light, I don't think I'll even need to use night vision."

"Thanks, Billy. Wake me in an hour."

Gonzalez laid his head on his forearm and, like a good soldier, was asleep in minutes.

His companion studied the area below. The bunkhouse was on the left, fifty yards east of the stables. He could see the door at the front of the long, single-story structure, but he couldn't tell if there was another door to the rear. There was one window at the end of the building closest to him, and he thought there would probably be another at the other end. There were no windows along the front of the bunkhouse.

The stables were ahead of his position at eleven o'clock, a hundred yards from the bunkhouse. The paddocks for the horse stalls were empty, and he could look down the open center of the stables to about the middle of the building. There were two overhead light fixtures that lit the interior, and there was a dog that looked like a border collie curled up on a hay bale near the door.

To the right of the stables at two o'clock was the longest horse trailer he had ever seen. It was silver with black lettering that proclaimed it carried the polo ponies of Marco Vazquez. There were four windows at the rear of the trailer, and a door on the side near the front that opened into what looked like a small sleeping quarters and tack room. Unhitched nearby was an International RXT towing pickup. It was painted in the same silver as the trailer and had the same black lettering.

In the distance, sitting on a small rise overlooking the fenced pasture that ran along a small creek and single lane road, was the main ranch house. There were no cars that he could see and no indication that it was occupied.

Montgomery was surprised when Gonzalez suddenly raised his head and checked his watch.

"You let me sleep for two hours! It's almost sunrise. You want to grab a few winks before things get started down there?"

"Looks like it's too late for that. One of the guys on the ground is getting up."

Both men watched as the first horse groomer woke the others, then spread a prayer rug on the ground next to his sleeping bag. The others slowly followed, each man spreading a prayer rug and facing toward the southeast.

"This is their pre-dawn prayer, the *fajr*," Gonzalez muttered. "They're facing toward where they think the Ka'aba in Mecca is located."

Montgomery gave an almost soundless whistle. "No wonder they're sleeping outside. If they woke up the ranch hands each morning before sunrise, someone was bound to get hurt."

"Yeah. Keep an eye on them while I get the drone ready."

Gonzalez slid back out from under the camouflage netting until he was out sight from the canyon floor. The Draganflyer X8 drone was carried in a round, black, carbon fiber tube. After unscrewing the cap on the top of the tube, he pulled the drone out and laid it on the ground. With its four arms folded, it was just over twenty-seven inches long. Each arm had two rotors on the end, one above and one below. When the four arms were locked into place, the miniature aircraft was three feet long and three feet wide and had two landing skids and a bullet-shaped body packed with sensors, gyros, GPS, and a lithium polymer battery. Beneath the body of the drone was a mounting bracket for the video camera that was stored in the backpack Montgomery had carried. It also contained the handheld controller and the high resolution video glasses that would allow Gonzalez to see exactly what the drone was seeing.

When he had the video camera attached, he slipped on the video glasses and held the drone chest-high in front of him. When he switched on the rotors, he gently lifted it into the air and sent it on its way. Using the handheld flight controller, he flew the Draganflyer straight up until it was a hundred feet overhead, then he aimed it out over the rimrock. A minute later, he put the drone in a GPS position hold directly above the four men, who were standing in line waiting to perform their ablutions before they prayed.

One man held a hose as the others washed their right hands three times, then their left hands three times, then swirled water around in their mouths and rinsed their noses three times. Then they washed their faces, then their arms and hair, their ears, and last their feet. When the first three men had finished, one man held the hose for the fourth man until he was finished, and then all four returned to their prayer rugs.

Montgomery used the handheld controller to swing the video camera slowly around the area below, looking for anything that might explain what these Muslim so-called groomers were up to. There were no black Escalades in sight, no weapons lying around, no crate labeled *Nuclear Device, Danger*.

As he crawled back under the netting, he saw that Montgomery was watching the telemetry feed from the drone on a handheld ground control station that was recording the video it received in its internal memory.

"I'll keep the drone up for another five minutes or so," Gonzalez said. "I don't think we'll hear much from them until they've finished their prayers."

Montgomery nodded. "Might as well save as much battery life as we can. I think Drake expects us to watch this place until we learn something. Other than confirming these four are Muslims, there's nothing to report so far. Although I'm tempted to call in and see if anyone's up yet at the cabin."

"Not a good idea. The only person awake is likely to be Liz. You get her out of bed with nothing to report, and Drake might keep you out here until it snows in December."

"You think he likes her?"

"*Like*? I haven't been around him long enough to answer that. But he's trying too hard not to look at her like the rest of us do. That tells me he's trying not to like her, which tells me he does but doesn't want to allow himself to admit it."

"You learn to think like that in counseling or something?" Montgomery asked.

"Careful observation and a lot of experience. Keep your eyes on our friends. They'll be finishing up soon."

Chapter Forty-Two

Drake was awake early enough to see the rising sun shining through the slats of the rustic oak plantation blinds in the upstairs bedroom. He'd found an empty bed in Gonzalez's room and had stretched out fully clothed. But he hadn't been able to sleep much in the five hours since saying good night to Liz. His Kimber .45 was on the night stand to his right, next to the night vision binoculars he had borrowed from Casey. When he wasn't standing alternating guard duty, he had searched the area across the river several times to see if the sniper had returned, and when he wasn't kneeling at the window with the binoculars, he was lying on the bed with his eyes closed, seeing again that flash of reflected light from the sniper's rifle scope and shoving Liz down. Finally, an hour ago, he had forced himself to close the blinds and get a little sleep. Now, with the sun rising, he was alert and eager to move ahead. This was going to be the day he found out what Marco Vazquez and his friends were up to.

After a quick shower, he followed the smell of brewing coffee downstairs to the kitchen. Casey was breaking eggs in a large mixing bowl. He had a big smile on his face.

"Hope you're hungry," he said. "Because I'm fixing us the best scrambled eggs you will ever taste. Secret recipe, known only to a select group of men. But I'm willing to let you try it so you'll have the strength to win the day."

"What select group of men are we talking about?"

"Men who know what made 007 a special agent. This is James Bond's recipe for scrambled eggs. Twelve eggs, salt and pepper, six ounces of real butter, and *fines herbs.* Those are the ingredients. But it's all in the preparation."

"Does your wife let you eat eggs with that much butter?"

"She does not. That's why I'm having them today. Butter the toast for me and we'll eat."

"Want me to get Liz and Larry to join us?" Drake asked.

Casey shook his head. "Larry's only been sleeping for an hour, and Liz is showering. She said to go ahead, she'll join us in a minute."

With a bowl full of the scrambled eggs, a plate of crispy bacon, toast and jam, and cups of coffee in front of them on the breakfast counter, the two men sat on the nearby stools and started eating.

"These eggs are really good," Drake admitted.

"Thanks. It's the butter. Ricardo called a couple minutes ago. He used the drone to search the area at the ranch. Four men were sleeping outside on the ground when they got there. Sun comes up, and they go through their routine for morning prayers. Same thing we watched in Iraq and other places. Nothing looked suspicious, he said, except for the four guys sleeping out on the ground."

"Let's keep Ricardo and Billy out there a little longer," Drake decided. "These guys are involved with Vazquez. If we rattle him today, maybe we'll hear something if he goes out to check on his ponies for the match tomorrow."

Between forkfuls of eggs, Casey asked "How are you going to rattle Vazquez?"

"He's not." Liz walked into the kitchen. "I am." With her blond hair pulled back over her right ear, it was easy to see that the right side of her face and neck was splotchy and swollen. Her smile did nothing to conceal the trauma she had suffered the night before. "I'm going to tell him I know he's responsible for this," she said. "And when I prove it, I'll use everything in my power to make sure he spends the rest of his life in prison. I might even threaten to have him arrested so he'll miss his polo match tomorrow."

"That should do it," Casey said. "Latin men have a reputation for treating women badly, so seeing your face won't necessarily scare him. But keeping him away from playing polo tomorrow might. You feel like confronting him today?"

"Let me have some of those eggs, and I'll be fine."

Drake watched her carefully as she poured herself a cup of coffee and sat next to him while Casey brought her a plate of the scrambled eggs. The symptoms of a concussion were subtle, he knew, and not easy to identify. But she didn't appear to be dizzy or confused, and she wasn't showing any sensitivity to the bright lights in the kitchen area.

"You look gorgeous," he said. "I was right last night when I said you'd be turning heads at Pronghorn. How's the headache?"

"Better, thanks for asking. I'll be ready to go as soon as I eat something."

"I doubt Vazquez gets up too early, so there's no rush. If we catch him mid-morning working on his suntan, we'll be fine. You mentioned threatening the boy with arrest. Is that something you can do?"

"Actually, I can. When I first transferred to the Department of Homeland Security from the FBI, I was designated as a special agent. I still have that designation. It carries with it investigation and arrest authorization. I haven't had to exercise the power as the Secretary's executive assistant, but I can use it here if I need to."

"Liz," Casey said as he passed her a piece of toast that had just popped out of the toaster, "did you see if Vazquez has anything in his past that would make him nervous about talking with you? Does our playboy have a record in Argentina?"

"When Adam mentioned him, I checked with Interpol and the Argentine Federal Police. Other than noise complaints about some of the parties he's thrown after polo matches, he has a clean record. None of his known associates have records or ties to any of the terrorist organizations we track."

"He doesn't strike me as someone who would get involved with terrorists," Drake said. "He might be friends with Hollywood liberals, but that's as close as I can see him getting to terrorism."

"Ouch," Liz said. "There you go again, Mr. P.C."

Casey laughed. "Don't get him started."

"You know a man by the friends he keeps," Drake said. "That's all I'm saying. Vazquez obviously is a friend of Abazzano's, THE Hollywood lib, and his host at Wyler Ranch. Abazzano is known to be pro-Palestine, pro-Hamas, pro-Muslim everything with all the fundraising he does in Hollywood."

"Liz," Casey said, "do you have anything on Abazzano that might help?"

"His name has come up as a contributor to Palestinian causes, but nothing that's directly linked to known terrorist organizations. I'll call the head of our intelligence and analysis division and see if there's anything new."

Casey turned to Drake. "What do you want me to do while you're going to see Vazquez?"

"If your IT guy gets anything on O'Neil and the Escalades he rented, follow up on that. Otherwise, see if Ricardo and Billy need anything. If we finish by noon, I think it's time we paid another visit to Wyler Ranch. With Ricardo and Billy out there, they might see something when we come visiting. Plan on meeting us in Bend, and we'll go from there. And bring the hardware in case we run into our sniper friend."

"If we do," Liz said, "he's mine. He ruined a good glass of wine."

Chapter Forty-Three

SALEEM LEFT MICHAEL ABAZZANO'S VILLA AT WYLER RANCH and drove to the Pronghorn resort to collect Marco Vazquez. It didn't feel like it was going to be as warm a day as he was used to in San Diego, but temperatures in the mid-eighties were plenty warm by early afternoon in the high desert country of Central Oregon. The late morning air, however, was still crisp with the lingering coolness of the previous night.

Having watched the polo star lounging around the pool, Saleem thought of heading there first after he had parked the Escalade Barak had let him use while he was in Oregon. But as addicted as Vazquez was to tanning his lean body and strutting around in his Speedo swimsuit, Saleem couldn't see him being out this early. More likely, he would find him in the Trailhead Grill where Barak had found him drinking his breakfast.

Sure enough, he spotted Vazquez sitting alone at a small table next to a window looking out over the pool. He was sucking down a Bloody Mary, ignoring the hamburger and fries he'd ordered, and looking like it had been a rough night for him. Saleem hoped that it had been. It would give him immense pleasure to ruin the day for the pampered celebrity whose rough night had probably consisted of having to decide which fawning young woman to invite to his room.

Saleem sat down across the table from Vazquez, reached over and took a French fry from his plate and ate it. "Greetings, Marco. Have you been a good boy lately?"

The polo player frowned and set his glass down. "You some reporter? Leave me alone or I'll have you thrown out."

"I doubt that. I asked you a question."

"That I didn't answer. Now please leave."

"Have you talked with your father lately? He told you to be a good boy, didn't he?"

Vazquez scooted his chair back and leaned forward to stare at the smiling person eating his toast. "Who are you?"

"Let's just say that today I'm someone you do not want to anger. I will be your companion for the rest of your stay here. My duty is to make sure you do not disobey and get your family killed." Saleem helped himself to more of the French fries. "That's who I am."

"I'm not going anywhere with you and I'm tired of being ordered around. I have done everything I have been asked to do. I have a match tomorrow. I do not have time to escort you around."

"Marco, listen to me." Saleem leaned across the table. "You are this close to getting the people you love killed. You know who we are, just as your father knows who we are. Now give me your phone. I want you to listen carefully."

The two men sat without moving for a long minute until Vazquez slowly reached into the pocket of his silk shirt and handed over his iPhone.

Saleem dialed a number. "The Argentine needs to speak to you," he said to Barak.

Vazquez took the phone and put it to his ear.

"What is it Marco? Have you forgotten me already?"

"Why are you doing this?" Vazquez asked, recognizing the cold fear he felt in his stomach.

"Because I can't take any chances," said the voice. "And neither can you. Go with Saleem and do what he says. You will be our guest at the ranch with your ponies until your match. Saleem will call and say you are ill and need to rest if you are to ride tomorrow. You won't have to attend the dinner tonight. If you do as you are told, you will not see either of us ever again after your match tomorrow. And your family will be alive when you return to Argentina."

"Will this be the end of it?"

"This will be the end of it. You have my word."

Vazquez listened for the voice that made his stomach churn to speak again. After a minute, he realized the call had ended.

Saleem, sitting across the table with a cruel smile on his lips, held out his hand for the phone. "Go pack your bags and check out," he said. "When you are finished, return here to me. I'm going to order a lunch and put it on your tab. Tell the waiter on your way out that it's okay."

Vazquez stood up slowly and crossed the room to tell the waiter to take Saleem's order. His slumped shoulders and bowed head told his new keeper their time together was going to be a pleasure. Saleem was already enjoying the pain and fear he saw in the young man's eyes and began to think of ways he could increase the boy's fear in the hours ahead. He wouldn't be able to physically inflict pain on him, but Vazquez wouldn't know that. Besides, he thought as he studied the breakfast menu, mental torture could sometimes be as much fun as the physical methods he preferred.

Saleem was finishing a ranch burger when Vazquez returned.

"My bags are in front of the hotel lobby," he said in a sullen voice. "Where do you want me to put them?"

"Have the parking valet put them in my Escalade," Saleem replied. "Here's the key."

Saleem finished the rest of his fries, then followed his

charge to his Escalade that was idling in front of the hotel. Without a word to the valet, he got in and motioned for Vazquez to join him.

As they drove off, he began taunting his passenger. "You may as well relax," he said. "There's nothing you can do or say that will change this. Your stupid father got you into this, and he's not capable of helping you now, even if he wanted to."

"What are you talking about? Of course my father wants to help me!"

Like a cobra launching itself at its prey, Saleem's hand flashed across the center console and hit Vazquez in the mouth.

"You stupid fool! Your father's the reason you're leaving your precious resort with me right now. He's been working with us for a long, long time, just so he could keep his *estancia* and keep you playing polo. He's one of us. Just like you're one of us now. He takes orders from us. You had better learn to do the same."

As Vazquez wiped the blood from his split lip, Saleem laughed. Life is good when you're in the driver's seat.

Chapter Forty-Four

After Drake and Liz left to find Vazquez at the Pronghorn Resort, Casey called his white-hat IT hacker to ask for a little off-the-books help in locating the Escalades that had been leased by Timothy O'Neil. Kevin McRoberts, said white-hat IT hacker, was only twenty-two years old, but he was recognized as a rising star among Information Technology security professionals. At age fourteen, he had been caught exploiting a vulnerability in Microsoft's security shield, but instead of prosecuting him, Microsoft had offered to give him security training so he could work for them as a good guy, or white-hat IT hacker. After six years with Microsoft, McRoberts had let it be known that he wanted more excitement than the corporate world offered. That was when Casey's IT division chief had suggested they hire the young man and use him to test the security shields of their growing list of corporate clients. McRoberts had jumped at the opportunity and settled into his new role like a boy at Christmas with a new video game he couldn't wait to master.

His adaptation to life in Casey's company had not, however, been without challenges. The majority of the company's employees had military experience and were used to discipline and routine. Kevin, on the other hand, had been allowed by Microsoft to work whenever he wanted, any hours of the day or night, as long as he met the performance goals he had agreed on. So he worked at night or on weekends, from home or in his office, with his ever-present, noise-canceling iPod headphones in his ears. He had been granted the freedom Microsoft accorded a child genius.

Casey had had to work at developing a relationship with the kid. Kevin had made it a little easier dressing semi-appropriately, at least compared to the company's other employees. Although Casey had expected to see the young hacker in a hoodie, cargo pants and flip-flops, Kevin adopted jeans and a long-sleeve white shirt and purple canvas skate shoes to appease the Huskie fans in the office. But Kevin lived alone in his head with his music and his computer. He seldom spoke and didn't seem to share any of the interests his boss wanted to talk about. Except food. Kevin loved to eat and when Casey took him to lunch at his favorite BBQ shack, where the sauce was served in buckets labeled "Hot," "Hotter," and "Hottest," a friendship had developed over heaping stacks of baby back ribs. When Casey needed Kevin's undivided attention, he took him to lunch.

Now he found the young hacker's name on his iPhone contact list and called him.

"Kevin, it's Mike. How are we doing on the Patterson project?"

"They're not going to like what we have to tell them," Kevin replied. "They're completely exposed to modem mobile threats and cyber espionage. It was a piece of cake."

"Great. Go ahead and schedule a meeting with them next week. In the meantime, I have a new project for you. I'm trying to locate two SUVs for a client here in Bend that were rented from Enterprise Car Rentals at the Sunriver airport.

Both of the SUVs are Cadillac Escalades. I believe they have OnStar. Can you find out where those two vehicles are?"

"Sure, but I'll need the vehicle VIN numbers for the two Escalades. OnStar collects the GPS location data on all the GMC vehicles. You want me to, um, *borrow* that information?"

"Get the VIN numbers for the two SUV's from Enterprise," Casey told him. "The rental agreements will be in the name of Timothy O'Neil. Then see what OnStar can tell us. This is semi-official for now, but untraceable would be best."

"It's what I do best! We going to do lunch anytime soon?"

"Soon as I get back. Call me as soon as you have something."

Before Casey even had time to finish cleaning the mess he'd made in the kitchen fixing breakfast, Kevin called him back.

"One of the Escalades is on the road north of Bend. The other is at Sunriver near the airport."

"Can you tell where at Sunriver?"

"From what I'm seeing, it's stationary and approximately three hundred yards south of the airport terminal."

"Thanks, Kevin. I'm on my way to check it out." He walked out to the deck where Green was cleaning his handgun and talking with Gonzalez at the observation post at Wyler Ranch.

"We need to go, Larry," Casey said. "In less than five minutes, Kevin located the two Escalades. One's on the road, the other's just south of the airport at Sunriver. Let's go take a look."

They picked up their black tactical responder equipment bags, into which they had stuffed two handguns each, loaded magazines, vests, binoculars, flashlights, and every other necessary item they could think of, and loaded them into the Yukon parked outside. Both men were also carrying their favorite concealed handguns.

"You got your camera bag?" he asked Green.

"In my room. Be right back."

While Green ran back inside to get his surveillance camera equipment, Casey called Drake.

"Good news," he said. "I think we have the location of one of the Escalades."

"Where is it?" Drake asked.

"Right under our noses. It's just south of the Sunriver airport. Must be in one of the houses along the golf course. Or maybe in one of the hangar houses."

"What's a hangar house?"

"It's a house with a garage big enough for an airplane. They build them near general aviation airports for civilian pilots who like to fly a lot."

"So you think O'Neil is a pilot?"

"He might be. It would explain why he rented the Escalades if he and his party flew in and needed transportation."

"Check it out," Drake said. "We're about twenty minutes away from the Pronghorn resort. I'll call you as soon as Liz convinces Vazquez she's someone he doesn't want to mess with."

Casey had to smile. "That should be worth the price of a ticket, seeing her in action."

"Agreed. Good luck at Sunriver."

"Shallow men believe in luck, to quote Emerson," Casey returned. "I believe in overwhelming firepower. Which I just happen to have with me."

"Shock and awe it is, then. But if you think for a moment that Barak is with O'Neil, I'd better be the one delivering the firepower."

"Deal. Wouldn't want you to miss the fun."

As Casey waited for Green to return, he thought about what it would mean if Barak were with O'Neil at Sunriver.

From what he knew about Barak and what he'd seen the terrorist's men try to pull off when they went after Drake's father-in-law and Secretary Rallings, he was sure there was going to be one hell of a fight. If Barak and Drake met, one of them would die. He had to make sure it wasn't his friend.

Chapter Forty-Five

It took all of ten minutes for Casey to drive north to the Sunriver Resort and follow River Road around to the airport. Three hundred yards southwest of the small airport terminal, he saw the cluster of large homes identified on his resort map as Lone Eagle Landing.

"This could be a problem, Mike," Green said, looking up from the maps application on his iPhone. "The GPS coordinates Kevin gave you put the Escalade in a hangar house on the far side of this development."

"Why is that a problem?"

"Drive on around and you'll see."

They drove past nine large resort homes until River Road swung around and turned north again behind the seven hangar homes with taxi access from the airport.

"It's the second house. Drive on past unless you want him to know we're looking for him. He can see us from any of the windows off the deck on the second floor," he pointed to the windows. "If the Escalade is in the garage, we won't be able to see it. If he has a plane around the other side in the hangar, we can't see that either. All we know for sure is OnStar says the Escalade is here. O'Neil doesn't have to be, though, and neither does Barak."

Casey gave this some thought. "So let's knock on the door and find out," he finally said. "I'll say I'm interested in renting the place. He's supposed to return the Escalades the day after tomorrow, meaning his vacation's over, so he might expect someone to be looking at the place."

The former L.A. cop wasn't so sure. "Mike, without knowing more about O'Neil and what he's doing here, we could start a war if he's involved with Barak and we walk in on him. This isn't the way I was trained to handle a situation like this. We need more information. Especially if there is a nuke stashed around here."

Casey had to agree. "You're right," he said. "I am rushing things. Drake and I used to watch targets for weeks. With the attempts on Drake and then Liz last night, though, we need to make something happen."

"Let's just think it through. That's all I'm saying." After they drove past O'Neil's hangar house and back toward the airport terminal, Casey had another plan. "Let's drive out to the parking apron where the Relentless is tied down," he proposed. "We can see the back side of his house from there. I'll act like I'm going through a pre-flight inspection while you use your binoculars. It's all we can do for now."

He drove on to the small terminal building, then out onto the asphalt parking apron, where he pulled up just south of his red and black Bell 525 and parked. Now Green had a clear view of the row of hangar houses three hundred yards away.

"I'll do a walk around," he said. "Then I'm going to ask the service attendant about fuel. Maybe someone knows if O'Neil is here with a plane. I won't be gone long."

He got out and slowly walked around the helicopter, carefully inspecting the doors and windows and running his hands along the seams of the panels. Although he didn't take time to check fluid levels, he knelt down and looked for leaks, as was his habit. A pilot familiar with his own pre-flight routine would recognize the procedure. When he had walked all the way around and returned to the passenger side of the Yukon, he pointed toward the service attendant and walked over to the Chevron fuel truck.

"Hi," he said as he approached the attendant. He glanced at the man's name tag. "Ramon, I need to refuel the Relentless sometime today. Have you refueled a helicopter?"

"Once. Don't worry, though. I've been trained."

"How long have you worked here?"

"A week. Guy that had this job had an accident. I transferred up here from California to take his place." He looked past his potential customer at the helicopter. "That the new Bell Relentless? It's a beauty."

"Flies even better than it looks," Casey bragged. "Okay, refuel it when you have time. By the way, those hangar houses down there…people live there year round?"

"A couple do. The others are rented out to vacationers who fly in."

"You know if there's one available now?"

"Guy down there just brought his Hawker 400 up for refueling. Said he was leaving tomorrow. Maybe his place'll be available."

"Thanks. Any chance you remember his name? In case I run into him?"

After flipping through the receipts on his clipboard, the service attendant said, "O'Neil. Timothy O'Neil."

With a nod, Casey walked back and climbed into his Yukon, repeating to himself the tail number for O'Neil's Hawker, which he'd glimpsed on the refueling receipt. With his hands on the top of the steering wheel, he turned to watch Green searching for signs of O'Neil.

"He's here, Larry," he said. "The refueling attendant just serviced his jet. He told the attendant he was leaving tomorrow."

"What do you want to do?"

"Let's go meet Drake in Bend. With the GPS coordinates Kevin has for the two Escalades, we'll know where they are. Drake can decide how he wants to handle this. He's pretty good at putting things together, especially when he gets one of his hunches. I want to think he's right this time and that O'Neil is working with Barak and Barak is involved with the missing nuke. Wrapping all that up in one neat package and sending it all to hell would make my day. Make my *year.*" He smiled. "It would also let Drake get on with his life."

"How would it do that?" Green asked.

"He's been having a tough time since his wife died a year ago. He was drinking too much and isolating himself out on his farm. Stopping Barak's assassination attempt last month seems to have snapped him out of his funk. He won't rest, though, until Barak's dead. When that happens, he'll be okay again." Casey put the SUV in gear and drove down the row of parked airplanes toward the terminal and the road leading out of the Sunriver resort.

Chapter Forty-Six

As Drake was helping Liz out of his Porsche in front of the clubhouse at the Pronghorn, he noticed her flinching a little as she turned her head to the right and reached for his hand.

"How's the head?" he asked.

"It's not my head," she replied. "It's my neck. I think it's sore from holding still so long while Ricardo picked the glass out of my face. Nothing a little time in the hot tub won't cure."

"The tub's all yours as soon as we get back. You sure you want to do this?"

"What? Pass on the opportunity to threaten this guy with a cell in Gitmo for the rest of his life? I wouldn't miss it."

"All right," Drake said. "Let's go find our boy."

He followed behind her a step or two as they made their way through the clubhouse and to the pool area outside. Most of the poolside chaise lounges and chairs were occupied. The men in several of them watched Liz carefully through the dark lenses of their sunglasses, while their wives watched them to see how long they would stare.

Drake himself wasn't immune to the effect Liz had on

men. He hadn't decided whether it was her natural beauty or her aura of confidence that caused it. She walked gracefully, with the light step of an athlete, the opposite of the stomping prance of a runway model, though it had much the same effect on the opposite sex. Her figure was full in the places it needed to be, and slender in the places where it didn't. And her eyes looked straight into the eyes of everyone she met, taking a quick reading of that person's intent and purpose and returning a small smile or a nod of her head. It wasn't that she demanded attention, he knew. She just knew that she would receive it.

She was looking around. "He's not here," she finally said. "Maybe he's at the bar."

But the polo player wasn't there either, and the bartender said he hadn't seen him since last night. When they looked for him in the Trailhead Grill, they were told he had checked out that morning.

"A fellow met him for breakfast," the manager said, "and he left to check out shortly after. They left together," he added.

"What did the fellow look like?" Liz asked.

"Young. Maybe thirty. Good looking. Maybe Hispanic. A little color in his complexion, anyway."

"I don't suppose you got his name," Drake said.

"Didn't ask. Vazquez charged both of their breakfasts to his room tab."

After thanking the manager, they walked outside and stood facing each other in the warm sun.

"Now what?" Liz asked.

"Now we think."

"Maybe Mike's learned something."

Drake pulled out his iPhone. "Let's see."

Casey answered on the first ring. "I have an outside table waiting for you at the Bend Brewery looking out on Mirror Pond. Do you want me to order something for you so it'll be ready when you get here?"

"It's not even noon," Drake said. "Are you eating already?"

"Just sampling while we wait for you."

"Did you find O'Neil?"

"Indeed we did. He's in one of the hangar houses at the Sunriver airport, a couple hundred yards south of where I parked the Relentless. He's a pilot, has his own jet, and is planning on leaving tomorrow."

"Is he alone?"

"That I don't know. I wasn't sure how you wanted to handle this, so we didn't pay him a visit."

"Vazquez checked out before we got here, so we have nothing new on our end. Have you heard from Ricardo and Billy?"

"Larry talked to Ricardo. They watched some Muslims sleeping outside the stables and then saying their morning prayers, but that's about it. You want to keep them at the ranch?"

"Vazquez is the key," Drake said, "and we don't know where he is. Tell your guys to meet us for lunch. We'll spread out this afternoon and see if we can find our polo star. Liz and I will be there in fifteen or twenty minutes."

When they pulled into the parking lot of the Bend Brewery, they saw Casey and Green waving at them from a table on the riverside patio.

"I have never met anyone as excited about food as your friend," Liz said.

Drake smiled. "He's been like that as long as I've known him."

"How long have you known him?" she asked as they walked to the patio.

"I met him in the army. We've been friends since then."

She glanced sideways at Drake, noticing the brevity of his answers. She already knew they were brothers in arms and that they had been together in several of the hell holes in the world. She had seen Drake's Delta Force file, the one that wasn't supposed to exist, and knew the broad details of missions he and Mike shouldn't have survived. They were more than friends and probably always would be.

"He's a good man to have as a friend," she said.

"Yes, he is," Drake said, letting her walk ahead of him through the scattering of tables on the patio.

When they reached their table, Casey stood up. "You're going to love the food here," he said. "Larry likes the brewery fries, but you need to try some of this spicy bean dip."

Drake shook his head. "If you like the dip, I know it's going to be too spicy for me." He sat down. "Ricardo and Billy on their way?"

"They had to crawl out with their gear, but they should be here before we finish the appetizers. Liz, what are you hungry for?" Casey asked.

"Something cold I can hold against my cheek. Iced tea would be nice."

"I'll try their IPA," Drake told Casey.

When Casey had ordered for them, Drake tried to focus his friend on the business at hand. "Were both of the Escalades at Sunriver?" he asked.

"Just one at the hangar house. Kevin said the other one was on the road north of Bend. Headed toward Redmond."

"And we don't know who's driving that one, right?"

"No clue."

"Is Kevin able to keep tracking these Escalades for us?"

"For as long as we want or until OnStar finds out they've been sharing information with us."

"Okay, let's keep Kevin on this. If we can't find Vazquez again, that's the only lead we have right now."

Green turned to Liz. "Could you find out where O'Neil's jet has been recently?" he asked. "It might tell us something about who's traveling with him."

"I can probably do that," she replied. "O'Neil can block

the Federal Aviation Administration from officially tracking his jet's flight. It's a routine request that's made to the National Business Aviation Association so corporate competitors don't know where each other are going and who they're seeing. But plane geeks track aircraft status messages sent to each other and to ground stations through ACARS. That's the Aircraft Communications Addressing and Reporting System." She smiled. "I think we have a plane geek or two at DHS I can call. Do you have the plane's registration or tail number?"

"Mike has it in the Yukon. I'll get it for you after lunch."

"Do we have any idea where Vazquez is?" Casey asked.

"No," said Drake, "but my hunch is he's going to turn up at Abazzano's ranch, where his horses are. I'd like to ask Ricardo and Billy to go back out there after lunch unless they've already spotted him."

Green was still talking with Liz. "Is there anything new from your office on the nuke? I called a friend in Los Angeles this morning. He said from what he's hearing at LAPD, they've called off the search."

"Your friend's right," she said. "Without something new to go on, NEST doesn't know where else to look. I checked in this morning, and other than informants saying the cartels are bragging about being able to smuggle anything you want into the U.S., there's nothing solid to follow up on. I told my secretary to tell Secretary Rallings that I'd had a minor accident and needed another day or so here. He wants me back in D.C. to coordinate a new approach to finding this thing. The White House is trying to keep everything quiet, but word is about to go public that someone smuggled a nuclear bomb into the country."

"Did you tell the Secretary that I think the bomb is here?" Drake asked her.

"Adam, you know I couldn't do that, and you know why. He trusts you. He'd send in the Army if you said he should. But where would you tell him to look? Besides, I think you have as good a chance as we have at finding some evidence if it's here. And as soon as you do, he's my first call."

"I think we have a better chance, too, but if it's here and we blow this, there'll be hell to pay. And you'll be the one who pays the price. Not me."

She nodded. "I realize that. But I know that if I set off alarms, and the full might of the government comes swarming in here, we'd close this town down and accomplish nothing. Look, Bend is what, seventy-eight thousand? San Diego is a million, three hundred thousand, plus or minus, and we nearly caused a panic there."

"She's right," Green said. "I saw what a terrorist alert does to a place when I worked in Los Angeles. That's why L.A. and New York City keep things quiet. There's only one main highway in and out of Bend, and if people saw the army on the streets or FBI agents and black helicopters overhead, nothing would move. Highway 97 would become a parking lot."

"Adam," Liz said, "we'll find the bomb if Vazquez is involved like we suspect. I trust you, but I don't want to put this in the hands of all the agencies that would have to be involved. It would take weeks for them to investigate the possibility that a nuclear device was smuggled all the way to Oregon, let alone find the thing."

"Well then," Drake said, "I guess we should have lunch and get back to work. I'd hate to make all those people work just to consider the possibility I might be right. Besides, here come Ricardo and Billy, and I know they're going to be hungry."

Chapter Forty-Seven

SALEEM DROVE DOWN THE WYLER RANCH ROAD FAST ENOUGH to scare the blackbirds from the trees and raise a huge cloud of dust behind him. He didn't care. He was tired of running errands for David Barak, tired of babysitting a plan that any fool could carry out with the demolition nuke his men had smuggled into the country and would deliver to the target. His name would never be linked to the thousands that would die. He would never be praised by his people as a holy warrior, never be extolled by the imam in his mosque.

As he steered the black Cadillac Escalade off the ranch road and up the driveway to the Tuscan-style villa his Hollywood host had built to replace the original modest ranch house, his ego screamed at the insult he was being forced to endure.

He hit the button on the overhead console to open the garage door and drove straight into the villa's four-car garage. Without a word, he got out and walked around and opened the passenger door for Marco Vazquez.

"We are alone," he said to the polo player, "and there is no one to stop me if I decide to end your miserable, spoiled life. So do not test me. Get out and walk to that door over there and go down the stairs to the billiards and rec room. Entertain yourself until I come for you." He stood back from the SUV and watched his captive turn in the seat and look at him before getting out.

"I don't know what you are planning," Vazquez said, "but if any harm comes to me or my family, I will find you and I will kill you. That is a promise."

Saleem laughed. "Aside from hitting someone by accident with your polo mallet, I doubt that you have ever hurt anyone, let alone killed someone. Do not make a threat you can't carry out. If you do as you are told, your precious family will not be harmed. Now get downstairs. I have to call your dinner hosts and tell them you're too ill to make an appearance."

After making sure Vazquez had followed his orders, Saleem locked the door out of the garage as he had done earlier with all the exterior doors on the lower level. Then he walked through the mud room and kitchen to the living quarters of the villa and the owner's office.

The walls of the office were covered with framed posters of the motion pictures and documentaries Michael Abazzano had directed or produced. Among the posters hung framed photos of the director with stars and starlets, politicians and people Saleem assumed were either rich or powerful. These were the celebrities that Americans worshipped and, worse, listened to. Why any thinking person cared what a beautiful movie star, with her cosmetically enhanced features, thought about anything, especially politics, was a mystery to him.

He stopped and peered closely at one framed photograph of a group of men standing on the rear deck of a large yacht. So that was Abazzano's connection. Four men stood facing a younger Abazzano and holding flutes of champagne in their hands. Two Saudi princes in traditional white *thobes* and headdresses; the Shia cleric and co-founder of Hezbollah, Abbas al-Masawi; and Yasser Arafat, the Fatah and PLO leader, who had his arm around Abazzano's beautiful wife, Nadine. It was rumored that Arafat had met her in a Palestinian refugee camp in Lebanon and started her on her career as a PLO operative. Saleem knew about the lovely Nadine, but he had not known of her husband's involvement in the cause of holy war.

Leaving the photo, Saleem made the necessary call to the woman in charge of the polo fundraiser and dinner that night and apologized for the star's temporary illness. He promised that Marco Vazquez would certainly appear tomorrow morning for the polo match. Yes, he assured her, the star would get a good night's sleep. With that out of the way, he walked back to the great room and poured himself four fingers of Abazzano's scotch, a twenty-one-year-old Old Pulteney single malt. The bottle was sitting on a bar near the covered patio that provided a view of the ranch in the canyon below. Swirling the amber liquid around in his tumbler, Saleem started to walk out to the patio when he heard someone walking through the kitchen from the garage.

"Pour me a glass, Saleem," Barak said without greeting. "I've wanted to try that. Abazzano swears it's the best single malt scotch in the world." He gave the room a cursory glance. "Is our boy down stairs?"

"Yes, and if I had my way, he would die downstairs. He promised he would kill me if we harmed his family."

Barak gave a thin smile. "Well, we don't need to worry about that, do we?" He tasted the scotch. "Citrusy lemon and pear," he said. "Do you enjoy scotch?"

"Not really."

"That's too bad. There are pleasures in the world we didn't invent. It doesn't hurt to sample them."

"Are you meeting with my men before their evening prayers?"

"Yes. I want to see if they're confident they can find the dam."

"They haven't been all the way to the dam on their practice runs," Saleem admitted, "but they've been to the turnoff from the highway that takes them there. They know how far it is from there. They'll get the bomb to the dam. Don't worry."

"They're your men. *Your* worry. We both know what will happen to the two of us if we fail."

"Like you failed last month? You're still here."

Barak set his tumbler on the bar and walked over to Saleem. Stopping inches in front of him, he said, "Do you know why you were selected to bring the bomb here, but not be in charge?" Before the younger man could reply, he went on. "It's because your blood is not pure. You're a half breed, half Arab and half Mexican. You're a warrior, they know that, but they aren't sure they can trust you with big plans. You have to prove yourself. Like I have. You have to prove that you can follow orders, that you respect those who give you those orders. And as you just demonstrated by insulting me, you have not proven that yet."

Saleem looked at Barak's eyes, which had suddenly become bloodshot and red, as if specks of dust had flown into them. At that moment, he knew he had pushed the older man too far.

He dipped his head and retreated. "I meant no disrespect," he said.

"Show me you mean that by doing what you are told. See if your men have returned. Go. I want to finish my drink." Barak's voice was cold.

BEFORE SALEEM COULD WALK past the door at the top of the stairs to the lower level of the villa, Vazquez quickly closed the door he stood behind and returned to the rec room. He had been playing billiards by himself before becoming bored. He had wanted to see if Saleem was still upstairs guarding him.

Chapter Forty-Eight

After feeding Casey and his men and enjoying a plate of grilled soft tacos and a Caesar salad that he shared with Liz, Drake dispatched his team with their afternoon assignments.

"Ricardo and Billy, go back to Abazzano's ranch and see if Vazquez is there taking care of his ponies. His polo match is scheduled for eleven o'clock tomorrow morning. I need to talk with him before that, if possible." He turned to Casey. "Mike, if O'Neil's leaving this weekend, why don't you and Larry see if the realty office that handles the rental of that hangar will give you a tour. Maybe O'Neil's there, maybe he isn't, but you might learn something."

As his team got ready to leave, he added, "I'll go back to Crosswater with Liz and see if her plane geek at DHS can tell us anything about where O'Neil's plane has traveled lately. We'll call when we hear something."

"Should I stop at the country store while we're at Sunriver and pick up something for dinner," Casey asked.

Liz laughed. "My turn, Mike. You cooked last night. Would linguine with white clam sauce work for everyone?"

"Mike's hungry already," Drake said. "You like to cook?"

"It's my hobby," she said. "My hours in D.C. are irregular

and I hate to eat out all the time. It's the only way I get comfort food when I need it."

Drake smiled at her. "Sounds like we're in for a treat tonight. Okay, guys, let's get going. Meet back at the cabin by six o'clock, unless we get a lead we need to move on."

After driving a dozen blocks or so through town to reach Highway 97 and turning south, with the sun in their eyes, Drake didn't have to see behind Liz's sunglasses to know if her eyes were closed. She hadn't said anything since leaving the restaurant.

They drove for several more minutes before she broke the silence.

"When I return to Washington next week, I'll be asked to explain how you single-handedly developed actionable intelligence about the missing nuclear device when we couldn't. We've spent several billion dollars to develop a system that pulls together state and local law enforcement resources to do what you're doing. And probably with better success."

"We haven't found the nuke yet," he reminded her.

"I think you will," she said. "But that's not the point. When the abandoned van was found next to the polo club in San Diego, someone should have thought to investigate everyone involved with that event. I should have thought to investigate it. If Marco Vazquez is involved, we should have known it a long time ago. We have to do better."

"You've stopped fifty or so terror plots since 9/11," he replied. "I'd say you've done a good job until now."

"Until now. Those terror plots involved homegrown threats that were much smaller in scale than what we're looking at now. We did do a good job stopping those people, but this is the big one, the unthinkable event we've worked hardest to prevent. And we don't have a clue where the bomb is. Or who's behind this."

"Liz, there are over two hundred thousand people

employed by DHS. You can't blame yourself for not seeing what none of them saw, either."

"Actually, I can. I was FBI before joining DHS. My job is to keep an eye on how the whole agency is doing. That's what the Secretary counts on me to do. I've let him down. I'm thinking of resigning, Adam."

"You can't do that! You're my liaison with DHS. I'm just getting used to working with you. Besides, you were the one who found Barak for me in Cancun. If it turns out he's behind this, you'll be the one who gets all the credit. I can't let everyone know about my arrangement with the Secretary. You're just going to have to tough it out and work with me a little longer. I'm starting to like my new role in life."

"You mean getting to be a cowboy again?"

"Maybe. Maybe that's what it is. Besides, I get to see Mike more often and have pretty women cook me meals. What more can a guy ask for?"

She turned her head to look at him and smile. "What other women? I like to know my competition before I cook a meal. In case I have to step up my game."

He smiled back. "A gentleman does not disclose that information. Just cook away and I'll let you know how you've done."

They had just turned off the highway and were driving into the parking lot of the country store at Sunriver to pick up the items Liz needed for her dinner. As they walked through the store, Drake began thinking about the banter he had just exchanged with her. It reminded him of better days, and, perhaps for the first time, he didn't regret letting a woman flirt with him. He followed her around the store, pushing a cart that she quickly filled with fresh linguine, an imported Italian extra virgin olive oil, garlic cloves, a tin of anchovy fillets, fresh thyme, three cans of whole baby clams, a lemon, fresh parsley, and four loaves of crusty French bread.

"Are we expecting company for dinner?" he finally asked. "You have enough food here to feed my old football team."

"Your friend eats like he *is* a football team," she said. "I just want to be sure there's enough for the rest of us."

Drake searched the wine corner until he found four bottles of 2008 Ponzi Tavola pinot noir to pair with the linguine with white clam sauce. The Senator had an ample store of wine in his thirty-bottle wine refrigerator he knew he could tap, but the Tavola was his favorite, easy-going, red wine with pasta.

With each of them carrying a large sack of groceries, they returned to Drake's Porsche, put the sacks in rear seats that were barely large enough to hold them, and drove on to the cabin at Crosswater. There, Drake put the groceries away while Liz went into the great room to call her favorite plane geek at DHS. When she returned, he was using his iPad to check the local news about the polo match the next morning.

"Vazquez isn't attending a fundraising dinner and auction tonight," he told her. "This report says he called in and said he wasn't feeling well and needed to rest so that he could ride tomorrow. What do you think that's about?"

"It might explain why he checked out," she said. "But where is he? I'd think he'd stay where he was and rest there instead of moving to a new location the day before the match. Too bad we can't trace his call and find out where he is now."

"Maybe we can," Drake said. "Law enforcement can track cell phone calls without a warrant. If you could get the local police to trace the call Vazquez made when he called in sick, we'd know where he's spending the night."

"The day before a big local event? I'm sure the Bend police department would drop what they're doing and run a trace for me."

"They would if you showed them your DHS badge, or whatever you carry. But it might not be necessary for you to make the call. My secretary's husband, Paul Benning, is a senior detective with the Multnomah County Sheriff's office.

He and Margo are coming over for the polo match. He's done favors for me in the past, and he knows what I'm doing here. He might be willing to ask his counterpart here in Bend to have the cell phone company trace the call. I'll ask him. Here, take my iPad and see if you can find the name of the person Vazquez called to say he wasn't feeling well."

At the same time, Drake found Paul Benning's number on his iPhone and called him.

"Detective Benning, how are you this fine day?" he asked when the detective answered.

"I was fine until I saw who was calling," he replied. "The only time you call me Detective Benning is when you want me to do something for you."

"No way to slip up on you, is there? Are you and Margo still coming to Bend for the polo match?"

"We're already here. We came over this morning, stretching the weekend for a mini-vacation. Why?"

Drake told him about needing to talk with Vazquez and not being able to find him.

"So you want me to request a phone trace on the call that was made to whomever this guy called to say he had to miss the dinner? Do you know who he called?"

"Liz, did you find out who Vazquez called?"

Reading from Drake's iPad, Liz said, "According to this story in the Bend *Bulletin*, a Mrs. Rebecca Harsh is the chairman of the local nonprofit raising money for breast cancer research. She organized the dinner and auction."

"Paul, the woman's name is Mrs. Rebecca Harsh. We think she's probably the one who took the call. If she didn't, she'll know who did."

"All right, I'll request the trace. There's no need to involve my friend in the Deschutes County Sheriff's office, though. I'll do it myself. I'm going to say I'm cooperating with the Department of Homeland Security. Is that okay?"

"Liz, can Paul say he's cooperating with DHS on this trace?"

"Fine. Have them call me if they need to," she said.

"Liz says it's okay, have them call her if necessary. Give them my number. I owe you, Paul."

"Yes, you do. Will we see you tomorrow?"

"Why don't you join us for dinner? Liz is making linguine with a white clam sauce for the crew here. There'll be plenty to go around."

Benning laughed. "I'll see if Margo wants to use one of her vacation nights eating with her boss. I'll call you."

Drake turned to Liz. "I hope you don't mind me inviting them for dinner."

"Not at all," she said. "I'll have a chance to get to know your secretary and hear all the gossip about you."

That's when it occurred to Drake that he might have made a big mistake allowing the two women to spend time together. One of them knew most of his secrets. The other seemed interested in knowing them.

Chapter Forty-Nine

Liz took the call from her plane geek at DHS while standing at the floor-to-ceiling windows and looking across the river to where the sniper had been when he shot her. When she turned away at the end of the call, she had a satisfied look on her face.

"I think we might be getting somewhere," she told Drake. "The tail number Larry gave me identifies a Hawker 400XP registered to an offshore Panamanian corporation. It flew from Las Vegas, where it was purchased last month, to San Diego, then here to Oregon. Panama has some of the strictest corporate book secrecy laws in the world, so we're not going to learn anything about the ownership of the corporation. At least not right away."

"How long has the jet been here?" Drake asked.

"It arrived here the same day the nuclear device was detected in San Diego."

"So it's possible the bomb was flown here. If we get a radiation detector on the jet, will we be able to confirm that?"

"There will be too many variables to be conclusive. The nuclear device could have been well-shielded. The jet could have been used to transport legitimate devices that are used for medical or industrial irradiation of blood or food items. If the source of radiation is still on the jet, we could x-ray the plane and see it. But you'd have to be pretty stupid to leave a nuclear weapon parked near an airport. Wristwatch sensors are now being used at larger airports and you would never know when one might accidentally walk by your plane on some pilot or some first responder."

"What about O'Neil himself?"

"Same kind of problem," she said. "Without knowing the physical factors controlling his exposure, plus the time, distance, intensity, source and type of exposure, all you could do is make a rough estimate. Medical x-ray examinations and airport body scanners all produce radiation exposure."

Drake gave this some thought. "Okay," he said, "let's forget about his radiation exposure. What about O'Neil himself? Maybe we can't prove he was around the nuclear device or whatever it is, but can we link him to terrorists or to David Barak or Marco Vazquez? Some connection that might lead us somewhere?"

She picked up her cell phone again. "I'll find out," she said.

"I'll let Mike know where the Hawker's been," Drake said. "If the realtor gives him a tour of O'Neil's hangar house, he might have a chance to talk with O'Neil, pilot to pilot, ask him about the Panamanian corporation he's flying the jet for." He walked out onto the deck and sat down in one of the cedar Adirondack chairs and made the call.

"Hey, amigo," he said when Casey answered. "Have you toured the hangar house yet?"

"We're waiting for the realtor to show up. We're sitting outside her office on the Sunriver Mall."

"If you get a chance to meet O'Neil, here's a few things you need to know about him and the Hawker jet he's flying." Drake told his friend what he'd learned. "See if he knows Vazquez or met him in San Diego. It's just too much of a coincidence that they both came here from San Diego," he added.

"What do you want us to do if we see him and don't like his answers?" Casey asked.

"Keep an eye on him. Liz is having DHS look into his background and record. If she finds something that will justify his arrest, I'll ask her to arrest him," Drake said.

"Have you heard from Ricardo and Billy?"

"They should be at the ranch by now. I'll call them and let you know. I've asked Paul Benning, Margo's husband, to try and trace the phone call Vazquez made when he called to say he's not attending the fundraising dinner and auction tonight. If we find out where Vazquez is, I'll want you and Larry to come with me when we visit him. I'm in no mood for another knife fight."

"Roger that," Casey said. "I've got to go now, the realtor just drove up."

A minute later, Liz joined Drake on the deck and sat down in the other Adirondack chair.

"Mr. O'Neil has no criminal record," she reported. "He was a Navy fighter pilot who separated from the service with an Other Than Honorable discharge. Seems he had a huge gambling debt and was discharged because of security concerns. That probably explains why he's not flying for one of the airlines and why he lives in Las Vegas. No known ties to terrorists, though. He flies in and out of the country frequently, Central and South America primarily, and it doesn't appear that he's ever flown for Marco Vazquez that we can tell. He seems to be a freelance jet pilot who will fly for anyone if the pay is good."

Drake nodded. "The kind of pilot who would fly a nuke into the country. Or fly for Barak. I don't suppose that's enough for you to detain him for questioning?"

"Not at the moment," she said. "The National Defense Authorization Act that was passed in 2011 allows for the questioning and indefinite detention of suspected terrorists, including American citizens. But a judge struck down the indefinite detention part as unconstitutional and it's on appeal. The best I could do is ask the FBI to interview O'Neil, but with what we have, that request wouldn't be granted anytime soon."

Drake stood up and walked to the end of the deck and back. "I feel like I'm back in the army, Liz," he said. "Fighting with rules of engagement that prevent me from doing my job. I took an oath to defend the Constitution, as a lawyer and a soldier, and I always will. But it makes no sense to pussyfoot around when we believe there's a nuke loose in the country. I'm not saying we have to torture the guy, but we should at least be able to detain him for questioning without the ACLU going nuts and suing us for violating his rights. We're going to lose this war because we're afraid to do what's necessary to protect ourselves."

"He's a citizen, Adam. The Constitution you took an oath to defend gives him the right of due process. Denying someone that right because he's suspected of involvement in terrorism violates the Constitution and takes the country somewhere I hope we never go."

He looked down at her. "A nation has the right to protect innocent civilians against those seeking to harm them, too. But I don't want to re-argue the whole counterterrorism-due process argument with you. I know the Fourth Amendment prohibits you from doing what I want to do." He began walking again, then stopped to face her. "But it doesn't prevent me as a private citizen from taking O'Neil for a little one-on-one private conversation somewhere."

"I hope you're not seriously considering that."

He shook his head. "No. I'm just frustrated, is all. When someone knowingly cooperates with terrorists to make a buck, he's an enemy combatant in my book. And he doesn't deserve due process. I don't know if that's what O'Neil is doing, but I'd sure like to find out."

"Do you have anything you want me to do right now?" she asked as she got up from her chair. "If not, I think I'll go inside and start preparing the meal I promised everyone."

"Go ahead," he said, turning to walk to the far end of the deck. "I'll give Ricardo and Billy a call and see if they've seen Vazquez out at the ranch."

He watched his conscience walk into the kitchen. On the battlefield, he told himself, decisions were not always clear-cut, but they'd sure been easier to make. Fighting the enemy at home was a new challenge. But it was one the country had better figure how they wanted to fight before it was too late. Still talking to himself, he walked down from the deck toward the river thirty yards away and sat on a large boulder to call his eyes on Wyler Ranch.

"Ricardo," he said when the connection was made, "any sign of Vazquez out there?"

"We haven't seen him," Gonzalez said. "Or the Muslims, either. It's real quiet here. You want us to keep watching for him?"

"No. Head on back. I have someone trying to trace a call he made. If we find out where he called from, we'll pay him a visit. Mike and Larry haven't been to the hangar house yet, but I'll head them back this way too when they're finished."

"All right," Gonzalez said. "We'll pack up and head back. See you there."

With nothing else he could think of to do, Drake sat on the boulder and watched a string of baby ducks following their mother upstream for a moment before he headed back to the cabin to see if he could help Liz with dinner.

Chapter Fifty

CASEY AND HIS MEN HAD RETURNED TO SENATOR HAZELTON'S cabin and were seated at the kitchen counter, enjoying a beer and watching Liz prepare a salad to accompany the linguine she had promised. Drake was carefully slicing fresh mushrooms for the salad when Paul and Margo Benning arrived for dinner.

After introductions and a quick tour of the cabin, everyone was in or around the kitchen and getting in the way of the chef. Margo shooed all the men out. "You boys go outside while I help Liz with dinner," she said. "That goes for you, too, boss. Can't you see she doesn't need your help?"

When the men were gone, she gently began her interrogation. "I don't mean to pry, honey, but what happened to your face? These men treating you right?"

Liz gave the best smile she could. "They're all gentlemen, Margo. They're taking good care of me. They had nothing to do with these cuts."

"From what I understand, my boss had *everything* to do with those cuts on your face," Margo replied. "If you weren't here trying to help him do whatever it is he's trying to do, I doubt you'd have those cuts. You mind telling me what happened?"

Liz looked up from the salad and studied the face of Drake's secretary. The concern she saw in her soft brown eyes, while definitely sincere, exceeded what the cuts on her face warranted. The concern wasn't entirely for her, she realized, but for Drake as well.

"How long have you worked for Adam?" she asked.

"Six years this fall," Margo said. "Five years when we both worked in the district attorney's office, and this last year when he decided to open his own office. Why?"

"Because I suspect you're more interested in knowing that he's not in any danger than you are in knowing how I got these cuts."

Margo had to smile. "Might be, honey. But you getting cut up hanging around my boss already tells me he's off doing his soldier thing again. Since his wife died and he got involved with that assassin last month, he's taking risks he doesn't need to be taking. Maybe I just wanted to know if you're over here taking those risks with him."

"Those risks are part of my job."

"Does your job include taking time off to be with him instead of being in Portland like your agency expected you to be?"

Now Liz had to smile. "You don't waste any time getting around to what's on your mind, do you? How did you know I was supposed to be in Portland?"

"I keep an eye on him for his mother-in-law. She finds out things when I ask her. The senator knew you were supposed to be in Portland but decided to take a few days off and spend them here in Bend."

"What is it you want to know?"

"You interested in Adam?"

As Liz turned away to refill her glass of wine, she felt herself blushing like a schoolgirl caught staring at the boy she hoped would ask her out on a date. She picked up the bottle of chardonnay and with a gesture asked if Margo wanted a refill as well. Leaning over to pour the wine, she shrugged her shoulders.

"In my job," she said, "I meet a lot of men. Most of them either want to see me socially or find a way to embarrass me professionally. Either way, they're all trying to use me in one way or another. I've never met one like Adam. He's a man's man, but a gentleman, too, and he could care less if I'm here or in Portland. He's on a mission. I'm just along for the ride because I'm beginning to trust his hunches." She set the bottle back on the counter. "But to answer your question…yes, I guess I am interested in your boss."

"Be careful you don't get hurt," Margo said. "Socially, I mean. He's had a rough year since his wife died. I'm just now getting him to focus back on his law practice. He is a good man, but he's still hurting."

"Who's hurting?" Drake asked as he walked into the kitchen. "You need Ricardo to get something for your cuts, Liz? They sent me in to see how soon we're going to eat?"

"Go back out there and tell them to have another beer," Margo said. "We'll call you when dinner's ready. The only thing that's hurting is your manners. You ought to be ashamed, working this poor girl when she's been injured. Don't any of you men know how to cook?"

Drake raised both hands in surrender. "We couldn't talk her out of it, Margo. Kind of like trying to talk you out of something. You two are a lot alike." He turned and left to rejoin the men on the deck outside.

"Looks like it's us girls in the kitchen again," Margo said. "Slaving away for the men."

Both women laughed.

OUT ON THE DECK, Drake announced that dinner wasn't quite ready. Then he pulled Paul Benning aside. "Have you been able to trace the call Vazquez made to cancel his dinner appearance tonight?" he asked.

Benning shook his head. "Not yet. The woman he called, Mrs. Harsh, has been tied up with the fundraiser and dinner and too busy to take any calls. That's what her assistant said. I have the number she uses at the polo club, but her assistant wouldn't give me her cell phone number. We can only trace the call from a cell phone to locate your guy's location. I'll pay Mrs. Harsh a visit tomorrow at the polo match and get her cell phone number."

"We won't need it if Vazquez shows up," Drake said. "Isn't there some other way to get her cell phone number?"

"Well, there are no cell phone directories, but I can try to find her on one of the social media sites. There's a couple reverse cell phone directories, too, but they may or may not have her listed. If you need it tonight and if I can use your computer, I'll try to find her number after dinner."

"Thanks, Paul. That would be great. Any idea what the women are talking about in there? There's more talking than cooking being done."

"My guess would be they're talking about you."

"Me? Why would they be talking about me?"

"Possibly because you have a woman staying with you that Margo doesn't know. Or maybe it's because your secretary wants to know what you've been doing here. Or here's another possibility: the woman who doesn't know you very well wants to hear all the secrets the woman who works for you knows about you. Take your pick."

"Hmmm. It's that last possibility that has me worried. Think I should go break it up in there?"

"No way. It would only delay our dinner. They'll find a way to finish what they're talking about even if you could break it up. Have a glass of wine and enjoy the evening. You lost control of things as soon as the women took over your kitchen."

When Casey walked over and asked how much longer until dinner was ready, Drake laughed. "That ice cream you had at the Sunriver mall didn't tide you over?"

"Temporary solution to a permanent problem," Casey said. "Sorry we didn't learn more about O'Neil when we toured his hangar house. He wasn't there, and the place hardly looked like it was being used."

"Was his Escalade there?"

"No, not in the garage."

"Was his jet there?"

"It was in the hangar. The realtor didn't let us look around, but the Hawker was there."

"Mike, we need to talk with him," Drake said. "Let's try again tomorrow after the polo match. He's involved somehow, and I want to know how."

At this point, the men's conversation was interrupted when Margo marched out onto the deck and summoned them in for dinner. The way she smiled at Drake as the men filed by made him wish he had stayed in the kitchen.

Chapter Fifty-One

DRAKE'S DAY BEGAN EARLY THE NEXT MORNING WITH A RUN ON the cart paths around the Crosswater golf course that crossed the Little Deschutes River seven times. When he got back to his father-in-law's cabin, the first rays of sunlight were reaching the meandering river and the mist was starting to lift. The smell of bacon cooking greeted him, and when he came into the kitchen, he found Casey humming to himself as he stood in front of the big gas range, watching the bacon sizzling in the cast iron skillet.

Casey looked up. "Hope you're hungry," he said. "Crack a couple dozen eggs for me in that bowl on the counter. The guys will be downstairs in a minute. I haven't seen Liz yet this morning. That sure was some dinner she fixed last night."

"Yes, it was." Drake picked up the first egg. "So why are you cooking bacon, eggs, and pancakes to go with that fruit bowl, granola, orange juice, and coffee you've already set out? You think that's enough breakfast?" He smiled to disguise the sarcasm in his voice. "I had to go running before I could even think about eating again."

"That's precisely why," Casey said as he turned slices of bacon over. "Who knows when we'll get to eat again? You have to be prepared for the unexpected, my friend. That's what my daddy taught me. On a ranch, you can wind up chasing stray cattle and be gone for days."

"With that new helicopter of yours, I doubt it would even take a day to find your strays. You want me to beat these eggs?"

"Please. And add a little milk and salt and pepper. So what are the plans for the day?"

"I'd like to see if we can talk to Vazquez before his match. And I think we should send Ricardo and Billy back to the ranch. Those are the only two places I know where to look. The polo field and the ranch."

Casey nodded. "Did your secretary's husband hear back on the phone trace he was asking for?"

"He tried to find the cell phone number for the lady Vazquez called last night," Drake said, "but he didn't find anything. He's going to see if the sheriff's office here in Deschutes County can help find her number before he meets us at the polo match today."

"What do you want me to do while you're at this polo thing?"

"Why don't you and Larry come with me to see Vazquez? If he has his men with him and doesn't want to talk to me, I could use some backup."

"He likes me," Liz said as she walked across the great room and took a seat at the kitchen counter. "Can I come too? I can always flash my badge and threaten to book a room for him in the Guantanamo Hilton."

Drake looked up. "Good morning, Liz. I thought you weren't going to deny anyone their due process until we had more to go on."

"I heard that you once threatened one of the ISIS goons with a parking ticket for sitting too long on a bench outside your office," she said. "I figured if it worked for you, I might want to give it a try. Widen my investigatory repertoire a little."

"It sounds like I might need a new secretary," Drake said. "One who knows how to keep my operational secrets to herself."

"Don't you dare! Margo and I are friends. I think it's the beginning of…"

"…a beautiful relationship," Casey completed the movie quote. "Care for some orange juice, Liz?" He nodded his head at Drake. "We'll talk some time when he's not around about the rest of his operational repertoire. I think you'll find it very interesting."

"Okay, that's enough," Drake said, forcing a smile. "First it's my secretary, and now it's my former best friend. *Et tu, Brute?*" When Casey only grinned, he added, "Cook breakfast and remember who once considered paying for you to be here."

As the eggs were scrambled and the pancakes were done, the rest of the team wandered in and found seats at the counter or the dining table to have their first cup of coffee of the day. Liz pitched in and helped Casey serve breakfast, whispering conspiratorially as she stood next to him.

Drake watched the two of them enjoying themselves, apparently at his expense. It made him think of the times he had watched men prepare for battle, joking around to lighten the mood. They weren't heading into battle, but it was clear the possibility of the missing nuke being in the area and the chance that Vazquez would be leaving soon was weighing on all of them. If he left and they didn't come up with something concrete soon, he was looking at a very expensive three days in the high desert of Oregon. There was no way DHS was going to reimburse him for asking Casey and his men to join the hunt if it turned out to be a waste of time.

By nine o'clock, the last few crumbs of their elaborate breakfast had been consumed and the dishes cleared away.

The men loaded their gear in the two Yukons, with Gonzalez and Montgomery leaving for Wyler Ranch and Casey and Green waiting for Drake to lead them to the polo match on the other side of Bend.

When Drake and Liz were seated in his Porsche, she put her hand on his shoulder. "We're going to find it, Adam. You were right last month about the attempt to assassinate the secretary, and I believe you're right this time, too."

"I hope you're right," he said with a sigh. "I hope you're right."

Chapter Fifty-Two

Traffic slowed to a crawl on Highway 97 as they approached the turnoff that led to the Red Lava Ranch, home of the High Desert Polo Club and host of the Pacific Polo Invitational. It was still over an hour before the Invitational started, but the county road that led to the ranch was already bumper-to-bumper from the turnoff all the way to the white-fenced ranch.

"Have you ever been to a polo match?" Liz asked as they idled forward to the ticket takers on both sides of the entrance to the ranch.

Drake smiled. "We don't have much polo in the Northwest, but I've seen polo played in the Middle East. Pretty tough sport, from what I've seen."

"It began as a training game for mounted warriors in fifth century-B.C. Persia," she told him. "They played it with as many as a hundred men on each side. It was a miniature running battle. My dad took me to polo matches in San Diego when I was a kid and wanted a horse. They didn't have women playing polo then, so after I studied the sport for awhile, I lost interest. It's a dangerous sport. And an expensive one."

"Expensive because of the horses?"

"That, and the training the top polo ponies require. A top polo pony sells for two hundred thousand dollars or more, and the best players will bring as many as a dozen ponies to a match. My dad was very successful in real estate, but you know what? I couldn't get him to buy me a polo pony."

"Smart man. So, are these polo players all rich boys?" he asked as he slowed to hand the ticket taker his ticket and a ten dollar bill for his passenger.

"Some are," she said, accepting her ticket. "But most ride for teams that have a *patron,* a sponsor. I think most of the players we'll see today do this as a hobby. They're not professional polo players."

Drake followed the line of cars, SUVs and pickups to the parking lot, which was a field on the west end of the long polo field. On the south side of the full-size polo field, three hundred yards long and one hundred and sixty yards wide, white party tents had been set up for spectators who wanted to be out of the sun and for vendors offering beverages. On the north side of the field, the horse trailers were parked parallel to the field, with each player's polo ponies tethered to the side of his trailer. At the ends of the polo field, collapsible white goal posts, set eight yards apart, marked the ends of the playing field.

After helping Liz out of the Porsche, Drake studied the horse trailers. "I see Vazquez's trailer," he said after a minute, "but I don't see him there with his ponies." They stood beside the car for a minute, deciding what to do. "Let's wait for Mike and Larry and then wander through the crowd," he said. "Our boy's probably signing autographs. We need to get him somewhere with a little privacy."

Liz decided this was a good time to continue her tutorial. "The match is divided into six chukkers, each seven minutes long," she said. "There's a little time between chukkers, maybe three or four minutes, and five minutes or more at halftime. We won't have a lot of time once the match gets started."

When Casey and Green walked up, Drake said, "Okay, let's find Vazquez and follow him over to his trailer before the match gets started. That should give us some privacy and the time we need to talk with him."

'It doesn't look like they're letting spectators over near the polo ponies," Casey said. "Liz, did you bring your badge?"

"Right here," she said, taking the black leather federal badge case with her ID in it out of the back pocket of her jeans. "I think I can get us over there to talk with him."

"All right!" said Drake. "Let's go find our guy." The four team members started walking down the line of vehicles toward the white tents and the crowd gathering along the south side of the polo field.

"Looks like this polo club allows people to bring their own food and drinks," Casey observed. "I see a lot of picnic baskets and tailgating going on over behind the tents over there."

"Help us find Vazquez first," Drake said. "He's the only lead we have right now. When we're finished, maybe someone will take pity on a guy that just had breakfast an hour ago."

Drake led the way through the clusters of spectators along the south side of the polo field until they reached the first white tent that was open on the side facing the polo field. The people standing under the tent were drinking champagne in plastic flutes they had purchased from a bar in the rear of the tent. A banner over the bar and an adjoining table covered with silver buffet warming pans announced the area as the domain of the High Desert Polo Club.

"Larry," Drake said, "why don't you see if Mrs. Rebecca Harsh is here. She's the lady who took the call saying Vazquez couldn't make the dinner last night. She's the organizer of the Invitational, so maybe she knows where he is."

On the other side of the polo field, polo ponies were being

saddled and readied for the match. Polo mallets were laid out next to folding armchairs for the riders, along with their helmets, kneepads, and gloves.

As Drake surveyed the field, Green walked up to him. "I found Mrs. Harsh," he reported. "She said Vazquez is in the clubhouse with the club's officers. They auctioned off a private session with him to make up for the dinner he missed last night. She said as soon as they finish there, they'll come directly here and get the match started. We won't get a chance to talk with him before then."

"Well," Drake said, "then it looks like we get to watch a little polo. Where's Mike?"

"Mrs. Harsh saw him looking at the food and told him to help himself." Green nodded his head as Drake grinned. "He said he'd find you in a minute."

"Adam," Liz began waving her hand in the air, "there's Margo and Paul."

Drake's secretary was walking smartly toward them, her husband in tow. She was wearing a floppy black hat, a black and white polka dot sundress, and white sandals. After giving Liz a warm hug and commenting on her outfit, she turned to Drake. "Boss, I hope you like my dress," she said. "Liz said you owed me for taking up so much of my husband's time this week, so I bought myself a new outfit and put it on the office account."

Drake looked from one woman to the other. "This friendship you two are developing is beginning to worry me," he said. "But I'll have to say you do the office proud in your new attire, Margo. You drug Paul here for the weekend, so I guess I did owe you."

"Actually," Margo confessed, "when I learned why you were coming to Bend, I Googled this Marco Vazquez and decided I had to come and see what a genuine international playboy looks like. Has he made an appearance yet?"

Drake looked toward the clubhouse and saw a small crowd

exiting the building with Vazquez in its center. When they reached the edge of the polo field, he continued on alone to his trailer, waving at the crowd along the sideline.

"He's doing that right now." Drake pointed as the buzz around the polo field grew noticeably louder.

Chapter Fifty-Three

AFTER THE TWO FOUR-MAN TEAMS WERE INTRODUCED AND Vazquez was enthusiastically welcomed as the only ten-goal polo player appearing in America at the time, the match began. Polo players rank each other, based on each player's importance to his team, and it was easy for the spectators to see why Marco Vazquez was a star. From the moment the umpire rolled the ball down the line between the two teams as they faced off in the center of the field, Vazquez and his light gray pony dominated the action.

He rode aggressively, checking opposing players with abandon and wielding his whippy mallet with deadly accuracy. By the end of the first seven-minute chukker, his team was leading 2-0, and he had scored both goals.

After a change of ponies between the first and second chukker, Vazquez scaled down his aggressiveness in recognition of the skill level of the amateurs he was schooling, but he appeared to be enjoying the match. If he was riding close to the edge of the boarded field after a score, he smiled at his admirers, especially the beautiful women. He also took time to compliment his amateur opponents when they played well, and joked with his new teammates.

By halftime, Vazquez's team was ahead by five goals, 6-1. He rode his pony to his trailer and dismounted. Spectators immediately stepped over the twelve-inch sideboards and began the traditional divot stomp to replace the turf torn up by the thundering horses.

Drake and Liz walked behind the main group of stompers, who were eager to get across the field and as close to the polo players and their ponies as possible. Some had their programs in hand to get Vazquez's autograph. He was checking the saddle on his fourth pony as Drake and Liz approached with the other spectators.

Drake kept his eyes on Vazquez in case he decided to slip away to avoid meeting with his fans. Instead of fleeing, however, the polo star finished cinching the saddle, then stepped around his pony to greet the closest stomper.

That step would be his last.

An explosion blasted through the chatter on the field. It was followed by a moment of shocked silence before the cries of the injured and dying began.

At the sound of the blast, Drake had instinctively thrown his arm around Liz's waist and pulled her to the ground. The explosion had sounded familiar to him, like roadside IEDs he'd heard in Afghanistan. As he looked at the carnage around him, he saw blood flowing from wounds in people directly ahead of him. The blast wave and the shrapnel that had cut through the divot stompers on the polo field seemed to have come from a location somewhere near Vazquez's trailer.

"Are you hit?" he yelled at Liz, his ears still ringing from the blast.

She shook her head and started to get up, but Drake pulled her back down. He could see she was disoriented, but he also knew terrorists liked to use a second blast to kill anyone surviving the first one.

To his left, he could see Casey searching the perimeter of

the polo field for a threat assessment. He didn't appear to have been hit and cautiously got to his feet, along with Green. A quick look over his shoulder to his secretary, Margo, and her husband, who were also getting up, told Drake they had all survived without suffering any major injuries.

Carefully rising to his feet, Drake looked toward where Marco Vazquez had been standing. The divot stompers nearest his trailer weren't moving. They were probably dead. The kill zone, vectoring outward from Vazquez's trailer, appeared to have reached almost half way across the polo field. Drake couldn't see the polo star, but the pony he'd been readying for the next chukker had been cut down by the blast.

"I'm going to find Vazquez," he shouted to Liz. "Make sure help is on the way."

He ran wide of the bodies of the dead and wounded, seeing mangled bodies and missing body parts as he got closer, until he reached Vazquez's dead pony. It was lying on its side with a massive wound the length of its body. Blood was flowing into a widening pool that darkened the green grass around the animal.

Vazquez was trapped under his pony, lying face down and struggling to breathe.

Drake knelt down. He could see that the young man's eyes were open.

"Vazquez, can you hear me?"

"Yes," came the response through clinched teeth.

"I'll get help. Hold on."

"Don't…go," Vazquez gasped. "Bomb…ranch."

"What?" Drake leaned closer to hear over the cries and noise around them.

"Bomb…ranch." A groan came, then pink bubbles slipping through his lips. "Dam…in mountains."

"Who has a bomb?" Drake shouted.

Vazquez's eyes fluttered, then fixed in a stare.

When there was no response to his question, Drake reached down. He couldn't find a pulse.

Standing up again, he looked for Casey and Liz across the field where he left them. Liz was kneeling beside a body near the middle of the field, waving for help from the growing number of surviving volunteers rushing to help. He saw Casey on his cell phone. He was standing in the worst of the destruction. Drake knew he was taking command and directing the responders who were needed so badly.

As he looked over the familiar scene of innocents suffering, Drake felt sickened by the waste. Those who survived would be scarred for life by their memory of this day, and if they lost loved ones or friends, the wounds might never heal. The dead were dead. But some had been so gruesomely cut down that those who mourned them would forever have nightmares after seeing what little remained of them.

Drake ran to Casey and waited for him to finish his call.

"Vazquez is dead," he said when Casey took the phone from his ear. "He was crushed when his pony fell on him."

"He must have been right at the blast's ground zero," Casey said. "I'm surprised there was anything left of him."

"His pony shielded him. But he was alive long enough to say there's a bomb at the ranch and something about a dam in the mountains."

Casey stared at his friend. "So he was involved in smuggling the thing here. I'll be damned. You were right."

"Yeah. We need to get to the ranch before the road is blocked by emergency responders and ambulances. Have Larry see if he can learn anything from Vazquez's trailer. I'll tell Liz what we're doing and meet you at my car."

Liz was still helping a young woman lying on her back with a partially severed right arm. She was being examined by a volunteer who must have had medical training, judging by the way he was working to stop her bleeding. The woman's eyes were fixed and looking up at the sky, as if she were trying to ignore looking at what the doctor was doing for her. She'd be lucky, Drake knew, if losing her arm was the worst that happened to her. He'd seen soldiers die in shock with that look on their faces.

"Liz," he said, kneeling down beside her, "I'm leaving with Mike. Vazquez's dead, but he told me there's a bomb at the ranch and something about a dam in the mountains. We may have found it."

Liz pounded the turf. "Yes! I'll call and get the place surrounded."

"Hold on," Drake said. "I said we *may* have found it. Let me check with Ricardo and Billy. They're out there. Maybe they've seen something. We can't send in the cavalry on a wild goose chase. I'm meeting Mike at my car. I'll call Ricardo from there. You find Paul and Margo and tell them to help Larry."

As he sprinted to his car he heard the approaching sound of sirens in the distance.

Chapter Fifty-Four

Saleem was watching the chaos from the safety of his black Escalade, which was parked near the west end of the polo field. He had arrived early so he would have a clear view of Vazquez's trailer when the time came. Then, when the polo match was half over, and the silly divot stompers were marching around stomping divots (as if the horses really cared if there were divots), he waited until Vazquez was standing beside his horse trailer. He had placed the C4 charge in an outside storage compartment under the recessed D rings where Vazquez tied his polo ponies. The charge had been shaped to maximize its shock wave in the area where Vazquez was likely to be standing and to carry on from there, shooting out enough shrapnel to kill as many people as possible.

All Saleem had to do was wait for the right moment to enter the three-digit code on his cell phone. *Good riddance, pampered playboy.*

His only regret was that no one would ever know that his group had carried out this attack. It was not yet time to announce that Hezbollah was poised and ready to strike. That time would come, however, when there were bigger issues involved, when the leaders decided to show the America just how vulnerable it was. This was a joint operation with Barak and the Brotherhood, he told himself, so let them take the credit, and the blowback if their plan with the nuclear device was carried out. He knew how America had reacted after 9/11. Let Egypt be the next Afghanistan and Barak the next bin Laden. He would like to stick around for awhile.

When he saw the attorney run to his car in the parking lot, he decided it was time to report to Barak. He could hear the sound of sirens in the distance, so he closed his car window.

"It's done," he reported.

"Describe the scene for me," Barak said.

"Vazquez is dead. He should have been vaporized, but he moved around his horse at the last moment, so he was trapped under it. There are lots of dead and wounded and people are running around trying to help the survivors. I can hear the sirens coming. I expect the first responders will arrive any minute."

"Are you sure Vazquez is dead?"

"That attorney I followed rushed over to him. I watched the whole thing. He left Vazquez when he couldn't find a pulse." Saleem waited for Barak to say something.

"What is the attorney doing now?" Barak finally asked.

"He just ran to his car. He's standing beside it using his phone."

After another pause, Barak gave Saleem his final instructions. "Call your man at the ranch and make sure the team has left. Go meet him as we planned. Abandon the Escalade before you leave for Reno. You have done well, Saleem. This diversion will keep everyone looking north while we strike to the south."

"Thank you, Barak. Allah willing, we will work together again. When are you leaving?"

"*Inshallah*, my young friend. *Inshallah.* I will leave as soon as I hear the device has been delivered."

Before Saleem left the polo ranch and just before the first

of the EMT fire engines pulled in, he made a call to report when Barak would be leaving.

Chapter Fifty-Five

WHILE DRAKE WAS WAITING BESIDE HIS PORSCHE FOR CASEY, he called Gonzalez.

"Yes, sir," the former sergeant answered.

"Ricardo, Vazquez has been killed. Before he died, he said there was a bomb at the ranch. Have you seen anything that would support that?"

"We haven't seen anything that looks like a bomb. Or the nuclear device you've been looking for. The only activity here has been those four Muslims taking off on their Harleys twenty minutes ago."

"Could they have the bomb?"

"Only if it would fit in the trailer one of the Harleys was pulling."

"Vazquez also said something about a dam in the mountains. You're familiar with demolition work. Could they have a demolition device in that trailer that would take out a dam?"

"If they had a Special Atomic Demolition Munition, a SADM," Gonzalez said, "like the ones the army developed in the 1960s, it might fit in that trailer. The army used to train troops to parachute into Soviet-occupied Eastern Europe to take out power plants, bridges, and dams. But there's no way these guys could get their hands on a SADM."

"It doesn't have to be one of ours," Drake said. "Something set off our nuclear detection system in San Diego, and I'll bet that's what they have in that trailer. How long ago did you say the bikers left?"

"They left at eleven-thirty. Twenty minutes ago."

"That's exactly when the bomb here exploded," Drake said. "Which direction were they headed in?"

"They turned south when they left the ranch."

"Follow them, Ricardo. We'll use Mike's helicopter and see if we can get ahead of them."

Drake waved at Casey, who was jogging toward him. "Double time, partner!" he shouted. "We need to leave. Right now."

With Casey still fastening his seat belt, Drake explained his plan as he drove as fast as he could, between the rows of parked cars in the field that served as the parking lot. "Ricardo says Vazquez's Muslim groomers left the ranch on their Harleys twenty minutes ago, right when that bomb exploded. One of the Harleys was pulling a trailer big enough to conceal a nuclear demolition munition."

He glanced back at the chaos on the polo field. "This was all a diversion, Mike. If Liz can find out what dam they might be targeting, we can use your Relentless and head them off."

"They're going to have quite a head start," Casey replied. "We're thirty minutes north of the airport at Sunriver."

"Then call Paul," Drake said. "See if he can get someone in the sheriff's department to escort us to Sunriver. Following a set of flashing lights will cut the time in half. I'll call Liz and have her try to locate the dam they're headed for."

While Casey was calling Benning, Drake put his iPhone in its black leather mount on the dash. As soon as Casey hung up, he put them on speaker and called Liz.

"Liz," he said as soon as she picked up, "Ricardo says

Vazquez's so-called groomers left the ranch on their Harleys twenty minutes ago. At the same time as the bomb went off. One of the Harleys was pulling a trailer big enough to conceal a demolition nuke, the kind our army developed in the 1960s. The Russians have the same kind of munition. Can you get someone in your shop to locate the dam they're most likely targeting?"

"Which way were they headed?" she asked.

"Ricardo said they turned south. He and Billy will try and catch up with them, but they'll be way behind."

"If the dam is in the mountains, that will narrow it down. But why are they going after a dam? I expected them to hit a populated area, not something in the mountains."

The answer came to them both at the same time.

"Oh, my God," Liz said first. "They're going to blow a dam and flood everything below it."

"Can that happen if they just blow one dam?" Drake asked.

"If they cause the right dam to fail, yes, it certainly can. The wall of water would hit the dam below it and cause that dam to fail, and the next one, and so on. We've done inundation studies that identify the areas that are most vulnerable. That may help us narrow things down."

"Call me as soon as you have the dam located," Drake said. "We're racing to Sunriver. We'll head 'em off in Mike's helicopter."

"And then what? Will you be able to stop them?"

Before Drake could reply, Casey spoke up. "Liz, this is Mike. I have some weapons on board, we'll do our best."

"All right," she said. "I'll get back to you as soon as I can."

Drake drove south on Highway 97 flashing his headlights to clear the road, but most of the drivers didn't pull off the road like they would for the flashing lights of a police car or ambulance. As they approached the outskirts of Bend, they were averaging only twenty miles an hour above the posted speed limit.

"Look up ahead," Casey said.

Two patrol cars were pulled off the side of the road. When Drake's Porsche came into view, the first of the two laid down two long black streaks of burnt rubber as it pulled out. The second car also pulled out and fell in behind them.

In less than ten seconds, the three-car convoy was traveling ninety miles an hour. When they were clear of highway traffic, their speed was closer to a hundred and ten miles an hour.

"Damn, these boys are good," Casey said.

"They are," Drake said as they passed two sixteen-wheelers that had pulled as far as they could onto the shoulder to let them by. "Paul came through. Let's hope Liz does, too. We have to find the dam."

When they left the city's southern limits, their speed increased to nearly a hundred and thirty miles an hour. Despite the circumstances, Drake had a smile on his face. Speed was his secret addiction. His buddy seemed to be enjoying the ride as well.

"Next year," Drake casually remarked, "I'm thinking about entering the Silver State Classic Challenge. You interested in riding shotgun?"

"Is that the race in Nevada where they close ninety miles of the highway and let you drive as fast as you can?"

"That's the one."

"Sign me up. I might even bring the 1970 Hemi 'Cuda I'm restoring. Probably have to enter it in a faster class than you can enter, though."

Before Drake could respond to the challenge that had just been laid down, his cell phone buzzed.

"Adam," Liz began, "we think the dam is eighty-five miles southwest of Bend in the Cascades. Inundation maps from the Army Corps of Engineers predict that if the highest dam fails, two other dams below it will also fail. There will be a wall of water rushing down that will be a hundred feet high by the time it reaches the valley floor. It'll be like a tsunami. Worst-case scenario is that a hundred thousand people will die in the flood."

"We're almost to Sunriver," Drake replied. "As soon as we're airborne, we'll need the GPS coordinates for the dam. Is the dam defended in any way?"

"There are two employees there. There's a security fence, but that won't keep anyone out who's prepared to get through it. Those guys and their dam are sitting ducks."

"If we don't get there in time," Casey asked, "how much warning will the people down river have?"

"The first city will have an hour. Maybe four hours for the cities on the valley floor. It's not enough time to evacuate those cities. This will be a catastrophe!"

"Well, then," said Drake, "we'll just have to get there in time. Warn the guys at the dam we're coming. Have someone ready to collect that nuke. That's one bomb I don't want to have anything to do with."

Chapter Fifty-Six

THE WHITE INTERCEPTOR PATROL CARS DROVE THROUGH THE twisting lanes of the Sunriver Resort with their flashing lights warning vacationers along the way that an emergency was in progress. When the convoy reached the airport, Drake took the lead and drove out onto the airport apron to Casey's Bell Relentless helicopter. He skidded to a stop mere feet from the aircraft. As Casey jumped out of the Porsche, Drake thanked the deputies for the escort to the airport.

"Our pleasure, sir," the senior deputy said. "We don't get to drive this fast very often. Where are you flying to? Does this involve the explosion at the polo match?"

"We think it does, but that's all I can say right now," Drake said. "If we're right, you'll read about it tomorrow. Thanks again for your help."

Casey had already done his visual inspection of the helicopter and was now going through his pre-flight checklist when Drake joined him on the flight deck.

"Buckle up, buddy," Casey said. "This baby's ready to fly." The five-bladed, main rotor system started turning overhead.

As he took his seat, Drake took a close look at the all-glass instrument panel in front of him. The four twelve-inch color display screens reminded him of the cockpit in an F-35 stealth fighter.

"This thing fly itself?" he asked.

"Almost," Casey said. "Call Liz and get the coordinates for the dam and I'll show you."

As the two eighteen-hundred horsepower GE engines lifted the helicopter off the ground, Drake called Liz to get the coordinates. When he repeated them to Casey and they were entered into the state-of-the-art avionics system, Casey pointed the Relentless toward the distant mountains and sat back with a broad smile on his face.

"We're flying at 150 knots per hour," he said. "Won't be long now."

"How fast is that?" Drake asked.

"One hundred and seventy-three miles per hour. We'll be there in twenty minutes. What's the plan when we get there?"

"Simple. First we find a place to land. Then we stop the bad guys from using the bomb."

"Your planning still sucks."

"But the execution of said plan will be a thing of beauty," Drake said. "You'll see. What weapons do we have here?"

"What my team carries. Four HK416 assault carbines, four Glock 21s, and my Remington M24 sniper rifle."

"That'll do," Drake said. "Let me check in with Larry and see how they're doing at the polo field."

Greene's report wasn't what Drake hoped to hear.

"Including Vazquez," the former L.A. cop said, "there are twenty-seven dead and twelve who are critical and probably won't make it. The EMTs are triaging another forty or so injured and traumatized. This is worse than some of the suicide bombings I saw in Iraq."

"Did you find anything in Vazquez's trailer?" Drake asked.

"Nothing except his cell phone and a change of clothes in the sleeping compartment at the front of the trailer."

"Find Paul and give him the cell phone. Ask him to find

out who Vazquez was talking to here in Bend. If this is a suicide mission for these guys on the Harleys, the leaders have to be somewhere close. If they haven't already bugged out."

"Got it. Where do you want me after that?"

"Stay with Paul and help Liz if she needs anything. When we find the nuke, we'll need someone coordinating our role in all this with law enforcement and the feds. I don't want us spending the next month explaining how we found the nuke when the government couldn't," Drake said.

"Good luck with that," said Green. "When you make the government look bad, you become the enemy."

"That's why we need to keep our names out of this. Make sure Liz gets the credit. She can say it was her hunch that the nuke was headed to Oregon. DHS won't argue with her story."

"I hope you're right. Good luck at the dam."

"How bad is it?" Casey asked Drake, who was staring at the mountains ahead.

"Bad," he said. "Thirty-nine dead or dying. Another forty wounded."

"What a sick, twisted way these guys fight a war."

Speeding toward what both men hoped would be another chance to stop the killing of innocents by an enemy they knew all too well, their minds flashed through other grisly scenes they had witnessed.

"Do you think we'll see the end of this war in our lifetime?" Casey asked several minutes later.

Drake sighed. "We won't ever defeat evil, you know. All we can do is kill as many evil-doers as possible. Starting with these pukes today. Are the weapons in the rear storage locker? I'm feeling the need to have a gun in my hand right now."

"Rear locker, right side. Lock and load them all. The dam is ten minutes away."

Chapter Fifty-Seven

Cresting the Cascades southwest of Bend, Casey flew the Relentless five hundred feet above a dark green carpet of Douglas firs. Dead ahead, the waters of the six thousand-acre reservoir behind the dam shimmered silver, reflecting the afternoon sun. The reservoir, which was seven and a half miles long, controlled the runoff of a three hundred ninety square mile drainage area.

"That's a lot of water," Casey said.

Drake finished loading their armory. "I've fished there," he said. "The earthen dam is fifty years old. It's not hard to understand why it's their target. Follow the highway and look for those Harleys. If we get there first, find a place to land so we can surprise them. I want to be sure they have the bomb and intend to use it here before we do anything."

Drake moved forward, tightening the straps of the drop-leg tactical holster on his right thigh and took his seat. "The area around and above the dam is heavily wooded, as I recall. You may have to set down on the highway beyond the dam and let me run back."

"I'll find some place close," Casey said. "We'll do this like we used to. Together. You're not going it alone."

"Only if I have to," Drake answered as he began searching ahead with the binoculars he'd found in Casey's gear bag. "Head north just a bit. I think we may be in luck. There's a clear-cut area on the top of that ridge above the dam. If you can set down there, it's only a couple hundred yards or so down to the highway."

The Relentless swung right and approached the logged-off top of the ridge.

"Looks like they've cleared the brush and slash for replanting," Casey said. "I should be able to set it down on that flat area at the top of the slope."

Drake was searching the highway to the east. "I don't see the Harleys," he muttered. "I'll try to get to the dam before they get here. Get as close as you can and cover me." He pulled the shoulder strap of his HK416 over his head and positioned it across his chest as he prepared to jump out of the helicopter as soon as it touched down.

When Casey landed the Relentless in a swirling cloud of dust and debris, Drake moved to the door behind the flight deck, opened it, and jumped down to the rough and uneven logging site and took off running down the slope.

When he reached the trees at the edge of the clear cut, he saw that the ridge sloped precipitously for a hundred yards to the highway below. Reaching out to the rough bark of the fir trees to slow himself, he ran a slalom course between the trees until he started to outrun his feet. With a lunge to his right, he slammed against the broad trunk of a tall fir and stopped, only ten feet from the edge of a twenty-foot drop to the roadway below.

Taking a deep breath, he moved laterally to his right around the sharp drop-off, and then surfed down a loose gravel embankment to the edge of the highway. When he regained his balance, he ran toward the dam, which was a hundred yards away.

CASEY WAS ALMOST at the edge of the clear cut when his cell phone buzzed. Stopping briefly under the branches of the first tree he reached, he listened as Montgomery reported in. His voice was barely audible over the roar of the Yukon as it raced on the road to the dam.

"Mike, we have four Harleys in sight. Two hundred yards ahead of us. Four bikes and one's pulling a small trailer."

"How close are they?"

"Well, we've driven three miles along the reservoir. I'm not sure how close to the dam that makes us."

"You're half way to the dam," Casey said. "Keep them in sight, but don't close in yet. Drake's on the highway, running back to the dam. I'm on a ridge overlooking the dam. Let's make sure the dam's their target before we act."

"Roger that. We'll hold back until you tell us to engage."

Pocketing his phone, Casey ran diagonally through the tall trees until he reached a point at the edge of the drop-off directly across from the dam. Unslinging his sniper rifle, he looked through the lens of the scope at the scene below.

The spillway of the long dam was near the highway. The control building was fifty feet on the other side of a razor-wire fence. Running along the fence was a small gravel parking lot large enough for a car to pull off the highway or a service truck to turn around and head back down the mountain. There were no cars in the parking lot right now, and no Army Corps of Engineers employees visible through two windows facing the fence and the highway.

Looking east, he spotted the four motorcycles half a mile away and heading toward the dam. They were riding single file, with the bike towing the trailer third in line. As he watched, the first two Harleys pulled beside each other, as if they were motorcycle officers leading a funeral procession. With a grim smile—*your funeral, guys*—and a quick glance back to the west, Casey saw Drake slow to a walk as he entered the parking lot and continued toward the gate to the control building. The assault carbine was hidden from view by his right leg.

Casey phoned Montgomery.

"Billy, there's a small graveled parking lot at the dam. Drake just got there. He's at the west end. I'm on the hillside above with my M24. Pull off the highway and get out and stretch your legs. Wait until they make the first move. Once they're down, secure the nuke."

"Roger that. Do we know if the thing is armed?"

"No, but they probably wouldn't drive all this way with it armed. If it's hot, we'll think of something. Pray God it isn't."

Explosive ordinance disposal was the deadliest job in the military, Casey knew, and it wasn't something he wanted any part of, especially if this particular ordinance was a nuclear device.

He focused his rifle scope again on the convoy of Harleys and watched as it neared the dam. When the four motorcycles reached the parking lot, one of the lead Harleys rode on to the west end, stopping behind Drake. Another pulled into a position at the east end. The Harley pulling the trailer pulled up next to the gate in the razor-wire fence that led to the control building, and the last Harley stopped beside it, shielding it from the view of passing motorists.

Casey watched Drake approach the Harleys near the gate and greet the two men with a casual wave of his left hand.

Chapter Fifty-Eight

DRAKE LOOKED AT THE TWO MEN SITTING ON THEIR HARLEYS. Neither had dismounted, which would give him an advantage when they recognized him, as they surely would.

The only sounds he could hear over the rushing water in the dam's spillway were the crunch of gravel under his Nikes and the clicking of the motorcycle engines as they cooled. Neither man returned his greeting, even when he came to within fifty feet of them. Their eyes were hidden behind the tinted visors of their matte black motorcycle helmets, and their gloved hands still gripped the handle bars in front of them.

Then, as both men slowly reached back with their right hands to the saddle bags on their Harleys, Drake knew he'd been recognized. When the man closest to the highway brought up a Micro-Uzi, he was sure of it. The little submachine gun, with a magazine of twenty nine-millimeter rounds that could be fired at a rate of twelve hundred and fifty rounds per minute, was one he was familiar with. He had to smile at the irony of its being in this Muslim terrorist's hand. The Uzi had been a favorite of the Israelis before it was phased out.

Almost faster than thought, Drake raised his HK416 and

fired two rounds into the chest of the first terrorist to draw on him, knocking him off his motorcycle. Before he could swing his weapon toward the man on the other Harley, the man's visor flashed red as he was knocked sideways off his motorcycle. Casey's shot from the hillside had penetrated the side of the man's helmet and exploded his head, killing him before he could level his Uzi at Drake.

Spinning around, Drake saw that the man at the west end of the parking lot was gunning his Harley in his direction. He fired four rounds at center mass and saw the rider jerk as the rounds struck him. The Harley came on, even as its dead rider tumbled back onto the gravel, and crashed into the razor-wire fence, where it slid sideways in the gravel before coming to rest.

That left the man fifty yards away at the east end of the parking lot. He was now crouching down behind his Harley, which blocked a shot from either Casey or Drake. All Drake could see was a bit of the man's left shoulder.

Looking for a way to make the shot, he suddenly saw the white Yukon pulling slowly off the highway behind the crouching terrorist. When the man raised his head to see if the vehicle was a threat, Casey took the shot from above, killing him with another headshot.

Drake made sure the four men were dead before he walked to the small trailer that had been towed behind the black and silver Harley Softail. Painted black with red flames on the rear panel, it was the type of lightweight cargo trailer he'd seen pulled by motorcycles before. Seven feet long, four feet wide and almost four feet high, it was big enough to hide an atomic demolition device.

What Drake didn't know was if the trailer was booby-trapped or rigged to explode if the locked hatch was opened. There was a single keyhole at the rear of the trailer. It was in the nose cavity of a chrome skull and cross bones ornament.

Gonzalez and Montgomery sprinted across the highway

and stopped on the other side of the trailer Drake was studying.

"Before we have a motorist wondering why four dead bodies are lying on the ground here," Drake looked up and said, "bring the Yukon over and hide them in the back. Then we'll see if this trailer's holding the nuke Liz is looking for."

While the bodies were being stowed away, Casey traced Drake's path down the ridge and jogged to his side. "Now what?" he asked.

"Now we wait for Ricardo to show us how much of his explosive ordinance training he remembers."

"I'll get the emergency tool kit in the Yukon," Casey said. "He'll need some tools. While I'm doing that, you might want to explain what just happened to the guy watching us from the window in the control building. He's on his phone."

"Tell Billy to go see him. He hasn't seen Billy shoot anyone."

Drake got down on his hands and knees to look for anything suspicious under the trailer. The sidewall substructure was made of one inch by one inch tubing that probably housed the wiring for the turn signals and brake lights on the trailer, but there didn't appear to be anything added to the bottom of the trailer that didn't belong there.

As he was standing up again, Casey returned with the tool kit, Gonzalez right behind him.

"I don't see anything that screams 'bang, you're dead' if we open it," Drake said. "But you're the expert."

"If there's a nuclear device in there," Gonzalez said, "I don't think whoever planned this would risk letting one of these nut jobs blow it up when they forgot how to defuse a booby trap. You guys stand back and I'll open it up." He pulled a large flathead screw driver out of the tool kit Casey was holding open for him.

Drake and Casey quickly stepped back as he looked carefully at the keyhole at the rear of the trailer. Inserting the head of the screwdriver into the nose of the skull, he hit it hard with the palm of his hand, then twisted the screwdriver hard to break the lock.

The strut-activated hatch opened slowly.

Drake and Casey stepped forward again, and the three men saw the brown canvas transport container of a Special Atomic Demolition Device with Cyrillic lettering on it.

"I'll be damned," Casey said. "I knew one of these would make it here one day. But I never thought I'd be there to see it."

"Is it armed, Ricardo?" Drake asked.

"No. These SADMs require an arming device that has to be attached with a timer. This timer," he said, as he removed it from a pouch on the front of the canvas container. "It's not attached. We were lucky, though. They could have armed this thing in a couple of minutes."

"And then what?" Drake asked. "How were they going to blow this dam?"

"If they did their homework, they probably found a spot out on the dam they figured would cause the dam to fail when this thing went off. Break through the fence, kill anyone in the control building, set the timer, and get out of here."

Gonzalez brought the arming device closer to his face to inspect it. The size of a baseball, it had a set of rings used to set the delay time.

"Only they wouldn't have made it off the dam," he said with a grin. "These rings are set at 'Instant.' And they won't turn. As soon as they attached the arming device, it would have detonated." He paused. "It looks like whoever sent these four out didn't want them coming back."

"It was a suicide mission," Casey said. "Well, I'm glad we helped them with the suicide part."

"I'd better let Liz know we got here in time," Drake said, taking out his cell phone. "Mike, see if you can convince the guy Billy's talking with over there to let DHS handle this. Liz might have a team on the way, and I'm sure she'll want to limit local law enforcement involvement as much as possible."

"On my way." Casey gave him a two-fingered salute.

Drake smiled and walked to the side of the Yukon and leaned against it, where he took a moment to breathe deeply through his nose and relax his muscles. The adrenaline dump was still racing his heart and raising his blood pressure. He was familiar with the boost his body had given him in the face of danger, and he also knew how to ride out the return of the neuropeptide Y level in his brain to normal. After a minute, he found Liz's number in his contact list and waited for her to answer.

"We got it, Liz. It's a Russian atomic demolition device. We also have four dead terrorists in the back of Mike's Yukon."

"Are you all right?"

"No casualties here. Just a nervous Corps of Engineer employee we're trying to calm down. You'll want to let him know everything's all right before he gets the state police up here."

"Will do. I've just borrowed a new Lakota helicopter from the Oregon National Guard, and a DHS team from Eugene is on its way. I'm coordinating the operation to recover the nuke from here with the governor's office. We're trying to keep this out of the press."

"You should be able to," Drake said. "The four of us here at the dam are the only ones who know what we've recovered. You might have to create a story about the four dead terrorists, though."

"Yeah. We're working on it. The massacre at the polo field is being linked to drug traffickers and a cartel dispute over drug routes to Canada. We could say the four at the dam were tracked down by undercover operatives whose names will not be released."

"Thanks. We don't need the publicity."

"You're welcome. Before you go, the Secretary says thanks, job well done, and Larry needs to talk with you."

Drake heard Green being called over the noise of what sounded like a hastily assembled command center.

"Drake, I worked with your friend Paul and the Bend PD," Green told him. "We traced calls on Vazquez's phone to the hangar house at Sunriver. Calls were made from there to Vazquez at the Pronghorn Resort and a number of calls to someone at Wyler Ranch. That's gotta be where they ran this operation from."

Chapter Fifty-Nine

Sitting comfortably in a brown leather armchair next to a picture window looking toward the mountain range to the west, Barak caressed the bottle of his favorite single malt scotch he was holding. An empty crystal tumbler sat on the glass-topped end table next to him.

He had waited patiently for a call. His man riding the last of the four Harleys had been instructed to call once the demolition device was out on the dam. He'd been promised a nice reward for making the call, a payoff Barak knew he would not have to make. Still, he thought, the sum was large enough that he felt sure the man would call him shortly before the detonation took his life.

But the call had not come. Had he failed again? He had waited twenty years for the green light to start working down his assassination list of prominent Americans. He had begun a month ago, but he had failed at the last moment to kill the Secretary of Homeland Security. And now the *coup de grace* that he'd designed to panic America and earn him respect as the leader of the worldwide jihad might not have happened.

How could he have failed? No one could have known the nuke they had purchased from Venezuela, courtesy of Iran and Russia, was in Oregon. No one except the men who'd brought it here for him. No one knew the dam was the target, either, except for those same men. And of those men, only Saleem had the opportunity to betray him. But there was no reason he could think of that the young Hezbollah leader would disobey him. Nothing would be gained by doing so.

If Allah had allowed him to fail again, Barak told himself, it surely must be that his years living in Las Vegas while he developed the security firm that concealed his team of assassins had corrupted him. It was true that he had enjoyed some of the pleasures of the West his religion despised—he abruptly set the bottle of scotch on the end table—but he had decided it was necessary to hide his mission and his true identity. He didn't know how else he could have developed the business clientele he had without pampering and hosting all the American businessmen, plus more than a few Muslims who supported the cause.

With a shout of hot rage and icy despair, Barak rose from his chair and threw the bottle of Glenmorangie against the face of the river rock fireplace.

"Get the Hawker ready to leave," he shouted at his pilot, who was watching TV in the next room. "I want to be airborne in fifteen minutes."

Then he calmly walked to the closet in the master bedroom and retrieved the two black duffle bags of Semtex, the detonator caps, and a disposable cell phone. Each duffle bag held five pounds of Semtex. That was more than enough to level the two-story house and its hangar. When he was safely out of the house and ready to takeoff, he would dial the pre-set number and detonate one duffel bag of pre-wired Semtex. The explosion that would eliminate any trace of evidence he'd ever been in Oregon. The other duffel bag would travel with him for the next battle.

He carefully set both of the duffle bags on the floor in the middle of the great room, then returned to the bedroom to load his travel bag and collect the nylon range bag with his other weapons. His next stop was going to be Toronto, Canada. Its cooler climate would require a different wardrobe, so he tossed just a few items of clothing in his bag along with his leather shaving kit.

He had a safe house in Toronto that was three adjoining apartments in one of the densely populated, high-rise buildings that were overwhelmingly occupied by Muslim immigrants. He would have no trouble hiding in Toronto. The city had the highest concentration of Muslims living in North America, but he thought he would grow a full beard…just in case.

For now, though, it was just a matter of getting out of Oregon and in the air before anyone knew he was involved with trying to blow up the dam in the mountains.

Taking a last look around the master bedroom, he carried his travel bag to the top of the stairs leading down to the hangar.

"Tim," he shouted to his pilot, who was cleaning out his own bedroom, "Take my two personal bags to the jet and get ready to leave. I have one last chore to complete here, and then I'll join you."

When his pilot acknowledged the order, he walked to the window and looked out at the airport runway. This small airport didn't have a tower, and there were just a few planes below him that looked like they might be leaving any time soon. Well, he thought, leaving as soon as they were ready shouldn't be a problem.

His immediate concern, aside from leaving the resort, was whether he should let anyone know where he could be reached. He had no intention of calling Ryan, his contact with the Alliance who had brokered the delivery of the nuclear demolition device from Venezuela, or his sponsor at the Brotherhood in the Middle East. All three would know of his failure soon enough and expect an explanation he was unwilling to provide until he was safely out of their immediate reach.

He also briefly considered alerting Saleem to be extra cautious on his way back to Tijuana. While he wasn't altogether sure he could trust the younger man, he had delivered the nuke from Mexico to Oregon successfully. Perhaps it was only the difference in their ages that made him wary of Saleem's loyalty, that and his mixed Lebanese and Mexican blood. He concluded that Saleem had enough of a head start and would be fine.

Grabbing the duffel bag of Semtex that was going with him, Barak walked downstairs to his Hawker . As he always had, he would trust his fate to Allah.

Chapter Sixty

After a sprint back up the ridge above the dam, Casey prepared the Relentless for a dash back to Sunriver. Seated next to him, Drake waited until they were in the air before asking for help in using the helicopter's Garmin avionics to acquire satellite images of the hangar house.

With a touch of the display screen in front of him, Casey switched the touch screen in front of Drake. "This'll give you the global connectivity option," he said. "Touch the icon for Internet access and select Google Earth, then enter Sunriver Airport. It won't be a live shot, but it will show you our options when we get there."

After following these instructions, Drake leaned closer to study the shot of the southern end of the runway and the adjacent row of hangar houses. "Looks like the only place to land is right next to the house on the taxi way," he said. "The other side has houses for a hundred yards, then trees. The good news is the noise we make on approach won't be unexpected at an airport."

"The house faces a street on one side and the airport taxi way on the other," Casey said after a glance at the display.

"Do you want to wait for Larry to block the street if Barak's there and makes a run for it?"

"I think we'll get there before Larry does. He's with Liz at the command center she set up in Bend."

"Adam, if Barak is there, he's not going to just sit around and wait to be caught. Remember how he slipped out of that resort in Cancun? And then the villa south of Tijuana? I think we should lock the place down and then go after him."

It was good advice, and Drake knew he should listen to his friend. They had survived more than one close call by playing it safe. But he also knew he didn't want to chance letting the man get away again. In a month's time, Barak had tried to kill him, a sitting cabinet member, and what remained of his family. If Barak was behind the massacre at the polo field and the attempt to blow the dam and kill a hundred thousand innocent people, he needed to be stopped. It was a risk Drake was willing to take.

"Let's see what it looks like when we get there," he said. "The last thing I want is to let this guy live to kill another day."

They flew low and fast down the eastern slope of the Cascades toward the Sunriver Resort without talking for several minutes. Both men were thinking about the actions they might have to take shortly.

Casey touched the communication icon on his display screen and called Green at the command center in Bend. "Larry," he said, "we're five minutes from the Sunriver Airport. Let Liz know we're hoping to make a surprise visit to our friend with the jet. If we find him, she needs to be ready with a story to match the other stories she's putting out."

"Just you and Drake? I heard from Ricardo. He's still at the dam."

"Just the Lone Ranger and Tonto," Casey said, "and the element of surprise."

"Hope you find him, boss. Good hunting."

Drake looked down ahead and to his right and saw the golf courses ahead that crisscrossed over the Little Deschutes River at the Crosswater Resort.

"We chase Barak to the Mexican Riviera and back and find he might be less than a mile or two from where we've been staying," he said. "Amazing."

"You think he came back to Oregon to get revenge?" Casey asked as he dropped down to five hundred feet and touched the display panel to activate the Nav/Com functions and make sure there weren't any other planes landing or taking off from the small airport that he needed to avoid.

"He had to have been planning this for longer than a month," Drake replied. "Arranging to get a nuke smuggled here had to take awhile. At least I hope it did." He got up and walked back through the passenger cabin to the storage locker and switched out the magazine in his HK assault carbine for a fresh thirty-round one. Then he returned to his seat beside Casey.

"Veer to the west of the hangar house over those other homes," he said after taking another look, "and then flare around and set down on the taxi way so we block his plane from coming out. I'll make my way to the side of the house next to the hangar door. I'll cover you as you move in." Casey nodded. "It looks like you can boost me up to reach the bottom of the railing on that deck. I'll enter through the sliding doors up there. You make it around to the front door on the other side. If I take fire, shoot your way in."

"What about his pilot?"

"If Barak's pilot is here, he's been helping the wrong side. He'll have to make a choice."

Casey dropped the Relentless down until they were flying just above the tree tops for the last three hundred yards. As he swung around to land on the other side of the hangar house, they saw there were no vehicles in the driveway.

As soon as the helicopter's rear wheels touched the

tarmac, Drake sprang for the door behind Casey and jumped to the ground, fifty yards from the hangar house.

AT THE OTHER end of the runway, Barak stared out the window next to the copilot seat in his jet. His pilot had just turned the jet around for takeoff at the north end of the runway when he'd seen the red and black helicopter come in low and swing around to land beside the hangar house.

Allah was on his side. Another ten minutes, and they wouldn't have been able to pull the Hawker out of the hangar and onto the taxi way. He didn't know who was pursuing him in the sleek helicopter, or how they had found him, but he didn't really care, either. Another minute, and they weren't going to find a trace of him in this cursed land.

He gestured for the pilot to takeoff and watched as a man ran to the side of the hangar house and turned to wave back at the helicopter. With his cell phone in his hand, Barak waited until they had raced down the runway to liftoff. As he flashed past the hangar house, he sent the message to the disposable phone inside the house to detonate the Semtex surprise he had left there.

Turning to look back as the Hawker gained altitude, he saw the hangar house explode. Then he felt the shock wave hit the plane.

CASEY STEPPED DOWN from the Relentless and saw Drake wave him forward. As he ran around the red nose of the helicopter, the hangar house erupted in a flash of fire. Instinctively, he turned his head away from the blast. When he looked back, the side of the house where Drake had been crouching was now a just a pile of debris.

He was running to the place where he had last seen his friend when the jet that had just taken off exploded in a burst of flame and began falling to earth just past the end of the runway.

A HISPANIC MAN in his late forties and smoking a fat Cuban cigar was standing beside a black Chrysler 300c. He held a cell phone in his left hand. As he watched the white Hawker jet explode and burn before his eyes, he raised his right hand in a universal salute of disrespect. A just and fitting death, thought Hector, brother of the Architect, for the assassin who killed the head of his cartel.

Chapter Sixty-One

HIS FIRST SENSATION WHEN HE REGAINED CONSCIOUSNESS WAS that his head hurt and the light was too bright. When he tried to lift his head, dizziness was added to the list, as well as a throbbing pain in his left arm and most of the rest of his body.

A familiar voice told him to relax.

"You're in the emergency room," it said. "You have a concussion, a broken arm, contusions, and lacerations. And you look like hell." The voice turned into Mike Casey. "But you'll live because I've seen you hurt worse than this.

Drake tried to open his eyes again, but promptly decided it wasn't worth it. "What happened?"

"The house blew up and fell on you."

"Whose house?"

"You don't remember?"

A voice he didn't recognize saved him from admitting that he didn't remember.

"Let's let Mr. Drake rest now," someone said. "We're almost finished here. He'll be moved to Ortho-Neuro, third floor and you can visit him there."

Other voices, different smells, and a ride in an elevator to a room with dimmer lights brought Drake to a place where it felt like it would be a really good idea to sleep for awhile.

Soft voices in the room woke him later. Looking up very carefully, he saw Mike and Liz standing on one side of the bed and his secretary and her husband standing on the other.

"How are you feeling?" Margo asked as she straightened the blue sheet that covered him.

He managed a smile. "Two aspirin and a good shower and I'll be fine. I might not be in the office tomorrow, but I'm fine."

She shook her head. "The doctor said it might be longer than that. He wants you to rest for a day or so, then he'll run some tests. You were unconscious for close to half an hour. I told him to keep you as long as he needed to, that I'm used to running your office by myself."

Drake looked at her husband. "Paul, you're married to her. What does a guy have to do to get a little sympathy?"

"I haven't been married long enough to find out," Paul said with a smile.

Drake carefully turned his head. "Mike, you asked me if I remembered what happened. Last thing I remember is landing at the hangar house...."

"You ran to the house and stopped against the wall under the deck. When the house exploded, the shock wave blew the wall out. When we dug you out, you were unconscious. You stayed that way till we got you to the ER."

He considered this for a minute. "Was Barak in the house?"

"No. We think he was in his jet at the other end of the runway. He flew over just as the house exploded. We think he detonated Semtex in the house. Enough to bring down a building three times that size."

"So he got away?"

"Not exactly," Casey said. "His jet climbed to maybe five hundred feet and then it exploded, too. Liz and her people haven't confirmed from what remains they found that Barak was on board, but I think he was. Preliminary report is someone rigged Semtex under the copilot's seat."

"It's over then," Drake said. He closed his eyes, then asked. "What about the bomb at the polo field?"

Liz took a turn answering his questions. "It was Semtex, same as the hangar house. It was a shaped charge planted in a storage compartment on the side of Vazquez's horse trailer. We think Barak was tying up loose ends and creating a diversion so they could run the nuke to the dam."

Drake opened his eyes again. "If Vazquez was the target, someone had to wait for him to get next to his trailer. Do we have a suspect for that?"

"No, but we've collected everyone's cell phones and we're hoping there are pictures that will help identify the bomber. We have a team at Wyler Ranch, and we're also interviewing Mr. Abazzano in Los Angeles. It all leads back to that ranch and the people there. It might take some time, but we'll put it all together."

"While they're doing that, ole buddy," Casey said, "I'm going to fly my guys home and get reacquainted with my wife. Liz has been gracious enough to ask for my bill for all the help we provided you. She's also offered to stay over while they continue the investigation here, then drive you home." He reached across the bed to give his friend their secret handshake.

"Okay. Tell your kids Uncle Adam will visit them before Christmas."

"I expect I'll see you before then, if you continue working with this lady." Casey nodded toward Liz, then walked out of the room with a wave to Margo and Paul Benning.

"We should be going, too," said Benning. "Margo's had

enough excitement for one weekend, and I need to get back to work."

"Thanks for running down that license plate for me," Drake said. "And for working with Larry at the polo field. Burgers and beer on me when I get back."

Margo leaned down and kissed him quickly on the cheek. "I don't like seeing you in a hospital bed. Come back to work. Your desk is a mess," she said. There was a trace of moisture in the corners of her eyes when she turned to leave.

"I should go, too," Liz said. "Paul got the sheriff to let me use an office. I need to make a full report to the Secretary on what we learned about the nuke and Barak. He'll want to talk with you when you're feeling up to it. He also wants to update you on the company he wants you to visit in San Francisco."

"Stay at the Senator's place tonight, if you want," Drake said. "And use my car. If you're sure you want to drive me home, you should get use to the racing clutch I put in it."

"All right, I will. Now rest, enjoy the Jello and juice, and I'll see you tomorrow." She gave his left hand a squeeze.

Drake watched her leave. He had never let anyone else drive his Porsche.

After a moment, he raised his right hand and opened his fist close enough to his eyes to see the challenge coin Casey had passed to him with the secret handshake. It was from his old Night Stalkers unit, the 160th Special Operations Aviation Regiment, that provided helicopter aviation support for their special operation forces. Under the unit insignia on the shiny medallion was the Night Stalker motto, *Night Stalkers Don't Quit.*

If you wore a military uniform, you carried a challenge coin and could produce one immediately when you were challenged drinking inside an NCO or officers' club on any military post or base anywhere around the world. Once the coin was slapped down onto the bar, tradition demanded that everyone else had to quickly answer the call by slapping down their own coins or pay the price and buy drinks for everyone.

Drake smiled and closed his hand over the coin. With the secret handshake and the unseen exchange of the challenge coin, his friend had acknowledged their victory that day and thanked him for not quitting. Casey knew he couldn't quit. They had both taken the same oath to protect the country, and it was an oath that never expired.

Author's Note

The Department of Homeland Security issued a report in 2012 that examined twenty-five terrorist attacks on dams around the world between 2001 and 2011 that were similar, although fortunately not as destructive, as the attack depicted in this work of fiction.

It's an age-old tactic that has been rediscovered by today's terrorists. The projected casualties mentioned here are based on existing and current assessments made by the U.S. Army Corps of Engineers.

Next in the Adam Drake series

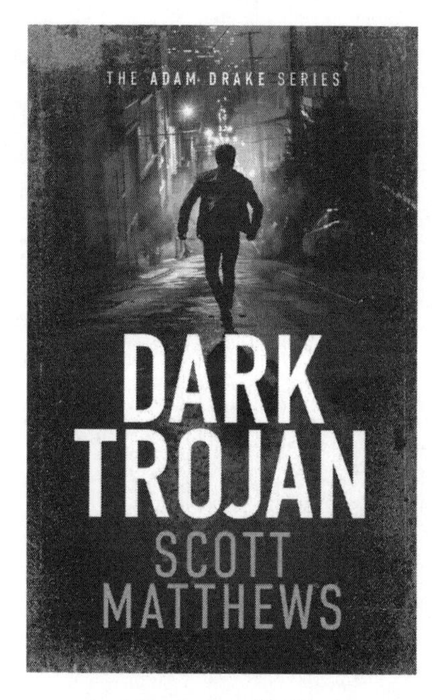

vinci-books.com/darktrojan

America's electricity grid is under attack, if successful, the nation will plunge into anarchy.

Domestic terrorists have the grid in their sights and they've already planted their malware.

What they don't know, is their operation is being sold to the highest bidder. And America's enemies have deep pockets.

The countdown has begun to keep United States lights on and hunt down the dark forces ready to make their move in the chaos.

Made in the USA
Columbia, SC
23 September 2024